Dead

Tomorrow

Tony McFadden

If you purchased this paperback and feel like re-gifting it, go right ahead. Just do the author a solid and leave a review somewhere first. If you're interested in more titles by this author, a list can be found at the end of this book.

DEDICATION

For Linda,

Who has been having one hell of a year so far.

DISCLAIMER

All characters in this book are fictitious. Any resemblance to real people is entirely coincidental.

This book is set in Australia and written in Australia. It has Australian sayings and spellings.

And swearing. A decent amount of swearing.

Proceed at your own risk.

ACKNOWLEDGMENTS

The journey I've followed over the past slightly more than a decade is on the back of the feedback I get from you, my readers.

Thank you so much.

Chapter One

The full moon reflected off the small waves lapping Narrabeen Beach, and the air was sweet with the smell of Orange Jessamine flowers.

Nick's trousers were rolled up to mid-calf. He carried his shoes, socks stuffed in them, in one hand and held Lucy's hand in the other. "You," he hesitated, "have one hell of an appetite."

She punched his arm. "Do you normally date your clients?"

"Ex-client. Your company paid my invoice. This is extra-curricular."

"What, like a hobby?" Her smile was real. The moon illuminated her freckled, alabaster skin. Her curly red hair was in a loose bun, showing off her long neck.

Nick was smitten.

"Are you enjoying yourself?"

Lucy shrugged. "I've had worse dates." She smiled. "Paddle-boarding this afternoon in the Narrabeen Lagoon and dinner on the beach? What's a Bondi boy doing on the Northern Beaches?"

"Grew up in Warriewood, just up the road. As far as I'm concerned, Australia's best beaches are up here. As dad's law firm grew, we moved to Rose Bay. But I still love it up here. Don't get enough chances." He smiled at Lucy. "Thanks for giving me an excuse."

"So," said Lucy. "Are you an only child?"

"That's me. The parents quit at one."

"Are they still working?"

"Mum was an ER Nurse. She left that a few decades ago. My father has just started backing away from his law firm. They're both in Italy looking for a villa in Tuscany to use as an intermittent retirement home."

Lucy raised her eyebrows. "Wow. Serious family money."

"He's promised he'll spend the last dollar on his deathbed. What about you? Only child?"

"A younger brother. Bobby. By three years. He's a telecommunications engineer at one of the carriers. He's bounced around a couple of times. INot sure which one he's at this month." Lucy stepped over a piece of driftwood. You've got to tell me how you managed to convince what's his name—Tom Goulding—to make full restitution to my company."

"He offered. He needed to wait until the executor sorted his father's estate, but he told me he'd ensure all of it was accounted for and returned. Drop in his financial bucket. I'm glad he came through."

"Got me a promotion."

"Congratulations. So you should have paid for dinner."

They turned to walk back up the beach toward the

restaurant. Nick turned and swapped sides with Lucy.

"Trade sides," she said. "You're getting all the surf." She changed her shoes to her other hand and moved to the downside of the beach. The waves lapped around their feet.

"You ever surf?"

Lucy looked up at him. "Are you kidding? My sports are indoor sports. I was cursed with Irish genes. I sit too close to a glass of orange juice, and I burn. I wear SPF1000. The lagoon this afternoon was way out of my comfort zone."

He chuckled. "What indoor sports? Badminton?"

"Various martial arts. Tae Kwan do, Karate, Wu Shu, Hapkido."

Nick stopped and turned and looked at her closely. "Really?"

"Why are you surprised?"

"I'm not falling for that. Listen, Miss Simpson, to what level of expertise have you reached in these acts of war?" He rubbed his no-longer straight nose with his thumb and smiled. "And where were you when I got pummelled while tracking down your missing money?"

She laughed. "Black belts in all. Different levels of black for each of them." She reached up and tapped him on the end of the nose. "Not that I would be any good to you in a street fight. Ours is a very controlled and disciplined sport."

He took her hand, and they walked back up the beach to the parking lot. "I don't know. I think you'd be an asset in the field."

She shook her head while she smiled. "Too rough for me. I want an official keeping an eye on the match-up, ready to step in if things got out of hand."

"Definitely could have used one of those officials."

"Hey. It all worked out in the end."

They reached Nick's car.

"The moment of truth, Lucy. And it's entirely

your call. Do I drive you home, and we plan for our next date? Or do I drive you to my flat and continue this discussion over a final drink?" He unlocked the car and held the door open for her. "I'm perfectly fine either way, but I'd be lying if I didn't say drinks at my place was my preference."

Lucy leaned in and took his hands. She kissed him and was enveloped by his arms. "Want to know my preference?"

A car door slammed shut, and Lucy was roughly pulled from Nick and tossed onto the pavement. As a large black sedan pulled behind Nick's car, she rolled and sprung to her feet. The back doors opened, and two men stepped out, grabbing Nick by his arms before he reached the man who threw Lucy.

He struggled against the grip. "Lucy, are you okay?"

Lucy fought to get past the man who had pulled her from Nick. The man was a head taller and had muscles on his muscles. He wrapped her up from behind, her feet dangling half a metre off the ground.

"I'm okay." She kicked back at her captor's knees, trying to connect. "If this arsehole would let me go."

Nick was pinned on either side. He couldn't move his arms. "Don't waste your energy, Lucy." He looked at the man on his left. "You want money, ask. We'll give you our money. No big deal. It's only money."

The man holding on to Lucy cleared his throat. "I apologise for the way this has turned out. We just want to talk."

Nick tried to wrench his arm free. "So let us go, and we'll talk."

"Rules of engagement, first. No screaming, no trying to run. You listen and comply."

"Comply? Like hell." Nick tried again to pull his arms free.

"Settle down. I'm here on behalf of a client. You're going to take a little ride with us—just you.

Lucy can take your car to her place, and after I deliver you to my boss, whatever happens, is between the two of you."

"That's not how it works, mate. I pick my clients. Lucy, call the cops."

"Hey Siri, call—"

The man holding Lucy dropped her and grabbed her bag. He managed to get her phone out and turned it off fast enough to stop the call. "Nope. No police." He slid it into his back pocket. "Anybody calls the police, and Nicky's going to get hurt. Just let it go. You can do that, right Lucy? Nick is fine if everybody plays along."

Nick shook his head at Lucy. "Let it go, Lucy. I'll be okay." His arms were pinned above the elbows. But he still had his keys. He underhanded them to her. "I'll call you as soon as I'm free." He looked at the big guy behind her. "Do you guys have names?"

"Of course, we have names." The guy from behind Lucy walked forward and stood in front of

Nick. "Why wouldn't we have names?"

"Are you going to tell us your names?"

"Hell no. You don't need to know them." He turned and looked at Lucy. "After we leave, you'll be busting to call the cops. Don't. We have friends there. We'll know if you call them. This needs to stay off their radar." He leaned against the black sedan. "We could have just dropped a sack over Nick's head and stuffed him in the boot. Popped you on the head and left you in the sand, prey for whoever—whomever? Never get that right—whoever might happen along. But we're not doing that. Asking for a bit of patience and consideration. Nick won't be harmed if you sit tight."

He pulled her phone from his back pocket and held it between his thumb and forefinger. "You'll sit tight?"

Lucy glanced at Nick, who gave her a quick nod. "I'll sit tight." She grabbed the phone. "For twenty-four hours. If I don't hear from him by then, I'm calling the police."

The big guy grabbed the phone back. "That's not how it works. Do not call the police. You'll hear from Nick soon enough. If you call the police, it'll get ugly. Do you understand?"

"Jesus. Okay." She held out her hand. "Give it."

"So you won't—"

"For Christ's sake, I said I wouldn't." Lucy grabbed the phone back and turned it on. "So help me god, if anything happens to him…"

Nick smiled. "These guys want to hire me for something. I'll be okay. Stay at my parent's house, if you want. The address is in my car's GPS, and the key is on the ring."

"See?" The big guy smiled at Lucy, then turned and smiled at Nick. "We're all getting along." He held out his hand to Nick. "Hand it over."

"What?"

"Your phone, mate. Don't make me ask again."

Nick frowned and handed over his mobile. "I'm

definitely not going to call the cops while you've got me jammed in the back of your car."

The big guy took a pin from his pocket and extracted the SIM from Nick's phone. He took a small glassine envelope from his shirt pocket, slid the SIM in and put it in his wallet. He handed the phone back to Nick. "I know you won't call the cops. But we can't have your little girlfriend tracking your location. You get the SIM back when you're finished."

"Finished?"

The big guy shrugged. "Finished. Whatever it is the boss wants you to do."

Nick took the phone back. The display, where it usually showed the name of his carrier, said 'SOS calls only'. "Just great." Nick opened the sedan's back door. "Let's get this over with. Lucy, don't worry. I'll call you as soon as I can. Tell Davie."

Lucy watched the other men get in the car: Two in the back, either side of Nick, and the third, the one doing most of the talking, in the front passenger seat.

Lucy took pictures of the receding licence plate as the car drove away.

Then she unlocked the phone and made a call. "Bobby. Wake up and put on a pot of coffee. I'll be there in fifteen minutes."

Chapter Two

Vladimir Petrovski sat at his table in the kitchen of *The Natalia,* a few miles northwest of Miami's city centre. He picked at his food. He had lost his appetite shortly after he heard Terri O'Shea was in Australia. It took him a year to recover from her theft. That year was rough. He almost lost his restaurant. This restaurant. His legitimate base of operations.

He had thought the events of a decade ago were the lowest point in his life. He'd been caught in a fire in the Florida Everglades. Somehow tables had been turned on him in a fight he'd thought he had won. He almost died in that fire. He ended up losing his right hand. The right side of his face, and most of the right side of his torso, was permanently disfigured.

Then three years ago, the O'Shea bitch disappeared with the ten million he'd entrusted her to clean.

Getting the money back didn't matter to him as much as making her pay with her life.

His phone was face down on the table. He tipped it up to check the time. Mikhail would be in LA by now, with a four-hour layover before the next leg of his flight. Mikhail's remit was simple. Find her, kill her, and leave before the police realise she is dead.

His phone buzzed with an incoming video call. He sighed and answered. "Martin, This isn't a secure device. I'll call you back from my laptop."

"No need. A quick message with no financial implications." Martin, Petrovski's money laundering contact, gave him an exaggerated wink. "Absolutely confirmed it's Terri in Sydney. She's travelling under the name Grace Rawlston. And she will be there less than a week. Banking business." The call terminated.

Six miles from *The Natalia,* FBI Special Agent James and Miami PD Detective MacCready sat back from a surveillance station in the bowels of the FBI offices.

"Martin is his money launderer," said James.

"And Terri O'Shea is in Sydney. How fast can you get approval for international travel?"

James laughed. "I'll reach out to the Australian Federal Police." He looked at his watch. "They're probably still open."

"You know anybody there?"

"A kid by the name of Nick Harding. I worked with him about five years ago. He's a whiz kid in the Financial Crimes unit."

"Sometimes you don't have to be good, just lucky. Most days Petrovski would never take a business call on that phone."

Chapter Three

Nick squirmed in the middle of the back seat. It was a tight fit. He made up maybe ten percent of the total mass in the car. "Can barely breath back here." He looked up at the man to his left. "This car looks like it should have been more spacious from the outside."

No response.

He looked to the man on his right. "Could you skooch over a bit?"

Still nothing.

"Where am I going?"

The guy in the front passenger seat half turned and looked at him. "They won't talk to you. Don't waste your time." He turned back to the front.

"But you will. Where are we going?"

"To our destination. You'll find out when we get there."

Nick shook his head. "Who is my client? I'm assuming I won't have much of a choice in the matter. And what's your name? I can't keep referring to you in my head as 'that big motherfucker'."

He twisted in his front seat again, a smile on his face. "I kinda like that name." He tugged on his earlobe. "I'm Reg. Lucy seems nice."

Nick scowled. "You've been watching me. Us. What the hell is going on?"

"Of course we were. My boss doesn't do anything without an annoyingly large amount of research. She was your client in your last case, right?"

"She stays out of this."

Reg raised his eyebrows. "She better."

They sat silently, the black car slipping through North Manly, over the Spit Bridge and into Mosman like a ghost. Traffic picked up by that point, and the stop-and-go seemed to shake Reg out of his stupor.

He turned in his seat again. "Hey, how'd you get into the PI business?"

Nick ignored him. He was tired, stiff and pissed off.

"Come on, mate. We're almost there."

Nick opened his mouth to respond, then exhaled, shook his head and adjusted himself, bumping into the man on his right.

The big guy grunted and pushed Nick back to the centre of the back seat.

"Jesus. Sorry." Nick rubbed his arm, leaned back and closed his eyes.

"Nah, mate," said Reg. "Open them. Look at this."

Nick opened his eyes and looked out the car window. They had just come off the Sydney Harbour Bridge and were on the Cahill Expressway, the Circular Quay and a lit-up Sydney Opera House in all its splendour on their left. "Nice."

"Just 'nice'? Mate, I've lived here on and off for

fifteen years, and I still love to see it."

"It'll be there tomorrow." Nick closed his eyes and leaned his head back. "I'm trying to rest. Trying to process the fact you've ruined what could have been a beautiful end to a perfect day." He yawned and slipped his phone out of his back pocket. He opened his eyes a squint and scanned for Wi-Fi signals. Then slid the phone back into his pocket. "Just give it a rest until we get to wherever in the hell we're going."

"Well, we're here. Look sharp."

The car entered an underground parking garage and pulled into an assigned spot. Nick waited until the mammoth on his right got out before he exited. He stretched and felt his back crack. The sign on the wall by the parking spot said 'Waterfall Properties'.

"This way," said Reg.

Nick, corralled by the two guys from the back seat and the driver, followed. "Like I've got a choice."

The lift door opened as they arrived. They stepped

in, and Nick turned back toward the door. The other four stayed looking at the back.

He looked over his shoulder and noticed the door on the back. "Right." He faced the back.

The lift eased to a stop, and the doors silently slid open. They stepped out into a private hall facing the double wooden doors to the apartment.

"This way." Reg pushed open a heavy oak door and motioned for Nick to follow. "You guys can go. Tell Jerry thanks." The three muscles got back in the lift and left.

Reg pushed him into the foyer facing a three-storey wall of windows looking over the city. The red light at the top of the Sydney Tower Eye spire blinked. The observation deck blazed green and gold. The World Cup was weeks away.

He tore his eyes away from the view. The main room was lit with evenly spaced sconces, throwing beams of light up to the ceiling and down to the white marble floor.

"Come on. Move it."

"Not so friendly now, mate." Nick followed him through the apartment and into a room and stopped. It was a stereotypical den. Mahogany furniture, thick carpet, priceless paintings on the walls and a man he hadn't seen in over five years puffing on a cigar, reclining in an over-stuffed chair.

"Fuck me." Nick took a couple of slow steps toward Terrance O'Shea. "I never thought I'd see *you* again."

O'Shea was a large man, but not the same kind of large as Reg. He wheezed as he stood and gathered his robe around him. Nick grimaced as his large white gut, hanging over his boxers, flashed him. O'Shea took another drag on the cigar, tilted his head back and exhaled. He dropped it in an ashtray and pulled the stopper from a crystal bottle. "Whiskey?"

"Jesus Christ. If I'd known you were behind this, I would have taken a run at Reg when I had a chance. Would have been worth it."

O'Shea poured two heavy glasses. "It's been five years, Nick. You're looking well."

"A bit over five, and you look like shit."

O'Shea chuckled and patted his stomach. "Life has been good."

Nick shook his head and dropped into a chair. "Why in the hell are you doing this, mate? You could have just called me."

"Would you have come?"

Nick thought about that for a second. "No. Probably not. This is ballsy, O'Shea. We were days away from having you for money laundering before you disappeared."

"Did you ever find the final piece of the puzzle?"

Nick shook his head. "You and your daughter cleaned everything out. Like you had advance warning."

O'Shea smiled and sipped his drink. He walked to Nick and handed him the tumbler of whiskey. "You'll never know."

Nick took the glass and placed it on the coaster on the table beside the chair. "Why in the hell am I here?"

O'Shea sat in the chair beside him. Clinked his whiskey glass with the one Nick had placed on the side table. "Cheers to your health, old chap, and may you have many more years. And the next time you talk to the lovely Lucy, please extend my profound apologies to her."

"Cut the shit. Why am I in your aerie, in the middle of Sydney at what time is it now, after midnight?" He pulled his phone from his pocket and checked the time. "12:18. In the motherfucking morning. Why?"

O'Shea scratched the back of his head. "I enjoyed our sparring back in the day. You're very clever. It was an enjoyable thrust and parry. You enjoyed it too, I'm sure."

Nick stared at him, not responding.

"Okay. Here's the deal. I need you to find my

daughter."

"Teresa?"

"The only one I have."

"Why me, why now and why didn't you just call me?"

"You wouldn't have come. You, because you're a good man and have a good reputation in the private investigator industry. And now, because she's back in town."

"Call someone else and screw up their evening." Nick stood and was pushed back into the chair. He looked back at Reg. "Easy on, pal."

Reg held his hands up and stepped back.

"I've already screwed your night up, Nick. Wouldn't be polite to do it to someone else."

"Oh, yeah. I forgot about your impeccable manners."

O'Shea chuckled. "I knew you'd understand. How long do you think this will take?"

Nick sat back and held his hands out, palms up, in

the universal 'what the fuck' pose. "An hour. A month. How in the hell would I know? Why do you think she's in town?"

"Ah, yes," O'Shea grunted as he stood and retrieved a TV remote. He produced a pair of glasses and poked a couple of buttons. A news program flickered to life on the large wall-mounted television. "Watch."

A blonde talking head was doing a location piece in Martin Square, just outside her studio. In the background, a popular K-Pop band was preparing to perform their latest hit. Throngs of hyper-excited teenagers were yelling something, and the reporter had to yell to make herself heard.

"So, what? Your daughter has joined a band? I don't get it."

"No." O'Shea looked frustrated as he rewound the clip. "Which button does slo-mo?" He peered at the remote over his glasses and pressed the right button. "Look. The girl in the red blouse walking right to left behind the reporter."

Nick watched the woman, knee-length blue skirt slowly billowing around long legs as she strode across the background in slow motion. Her face wasn't clear. She had shoulder-length blonde hair, a tan, and a pair of sunglasses. He walked closer to the screen. "Play it again."

The video scrubbed back and played again. Nick watched the woman as she walked. Her face looked slightly to her right, so not even a full profile was visible. Just before she walked out of frame, she turned her head to her left. "Freeze that."

O'Shea pointed at the screen. "Definitely her. Longer hair and a bit thinner, but that's her."

Nick took out his phone and took a picture of the television screen. "You sure that's Teresa?"

"Yeah. Goes by Terri, though."

Nick nodded. "I remember. So that's her, for sure?"

"One hundred per cent."

"When was this?"

"Today. Yesterday. Just before noon." O'Shea dropped back in his chair. "So you'll find her." It wasn't a question.

Nick locked his phone and slid it into his back pocket. He faced O'Shea and crossed his arms. "Why the fuck should I?"

"I'll pay you well. Two grand a day. Australian, not American."

"Not if I don't take the case."

O'Shea adjusted himself in his chair. "Perhaps I wasn't clear. You'll find her. I'll pay you fairly, but you will find her."

"Right. How in the hell do you expect that to work? I'm out of here. I'll bill you for the cab." Nick turned to leave and came face to chest with Reg.

O'Shea wheezed as he pushed himself from his chair. "Reg will be your escort until you find her. You'll go nowhere without him. If you need to make a phone call, you'll use his phone. If you need computer access, it'll be with one of mine in this place."

"I repeat. How in the hell do you expect that to work? I pop by here every time I need to access a crime database? Bullshit."

"You won't have to pop by. You'll be living here."

"You're nuts." Nick looked at Reg. "Your boss is nuts. You know that, right?"

O'Shea sighed. "Listen, Nicky. The case you worked on when you had a legitimate job with the AFP almost caught me. Now I'm pretty sure you guys didn't have enough to make a case, but I won't take that risk. I don't want anyone to know where I am until you find her, and I resolve my outstanding issues with her and then leave the country."

"Jesus. Not another reconciliation. They always go squirrelly. I'm a financial crimes guy. Missing persons isn't my strong suit. And you still haven't explained yourself."

"You're going to be my guest for the duration. I've set up a guest room. Toiletries and spare clothing have been supplied. You'll have run of the kitchen. I've got a pool on the roof. No gym," he patted his stomach," but that's probably not a surprise."

Nick stared at him for a beat. "You're serious. My god, you're serious."

"Make yourself comfortable. You're not going anywhere until you find her." He pulled the robe around him. "Reg will show you where you sleep. Early morning tomorrow."

Reg waited for him to leave the den and then motioned for Nick to follow him "Don't fight it, mate. He's serious. Don't try skipping out while we're sleeping. The place is alarmed. I'll catch you."

"I've got things I've got to do."

Reg laughed. "Least of your problems right now."

Chapter Four

David Sangster had just hit REM sleep when he was dragged from Morpheus' arms by incessant pounding on his front door. He groaned, wiped the drool from his mouth, and pulled his pillow over his head.

The pounding continued. "Davie. Open up."

He lifted his head out from under his pillow and sat up. It was a female voice, vaguely familiar.

"Hang on a tick." He rolled out of bed, grabbed a pair of boxers from the floor and pulled on his bathrobe. He looked through the peephole. A redheaded woman he recognised from the last case he worked on with Nick, and a man he thought was Nick in a baseball cap. Until he turned around. It wasn't Nick. He stepped back and opened the door.

"Lucy? It's Lucy, right?"

"It is. This is my brother, Bobby. Bobby, this is David Sangster, Nick's business partner." She looked past Davie into his apartment. "May we come in? I think we're disturbing your neighbours."

"Yeah, yeah. Sure." Davie backed up and let them enter. He checked the hallway after they were in. No doors open, but the biddy across from him was darkening her peephole. He smiled and waved before he closed the door.

"How did you find me?"

Lucy looked nervous. "I accessed credit reporting databases for personal use. Hopefully, it gets overlooked."

Davie nodded. "Nobody will hear it from me. How's my credit?"

"You don't know?" Lucy shook her head. "It never fails to surprise me how few people know how good," she looked pointedly at Davie, "or bad their credit is.”

“It’s bad? How bad?”

She smiled. “Call me after this, and I’ll walk you through setting up an account so you can check. I know some good credit repair organisations, too. If you need one.”

“Right.” Lucy and Bobby milled in the entryway. “Don’t just stand there. Sit. And tell me why you’re waking me up. Should I call Nick? Is Tom threatening you? Do you want coffee?”

“Take a breath. Coffee will be necessary. Don’t bother calling Nick. He’s been taken.” Lucy dropped onto his sofa.

“He’s what now?” Davie rubbed one of his eyes with the heel of his hand. “Taken where?”

“That’s the thing. He and I we walking on the beach at Narrabeen after a lovely day of paddle boarding and dinner when some big guys grabbed him and threw him in a car. But not after telling me not to call the cops, and after taking the SIM card from his phone, sticking it in a small plastic bag, and sticking it in his pocket."

"Maybe you should breathe, Lucy. The SIM is in who's pocket?"

"One of the big guys. The one who did all the talking."

"Where was this? Have you called the police?"

"No, no. They said no police. Said they had contacts inside the police department, and if I called them, I'd never see Nick again."

Davie took a deep breath and started the kettle. He spooned coffee into a large French press. "Start from the top. What was all the talking about?"

"They—he, the big guy—said that Nick had to go with him to meet a new client." She shook her head. "He didn't have a new client."

"I don't think he did, either," said Davie.

"I know he didn't. He told me at dinner he was between clients."

"Where was dinner?" He looked at Bobby. "You

eat with them?"

"Jesus, no. I was at training."

Davie raised his eyebrows.

"All-age team. Pre-season started a week ago. I'm getting long in the tooth. Need all the training I can get."

"Cool. What position?"

"Centre back, left back." He shook his head. "I'm emotional support for Lucy. She's got the answers."

"I don't need emotional support. I need to find Nick."

Davie poured cups of coffee, placed them on the counter and grabbed a litre of milk from the fridge. "No sugar, I'm afraid. Trying to cut down."

"Black for me," said Lucy. She took the cup to the sofa. "We had dinner in Narrabeen. That place on the beach. Then we walked along the surf, chatting—"

"Sounds romantic," said Davie.

"Don't get distracted."

Bobby took his coffee, a small smile on his face,

and sat on the other end of the sofa. "She doesn't distract easy, mate."

Davie sat across from them. "I'm getting that. So you were in Narrabeen when you were grabbed. Off the beach? Any witnesses?"

"It wasn't on the beach. We got to the parking lot. He had opened the door to his car and we were about to…" She paused. "The night was just beginning when this big guy jumped out of his car and grabbed me, and then the car blocked in Nick's Mazda. Two guys got out of that car and grabbed Nick."

Davie leaned forward and scanned Lucy's face. "Are you okay?"

"Light bruising on my arms. I'm fine. I've had worse after a tournament."

"A—never mind. They rough him up much?"

She shook her head. "Not that I saw. They held him while we talked, then shoved him in the back seat of the car and took off."

"I don't imagine you remember the make and

model of the car?"

"I've got photos of the licence plate. Does that help?"

Dave put his coffee down on the side table. "Can I see your phone?" He held out his hand. "Surprised you still have it, frankly."

"They were polite. Seemed to be more polite than they wanted to be. He returned my phone after he was explicitly clear about the ramifications of my calling the police. Which is why I'm here." She unlocked her phone and opened the photo album. "I'm not handing you my phone. I'll transfer the photos to you." She tapped a couple of keys, and Davie's phone chimed.

"Got them." He retrieved his laptop and sat back across from them. "You didn't answer before. Any witnesses?"

"No. And no, there were no cameras in that part of the parking lot."

Davie nodded, only paying half attention. "It's a

black Chrysler 300C. Not a hugely common car in Australia. Maybe a few thousand. Should make it a little easier." He zoomed in on the licence plate. "Nice, clear shot of the registration. Thanks. This makes things a lot easier."

Lucy moved behind Davie's chair to look over his shoulder.

He twisted and looked at her. "Not a fan of people standing behind me like that. I'll put it on the monitor." He mirrored his laptop to the screen on the wall. "You two don't know I have access to this site, okay?"

Bobby shifted forward in his seat. "Mum's the word." He smiled. "You know, Lucy, when I said you were a bit crazy to go looking for this guy? I apologise."

"Where else would she go? Can't go to the cops, and she knows I know Nick." Davie entered the registration and make of the car into the database. "Maybe not a lot easier."

"Damn,' said Lucy.

The car was registered to Waterfront Properties. Davie opened another website and entered the name. "This one is a public site." He looked at the results and shook his head. "And they're controlled by another company. Waterfall Properties." He checked the time and closed his laptop. "It's going to be shell companies all the way down. I suggest we reconvene in the morning when we've had a decent sleep."

"I would prefer if we continued tonight."

"The man makes sense, sis. It's late. I have work tomorrow. *You* have work tomorrow." He looked at his watch. "Later today."

"I'm taking some time off. For this." Lucy sighed. "You make sense. It pisses me off, but you're right. I'm exhausted. Mostly from the adrenaline, I expect. And the stress." She retrieved a set of keys from her pocket and handed them to Davie. "Hang on to these until Nick gets back." She unlocked her phone. "I'm calling a cab."

Davie looked at the keys, then took Lucy's hand and placed them in it. "Keep it. Drive it while he's not around. I'm sure he wouldn't mind."

She looked at them, then slowly closed her fist. "Okay. But I have a car."

"And so do I, and I only have one parking space. Better with you." He crossed his arms, closing off any chance of getting the keys back. "So are we reconvening here, or," he looked around his small apartment, "is your place bigger?"

"Do you have a job you need to be at?" Lucy slipped the keys into her pocket.

Davie shook his head. "Well, yes. But I'm taking time off also."

"My place is at least twice as big as this." She typed on her phone. "I've just sent you my address. 8:00 a.m.?

"Closer to nine. I'll bring coffee."

"Don't bother. I've got a machine."

Bobby looked back and forth between the two of

them. "I will *not* be taking time. This is on you two. I was moral support for Lucy, and it looks like that's not needed anymore. Drop me at my place on the way, okay, Luce?"

Nick stared at the ceiling. The guest bedroom had an ensuite, and the bedroom itself was almost as large as his apartment.

It was a sparsely decorated room. A few framed photographs adorned the wall. One was a large sailboat, its spinnaker in full puff. Another photo was the sun rising over Bondi. He knew that view. No way in hell he'd get on a sailboat. Only if absolutely necessary.

He reached over to the bedside table and tilted his phone. It displayed 2:13. He yawned but couldn't manage to sleep. "Jesus."

He got out of bed and pulled on the supplied bathrobe. He padded to the window. Checked the frame for latches and wasn't surprised there were none. He was on the 43rd floor. Insurance companies didn't like windows this far up in the air to be opened.

He tested the bedroom door. It was unlocked and swung open silently. The curtains on the wall of windows were open, casting blue city lights across the floor. He padded into the kitchen and opened the fridge, squinting at the sudden bright light. He grabbed a couple of beers and closed the door. Rustled around the kitchen until he found a large bag of salt and vinegar potato chips. He took the bag and the two beers into the lounge room, turned a chair to point to the view out the window, and sat. He fished his phone out of his pocket and scanned to see if he could pick up public Wi-Fi signals.

None. The only network picked up by his phone was a secured Wi-Fi signal called 'Waterfall'.

"The windows must screen radio signals." He looked around to make sure he didn't have an audience. His phone didn't have a SIM card, but phones without SIM cards could still call emergency numbers as long as they were in range of any carrier's tower.

He dialled 0-0-0 and pressed send.

And got three tones, indicating a lack of coverage.

"We thought of that, mate."

Nick twisted in his chair and nodded at Reg. "Of course you did." He picked the second beer from the floor and held it out. "Join me?"

"I need my sleep. So do you. Don't do anything stupid."

"Way too late for that." He looked out the window. "No chance of throwing a chair through it?"

"None." Reg retreated to wherever it was he slept.

Nick watched him leave. He sighed. "Okay." He crunched on a potato chip. He carefully looked at the corners of the room. He spotted a fisheye lens security camera in a corner. Raised his beer and saluted it. "Do your best, Davie," he said under his breath.

Chapter Five

"This is a nice place. How old are you?" Davie held up his hands. "Sorry, I didn't mean that the way you think. You've got a nice condo in an expensive area of town, and you seem kind of young."

"I'm twenty-eight. I'm smart with my money. Let's not talk about this again."

The condo was two-story, on the third and fourth floors of the complex. The lounge room looked onto a balcony overlooking a courtyard in the back. A small gas barbecue and a patio table with four chairs filled most of the balcony's space.

Davie slid the glass door open and stepped onto the balcony. He placed his laptop case on the table and pulled out a chair. "Nice place, though. Can't deny that."

Lucy joined him with two cups of coffee. "Black, right?"

"Thanks." He opened his laptop and navigated to a 'find my device' page.

"No, that's not going to work. The big guy took his SIM card, remember?" Lucy pulled out a chair and sat beside him. "What about the vehicle registration?"

"In a minute. Or three. If the phone tried to connect to a public Wi-Fi network, I might get a location."

"That's your field." She leaned her elbows on the table and sipped her coffee. "But if he was on a public network, wouldn't he have messaged you by now?"

"True, true. Hoping he kept his wits about him, though and at least tried." He tapped a couple of keys, and a map of the Sydney CBD filled his screen. Three blue dots appeared, one on the Cahill

Expressway, one on Bridge Street and one at the intersection of George and Margret Streets, in that chronological order.

Davie pointed at the dot at the George and Margaret intersection. "That was at about 1:00 am. Last location. He's around there somewhere."

"The rego."

"That's next." He switched to the corporate registration tab and started following the trail from Waterfall Properties.

Lucy frowned in thought for a second, then disappeared, returning a minute later with her own laptop. "I've got an idea."

"Sure," said Davie absent-mindedly. "This shell game of companies is intricate. Must be a tax dodge."

"Waterfront Properties, right?"

Davie nodded. "Owned by Waterfall Properties, which is owned by Puddle Jump Industries, and I'm still digging."

"Good luck." She glanced at him and smiled. "I've got an idea." She opened the same business registry site and checked for all properties in the Sydney CBD owned by Waterfront Properties. She copied the list to a blank document and then checked for all owned by Waterfall Properties. There were two. She copied those to the same document, and then one-by-one plotted the addresses on a map.

She glanced at Davie, who had been watching. She spun her laptop to face him. "Any of your dots line up with my dots?"

The laptop screens were side-by-side. Davie's glance flitted between them, then he used both index fingers to point at each laptop. "You've got a property at this address, half a block from the last ping location. Can you get more info?"

Lucy spun her laptop back and cross-checked the location Davie was pointing at against her list. "One of the two Waterfall properties." She opened the details from the Business Registry. "Three-storey penthouse suite. Private lift, private pool on the roof." She snorted. "More money than necessary."

"Smart. Hadn't thought of that. That's probably the 'where', I'll keep digging and find the 'who'."

Lucy closed her computer and stood. She reached over to Davie's laptop and closed his also. "We know the 'where', so we sit outside the 'where' until we see Nick, right?"

Davie grimaced and scratched behind his ear. "I'm the computer guy. Not the field guy." He lifted his laptop lid only to have Lucy push it back closed.

He sighed. "Okay, fine. You win." He swallowed a mouthful of coffee. "This didn't even get a chance to cool off."

"Pack it up. Let's go."

"Hang on a sec. Can you mirror your phone to your TV?"

"Of course." She crossed her arms. "Why?"

"Get a map up for that building and put it on the wall."

She narrowed her eyes. "I think you mean get a map up, *please*." She unlocked her phone, mirrored to the television and opened a mapping program. She panned, pinched, and zoomed until the building on the east side of the Sydney CBD was centred on the screen. "Okay. Now what?"

"We need to have even the briefest of plans before we run out there." He walked closer to the television. "Can you show me the street view in front of that building?"

She did.

"Now, slowly pan a full 360 degrees."

"What are you looking for?" The entrance to the building was secure. They could see a metal detector manned by a uniformed guard just inside the glass walls. She slowly panned to the left.

"Oh, stop there. Look." Davie pointed. "A cafe."

"A place to park our butts and watch."

Davie nodded. "It's a start."

Nick stepped out of the shower and towelled off. The steam did little to take the edge off the hangover. He drank a lot of O'Shea's beer the night before and felt it.

He opened the door to the walk-in closet and stopped. It was filled with cargo shorts and golf shirts. "Jesus."

He pulled open one of the drawers. Ankle socks. He shook his head and opened the drawer beside it. Boxers. He sighed and got dressed.

He padded sock-foot into the kitchen.

Reg was pouring a cup of coffee. He held it out for Nick. "You're late."

"Didn't know there was a schedule."

"The boss's daughter is only in town for a few days. We have to find her. Today, if possible."

Nick put the coffee down, untouched. "I need a computer, my computer guy and a phone to do what real private investigators do. Investigate. Walking around where she walked almost twenty-four hours ago is a complete waste of time." He looked down at his cargo shorts. "And trust me when I say, the sooner I return to my real life, the happier I'll be."

"Then drink the coffee, and let's get going. Get copies of local CCTV. Talk to the shop owners. You know, P.I. stuff."

Nick stepped close to Reg and looked up at his chin. "You're telling me how to do my job?"

Reg gave him a light push away. "I am. We're leaving in five minutes. Are you coming willingly, or am I dragging you out by a leg?"

Lucy picked a table on the sidewalk patio and ordered iced coffee for both. "So this is what detective work is like?"

Davie shrugged. "It's usually Nick doing this. I told you, I'm the sitting-at-a-desk-using-the-computers guy." He sniffed and squinted up at the blue sky. "This beats the office, though."

Lucy peeled the paper off the straw, stabbed her

drink with the straw, and tore the wrapper into long, thin strips. "What do we do if we see him?"

"Huh." He sipped on his drink. "I hadn't thought much beyond us getting here. What are our options?"

"We grab him and run." She held up a hand and shook her head. "No, no. Stupid. Unlikely to be successful. We can slip him one of our phones. We should do that if the opportunity presents itself."

Davie looked at his phone, face down on the table. "I just got this." He looked around and spotted a convenience store. "Wait here."

He trotted across the street and bought a pre-paid phone with the minimum text and talk plan. He waited for traffic to thin out and trotted back to the cafe.

"Pre-pay. Good idea." Lucy shifted in her seat, leaning her elbows on the small cafe table. It wobbled a bit, and coffee slopped over the edge of Davie's glass and onto the table. "Oops. Sorry."

"No worries." Davie mopped up the spill with a

handful of napkins. He placed the pre-pay SIM on the table and opened the box. He slid the SIM into the phone while Lucy read the number off of the SIM packaging.

She entered the number into her phone and handed the card to Davie. "How much charge does it have?"

"The SIM or the phone?"

"The phone. We're not going to be placing many calls."

Davie nodded as he powered up the phone. "Yeah, I got the smallest call plan they offered." The phone beeped, and he looked at the display. "Cool. It's at 85%." He entered his phone number and called. Terminated the call on his phone and stored the number in his contacts as 'Burner'.

Lucy picked up the burner phone and added her number to its contacts and Davie's. "It's highly unlikely he'd remember our numbers," she said gently, placing the phone gently back on the table.

"Everyone just uses the numbers in their phone's contact list, right?"

"Yeah, probably. Nick's got a good memory, though." A beeping started across the street, and an amber light flashed above the target building's garage door. "Hey, check it out."

Lucy turned in her chair and watched with Davie. The tightly meshed garage door rattled as it slowly rolled up. She sighed. "We're wasting our time if he leaves in a vehicle."

"We're not very good at this," said Davie. "At least we can get photos."

"Might be nothing, mate. Give it a minute."

The door raised with frustrating slowness. As the sun started illuminating the interior, the nose of a red sports car eased out. The sunlight reflected off the windscreen, blinding Davie. He winced and held his hand up to block the reflection. The tyres chirped as the car pulled onto the street and accelerated around the first corner.

"Shit. I missed them. Was that Nick?"

Lucy handed him his phone and nodded. "The big guy behind the wheel is the one who grabbed me. Have a look."

He scrubbed the short video to the beginning and tapped the play icon. The video showed the car pulling out of the garage and turning left onto the street. He paused the video as the car was halfway through the turn. He could see the driver clearly, and just beyond him, in the passenger seat, a white male who looked like Nick. He zoomed as close as he could until the passenger's head filled most of the mobile phone's screen. He could see three-quarters of the passenger's face.

He tapped 'play' again until the car turned left at the next corner. The back rego was visible. He paused the video, zoomed in, and used his phone to take a picture of Lucy's screen.

"Send that video to me, *please*. That was him. We've got the place he was in and confirmation that this is where he is."

"Was," said Lucy. She tapped out a couple of commands, and Davie's phone chimed when it received the file.

Davie shook his head. "This is his base for whatever they have him doing." He looked around. "No reasonably priced hotels around here, and I work better at my place. Let's go. I've got another rego to analyse, and dozens of CCTV cameras are around here that I can probably hack."

"I'm hungry. Let's get some food to go."

Davie's stomach rumbled. "Now you've done it. He heard you." He patted his gut and sighed. "They'll be gone for more than a minute."

Nick caught a glance at two people sitting in the cafe across from the Waterfall building. It was just a glance. A split-second flash of an image of two people he knew very well. He twisted in the passenger' seat as the car rounded the corner. Saw

Lucy and Davie. Confirmed. "Well done, mate."

"What was that?" Reg shifted the manual transmission into third gear and pointed at the Sydney CBD.

"Muttering to myself. Where in the hell are we going?"

Chapter Six

Reg parked at a meter on Castlereagh near Martin Place, less than a block from where Terri had been seen on camera.

"How in the hell do you find parking spots in this city?" Nick got out of the car and stretched. "Tight fit."

Martin Place was a pedestrian mall. A local news studio was on one side at the top of the hill, with glass walls exposing the studio to passers-by. High-end shops were hawking expensive watches, exercise bikes that killed famous TV characters and over-priced 'camping' equipment mixed with overpriced food stalls.

And banks. Every major bank in Australia. And a

handful of small personal banking establishments. Nick stood in the middle of the pedestrian mall and turned. "What are we doing here?"

Reg slid a photo from his shirt pocket. "A picture of Terri. Go find out what she was doing."

Nick slowly reached for the photo. "Would have been easier to take my phone with me. That had a picture of what she looks like NOW."

"Too many public Wi-Fi signals out here. You're supposed to be off the grid."

"O'Shea is paranoid.

Reg shrugged. "He pays me to do what he says. And he says you're not supposed to be able to contact any of your friends or colleagues."

"The guy's a nut job." He held the photo up and studied it. "Her hair is different. Shorter in this."

"So the picture is a couple of years old. The face is the same."

"She was thinner on TV. How many years?"

Reg waggled his hand. "About three years ago."

Nick nodded and grunted. He continued studying the picture. "Not a bad-looking woman." He slid the photo into his pocket. "While I'm looking for Terri, where will you be?"

Reg started laughing. "Nice try, champ. I'm going to be glued to you. I'm not letting you out of my sight. O'Shea would have my balls."

"Great." He looked along the mall. "She passed in front of the camera over there, right?" Nick pointed past the news studio.

Reg shrugged. "You're the PI."

"Wanker." Nick walked up the mall to the news studio and took his bearings. He pointed to the cafe across the way. "She walked past there, heading downhill…to somewhere downhill." He looked to his right, uphill. "So she was coming from somewhere up there."

He walked up the hill. More of a trudge than a walk. The sun was high enough to reflect heat off the pavement. He got to the top of the hill, Reg tight on his heels. He turned and faced the length of the pedestrian mall that was Martin Place.

Reg stood beside him. "What do you see?"

Nick saw dozens of CCTV cameras. And there was no doubt that there were just as many, or more, inside the businesses. He'd have a full timeline of Terri's movements with a laptop, Davie and half an hour. "I need a laptop."

"No. O'Shea was clear. You'll have to use whatever he has at his apartment if you need a computer." He crossed his arms. "Did Philip Marlowe have a laptop?"

"What? Jesus. Marlowe wasn't real. And I'm not that kind of private detective. I need electronic access to things. Might as well cut Usain Bolt's Achilles tendons and make him run. I need a laptop. One with some serious grunt. I guarantee you that whatever the old guy has won't do the job."

Reg sighed. "Fine. I'll talk to him about it when we get back."

"I'll talk to him."

"So this was a waste of time? You won't try to track her movements, see where she came from?"

Nick turned around and motioned for Reg to do the same. Pointed at the Martin Place train station. "She got off the train and walked down Martin Place to do something. I—we—can spend a couple of hours showing her face to the shop owners, or I can get on a laptop and scroll through the CCTV video from the shops." He looked up at Reg. "I can do the latter on your boss's balcony with a beer. Maybe poolside. And you don't have to tag along like a minder."

"*Like* a minder?" Reg grunted. "I *am* your minder."

"Must feel demeaning." Nick started walking briskly down the mall. "Keep up."

The pedestrian crossing at Philip Street was green. Nick's brisk walk accelerated into a trot. The crowd was getting heavier. He crossed against the light at Castlereagh, now into a run. He heard Reg yelling something behind him. He didn't have to hear the words to know the intent.

Reg was big but not fast. Nick kept a good distance between himself and his pursuer, but he didn't have the stamina for a long race. Reg would catch him eventually. Halfway to Pitt Street, Nick cut hard to his left and ran into a shopping centre.

He jinked around a couple of corners inside and slowed to a walk. The sweat that had beaded on his head was cooling and uncomfortable. He took a deep breath and let it out slowly. He needed to call Davie.

He found the interactive directory and searched for electronics shops. It showed that there were four in the shopping centre. The closest was around the corner, just past a kiosk flogging freshly squeezed juice. He filled out the necessary paperwork and purchased a prepaid phone. He thanked the sales lady and exited the shop.

Straight into Reg.

"Hi." Reg plucked the phone from his hand.

"Shit."

"You made me run. This isn't a cardio day. You've completely fucked up my training schedule." He plucked the cardboard envelope with the prepaid SIM from Nick's other hand and grabbed him by the upper arm. "What in the hell were you trying to prove?"

Nick pulled his arm free. "I need a laptop."

"I said I'd talk to him, right? Let's go." He took Nick's arm again and walked him to the exit. "Run again, and I'll rip one of your legs off."

Nick's chuckle died in his throat when he saw the look on Reg's face.

Davie used the last bit of toasted Turkish to wipe up the yolk from the poached egg. He crumbled his napkin, stood to leave, and then froze, staring at the building across the street. "That was quick."

"What?" Lucy swivelled and saw the same red

sports car stop in front of the rising garage door. "Well. What does that mean?"

Davie shrugged. "Hard to tell. Didn't go far. It hasn't been more than," he looked at the time on his phone, "forty-five minutes."

"Maybe they forgot something."

Davie slowly sat. "I'm going to hang around a bit." He leaned down and slid his laptop from its case. "Maybe nurse a coffee for a bit."

Lucy also sat. Then stood. "Black coffee, right? I'll be right back."

"Back so soon?" O'Shea walked into the shallow end of his rooftop pool. A substantial gut overhung his board shorts. He nodded at the chairs at the pool's deep end and started a slow back crawl.

"I'm finished walking. I need a laptop. I can walk up and down the streets of the Sydney CBD for days before I find what I can in three hours with a laptop and internet access." He slowly walked along the pool's edge, keeping up with O'Shea. The fat Irishman was moving barely fast enough to keep him from sinking.

"So you convinced Reg to come back so you could make your case?" O'Shea slowed to a stop and paddled to the edge. He tried pulling himself out and reached up a hand for assistance. Nick just stared at him. O'Shea gave up and pulled himself along the edge back to the shallow end. Nick walked back along the edge with him.

Nick looked at Reg and smiled. "Yeah. I convinced him. We're here, right?"

"The little shit did a runner. Caught up to him coming out of an electronics store with a prepaid phone." Reg crossed his arms and scowled.

O'Shea raised his eyebrows. "You made him run? And you're still upright?" He pulled on a robe and held his hand out to Reg. "The phone."

Reg slid it out of his back pocket and handed it to O'Shea, who glanced at it and threw it in the pool.

"Fucking hell, mate. You owe me eighty bucks." Nick dropped into a chair. "You're hobbling me. I can't do what you want me to do, pretending I'm Philip Marlowe."

O'Shea jabbed a finger at Nick. "I told you, I'm not here. I can't let anyone know I'm in the country. I can't have a single bit of digital footprint even remotely attached to me. Is that too difficult for you to understand?" He shook his head. "You made Reg run? Damn."

"I can't do this job the way you want me to. Terri will be long gone when I finish walking the streets and talking to the proprietors."

O'Shea sniffed. "Very, very bad people are looking for me. I've created a trail that leads to Saint Croix. It'll keep them busy until they realise I'm not *there,* and there are hints I'm *here*." He coughed. "And then I've got about twelve hours to live. I need you to find my daughter."

Reg grabbed him by the shoulder. "You heard

him. Let's go."

Nick pulled his shoulder free. "I'm not finished with my pitch."

"Yes, you are." O'Shea pushed himself up out of his chair. "Reg, get back to work."

Nick danced out of the way of Reg's outstretched hand. "No, I'm not. I can access what I need to access remotely. I can even make it look like you're in Christiansted, sitting on the Wi-Fi at Shupe's"

O'Shea cracked a half smile. "You've been there?"

"On my bucket list. I hear the seaplane in from St. Thomas is a trip."

O'Shea held up his hand to stop Reg. He scratched his chin. "Anonymous, how?"

"Piece of piss. Half a dozen different easy ways to anonymise my surfing."

"Like?"

"VPNs, TOR," Nick grimaced. "It gets pretty technical."

"Three hours?"

"What?"

O'Shea sighed. "You said you could find in three hours online what would take days of shoe leather."

Nick nodded. "Maybe even weeks."

"How?"

He grimaced. "Again, it's fairly technical, but if I can access the security cameras in the shops, I can follow her movement from shop to shop, inside and out. Track her movement and most likely find out where she is."

"He's bullshitting, boss."

O'Shea waved Reg away. "Let him talk. If he can do what he says, I need to let him do it."

"But…"

"Fuck off, Reg."

Nick clamped down to keep from smiling. He had no idea how Davie accessed the CCTV cameras. For now, though, he only needed a laptop and some time. Davie would come through. "I can do it." He tried not to sound like Rob Schneider.

"Tell Reg what kind of laptop you need, and he'll get one."

Nick thought about that for a second. He wouldn't know a high-end machine from a paperweight, but, he thought, neither would they. "Okay. A new model with Wi-Fi, fastest processor they have, max out the RAM," he looked at Reg. "You getting this?"

Reg glowered.

He smiled. "Okay. The largest screen they've got, also. Best resolution possible if you want me to be able to pick out Terri's face in the footage." He looked at O'Shea. "Okay?"

"Go, Reg. Get him what he needs. Don't be long."

Nick smiled and waved at him as he stormed out.

"Hey, the car is leaving again."

He looked where she was pointing. "Only the big guy. No Nick."

"Is that good or bad?"

He shrugged. "Again, who knows? At least we know where Nick is at this very moment." He tapped a few more lines in the code he was writing and sat back. "This might work."

"What is it?"

"I wrote a quick and dirty program to scan through IP addresses looking for security cameras. Most of them are unsecured. Some of the more expensive ones have stored video." He pointed across the street. "There's one at the garage door, one at the front door and, dollars to doughnuts, dozens inside that building." He closed his laptop and slid it into its case.

"What are you doing?"

"It will take a couple of hours to run through the networks. I'm heading back to my place. You coming?"

Chapter Seven

"Mikhail Sidorov, what brings you to Australia?" The immigration officer scanned the Russian passport. No flags. The appropriate visa was in the system, and all required documents were on file. He added an entry stamp to an empty page. The immigration card was properly completed, and the signature matched that on the passport.

"It is a beautiful city. I have seen pictures. I want to visit some of your beautiful beaches. Like Bondi." Mikhail looked at the stamped passport, willing the immigration officer to return it.

The immigration officer looked at the man in front of him. The Russian was pale and looked soft with small, dark eyes and a shaved head. "You flew in from Los Angeles. Do you live in the USA now, or was that just a stopover?"

"I live in Miami. Stopped over in LA for a couple of days to meet up with some friends."

"Miami?" He shook his head. "Would have expected a bit more colour to your skin, mate."

"The sun is not good for my skin. I burn easily."

The immigration officer nodded. He closed the passport. "Buy and use sunscreen, mate. The sun here is a lot hotter than in America. And get yourself a hat. Are you travelling throughout Australia or just staying in Sydney?"

Mikhail shrugged. "I do not know at this point. My return ticket is in a couple of months. If I run out of beaches here, I may head to Queensland."

The passport was slid across the counter, and the immigration officer turned his attention to the next person in line, waving them forward.

Mikhail slid the passport into his back pocket and followed the signs to the baggage carousels. He turned on his mobile and scrolled through the contacts. Dialled the number he was looking for.

"Da?"

"Picking up luggage, Dimitri. Tell me you are here. I do not like to wait."

"*I* have been waiting for almost an hour. Hurry."

Mikhail terminated the call and crossed his arms, waiting for the bags to come out. With a whine and mechanical clunk, the carousel started moving. He'd planned on travelling with only carry-on luggage, but Petrovski, the man he worked for, reminded him that he was supposed to look like he was travelling to Australia on vacation. You don't go on vacation with a single carry-on bag.

Noisy, tired tourists flocked around the chain of suitcases trundling in an endless loop. He pushed through the crowd, ignoring the protests, and grabbed his bag off the conveyor. He wheeled it to customs, satisfactorily answered standard questions, and rolled his case to the arrivals area.

It didn't take him long to find his soon-to-be partner in crime. Dimitri Popov was almost 2 metres tall and muscular. He had short brown hair and a few days' worth of stubble. He was standing, leaning against a pillar, engrossed in something on his phone.

Mikhail skirted the edge of the crowd waiting for incoming travellers and came up behind him. He stuck a finger in the larger man's back. "Your money or your life."

Dimitri raised his hands. "I work for Petrovski. I have no money nor life." He slid his phone into his back pocket and turned, smiling. "Long time no see, Mikkie."

"You fucking call me that again, I will hang you with your guts." Mikhail smiled and slapped his friend on the shoulder. "You have gotten bigger."

Dimitri involuntarily flexed his pecs. "Good food." He nodded toward the exit. "Let's get the hell out of here. We've got a job with a very tight timeline."

"You drove?"

"Yeah. We'll talk on the way."

Dimitri navigated out of the parking garage, paid the exorbitant amount at the exit and accelerated onto the motorway west. "What do you know about the job?"

"Find some *devushka*, get rid of her." Mikhail watched the trees go by the window. "Where are the kangaroos?"

The trees thinned to a golf course. "We're in the city, mate. A big city."

"Fair enough. I want to see some before we leave. What's the deal with this - this chick we are supposed to get rid of?"

Dimitri drove in silence for a few minutes. They were in stop-and-go traffic. He adjusted the air conditioning a few degrees cooler. "What were you told?"

"Nothing. Meet you at the airport, help you find someone, kill her. Why do we need two people to kill one woman?"

Dimitri sighed. "This 'one woman' is Terri O'Shea." He glanced at Mikhail. "You know the name? You know the significance?"

His passenger nodded. "Petrovski told me. That fat Irish fuck. Money laundering. He disappeared with something like ten million American dollars back in the day." He sat up straighter in his seat. "Do we get the money back from them? Hey, is the father in Australia also? Last time I heard, he was in the Caribbean somewhere. Too many little islands, too fucking hot."

"You going to talk this much on the job?"

Mikhail looked interested now. "Maybe we get her to tell us where the money is before we get rid of her. Where are we going?"

"Our place. West of the city. Regroup, and get yourself a place to stay. Get some armaments. You hungry?"

"They served breakfast on the flight. I am good for now."

Dimitri shook his head. "You're too skinny. Need to beef you up."

"Get me a knife. I do not need muscles, just speed."

He nodded. They sat in silence, traffic finally moving at speed on the M5 West. He took the exit at the A6 and travelled north. "We're almost there. Remember, you're just a visitor here. Behave, okay?"

Mikhail rolled his shoulders. "Absolutely. Just a tourist." He had a thought and stiffened. "The people do not know why I am here, correct?"

"Other than the boss. You're my cousin from America. Visiting. That's all they need to know." He pulled the car up to a chain-link gate. He nodded to the man behind it and waited while it slowly rolled open.

"Not much security."

Dimitri looked at the residential neighbourhood. "This is a local social club. Fully legit. The boss has an office in the back. Too much security gets too much attention. There's enough here." He pointed at the cameras above the gate and on the building. "We have eyes. Everywhere."

He pulled the car into the parking area behind a low, flat building and led him in.

The building was flooded with aromas that Mikhail recognised. his stomach started rumbling.

"I thought you weren't hungry.

"Is that *pelmeni*?" He veered off the path Dimitri was leading him into a large kitchen. Three middle-aged women sat at a long table, placing small piles of savoury minced meats on thin pastry disks and pinching them closed. A heated oven made the room almost unbearably hot. He looked in the glass door at the tray of cooking pastries and smiled. The women smiled back at him and continued talking among themselves in Russian.

"Babushkas, what is the occasion?"

Dimitri grabbed him by the arm and steered him back on track. "Leave them be. They've got a lot to do before this evening."

"Party tonight?"

"Season kick-off dinner for a local football club. We have work to do. The girl is a higher priority."

Mikhail took one last look over his shoulder at the receding kitchen. "Get them to save some for me. You were not clear earlier. Is the old man in Australia too?"

"O'Shea?" Dimitri shook his head. "There's been no indication." He bared his teeth. "And trust me, Petrovski has been looking for him for a long time. If there were the slightest stench of that fat arsehole in this country, he would have tasked a team."

Mikhail nodded. "So the daughter is to draw him out."

Dimitri shook his head. "He's not here. She's the

first sign of anyone from that family in three years. Since they failed to make the meeting and disappeared with the money." He opened the door to an office and stood to one side, ushering Mikhail in.

It was a plain office. Cheap wood panelling covered three walls. On the right, rendered brick with a cracked open louvred window. A grizzled man sat behind a desk facing the door. He had a lot of mileage on him. An unlit cigar jutted out of the corner of his mouth as he worked on a laptop. Grey stubble covered his face.

He looked up as the door opened. "You've arrived. Good flight?"

Dimitri pointed Mikhail to a chair and sat beside him, across from the old man. "Mikhail, this is Konstantin. Your host for the duration."

"Call me Kon." He stood and held out his hand. "Welcome to Sydney."

Mikhail rose to shake his hand. "Good to meet you, Kon. I need weapons and some information."

"Good, good. Right to business." Kon sat. "As you probably know, getting guns in this country isn't as easy as in your adopted country. But it's not impossible. You may not have as much selection as you're used to."

"No guns." Mikhail leaned forward in his chair. "But I want to know what knives you can get for me."

Kon's laugh sounded like thunder in a wooden cask. "Any kind of knife you want." He coughed, put his chewed-up cigar in an ashtray and wiped his mouth. "Knives, not a problem. What else do you need?"

"How do you know this bitch is in the country?"

"Your boss told me he was, to start with." Kon tapped a couple of commands on his laptop and spun it around so Dimitri and Mikhail could see the screen. He reached around and poked the space bar, starting a video. "And this was on television. Just happened to be watching. Normally don't."

Mikhail squinted as he sat forward. He pointed at the screen. "Does not look at all like her." He leaned back in his chair. "And you think she would be stupid enough to be a television reporter?" He stood and closed the laptop lid. "Waste of my time. Shame. I was looking forward to this. Dimitri, I need a car and directions to a casino."

"Sit." Kon stood and opened the laptop. "Not the reporter, you stupid." He turned the laptop back toward him, scrolled through the video to where Terri was looking left and paused the image. He turned the laptop back to face his visitors. "Her. In behind. That's her." He pulled a piece of paper from the printer on his desk. The screen grab from the video, at roughly the same time as he was showing on the laptop, was positioned beside a photo of Terri O'Shea from years ago. The similarity was undeniable."

Mikhail nodded. "I apologise for my hastiness. Where and when was this?"

"Two days ago in Martin Place. I sent this screen grab to Petrovski at his place in Miami as soon as I saw it. I am assuming he put you on a flight almost immediately after."

"The timing is about right. Where is this Martin Place?"

"Get a shower, some food in you, and we'll go immediately after." Kon pressed a button on his desk, and one of the three cooks opened the door. "Natalya, show Mikhail where his room is and where the showers are." He smiled. "And maybe some pelmeni and sour cream. Dimitri, you wait here."

Mikhail followed Natalya to the small room. It was at the back of the building, smaller than a motel room, and outfitted very much the same as one on the lower end of the budget.

"The bathroom with showers is here." She pushed open a door. Old but clean fittings. "Lock the door while you are in there, or maybe someone will walk in on you." She looked at Mikhail's thin arms. "I will get you some *pelmeni*. Come into the kitchen."

Kon waited until the door was closed. "This guy, he's good?"

Dimitri nodded. "He has me thinking. Petrovski's order was to eliminate her as punishment for the theft. I think we hold her, draw out her old man, get the money back, and eliminate both of them."

"The old man is in the Caribbean somewhere. We shouldn't piss off Petrovski."

"We'll have the girl. It's a no-risk scenario with a huge upside. Can you imagine how grateful he'll be when we have proof of death for both of them *and* the money?"

Kon thought about that. He wanted to get out of Australia and back to the US. He nodded. "Make sure your whippet friend doesn't kill her by mistake. I sense he's not very stable."

"First we have to find out where she is. You'll tell Petrovski?"

Kon re-inserted his cigar in his mouth. He looked at his watch. "Later. Let's go. We'll hit the CBD first."

Chapter Eight

She was in a youth hostel. Terri O'Shea owned a condo in Hong Kong, a chalet in the Swiss Alps and a beach house in Costa Rica. Shell companies owned them, but if anyone good at their job dug deep enough through the shells and trusts, they'd find her fingerprints on them.

Now she was one of six in a single room, in three bunkbeds in a hostel in the Sydney CBD. Anonymity came at a price.

She paid cash wherever she could and with a prepaid credit card when cash wasn't an option, an occurrence more frequent than expected.

By the end of the week, she'd be gone. A couple of months in Costa Rica de-stressing was on the menu.

There was a bank account she set up in Sydney six years ago. Many shells deep. Three years ago, she deposited ten million American dollars in $100 bills within the walls of that bank. Most of it was going to someone else, but a healthy chunk would finance a break from the rough and tumble world of money laundering.

But first, she had to get to the money.

She removed her personal effects from the hostel locker and stepped out into the harsh sunlight. She checked the map on her phone, oriented herself and walked north toward the waterfront. It was three hours before the bank appointment, and she needed to see the Sydney Opera House.

That day, three years ago, was a frenetic, panicked experience. This time, she had some time to explore.

She saw them almost a block into the four-block walk to the waterfront. She had stopped to look at a shoe display in the window of a shop on George

Street. They were nice shoes. As she lingered at the display, realising that this wasn't the time or place to fork over thousands of dollars for a pair of shoes, she saw him in the reflection on the window.

It was Mikhail Siderov. He was six years older, but it was him. The hair on the back of her neck raised. He was walking with a giant of a man, muscles on muscles, but it was Mikhail who scared her. She'd seen what he could do with a knife. And she'd been told he really enjoyed it. She ducked into the shop and watched them through the window. It didn't look like they saw her.

"May I help you?"

Terri turned to a saleswoman looking her up and down. "Just browsing."

Disdain oozed from the saleswoman's pores. "I doubt you could afford anything in our shop." She sniffed. "I suggest you try Target."

Terri looked down at her shorts, T-shirt and flip-flops. "Wow. I've walked into a 'Pretty Woman' scenario." She smiled at the woman. "I could buy everything in this shop many times over. Not really here for that, though. Avoiding an abusive ex. Saw him across the street. Give me a few minutes, and I'll remove my disgusting self from your hallowed shop."

The saleswoman seemed a little bit mollified. Not completely okay with the tramp in her store, but a little bit more accommodating. "Okay. A couple of minutes. No more." Her smile was brittle.

"You're a peach." Terri turned back to the window. The Russian and his giant friend were still walking north on George Street, on the opposite side, oblivious to her attention. They reached a sporting goods store, stopped and talked briefly, and then entered the shop.

Terri exhaled.

"Everything okay?"

She pushed past the saleswoman and headed to the back of the store. "There's a back way out, right?"

The woman ran in front of her and blocked her way. "If you go out that way, it'll trigger an alarm. The firies will be here in minutes, and I'll have a bill to pay if there's no fire." She saw the look in Terri's eyes. "No, I am not starting a fire."

"How much?"

"What?"

"For the false fire alarm. How much?"

The clerk shifted her weight. "Erm, I actually don't know."

Terri fished two bills from her back pocket and dropped them on the floor. "That'll have to do." She moved the clerk out of the way and hit the push-bar on the back door.

There was no alarm. Unless it was silent, which defeated the purpose of an alarm. She oriented herself and walked around to the front of the shop. She set her jaw and stepped back onto the street.

The sporting goods store was beside an arcade - a

narrow lane through the shops to the next street. Small boutiques lined either side of the arcade. If Mikhail and his friend continued in the direction they were travelling after they left the shop, they would walk right past it.

Terri trotted across the busy street, dodging traffic to get to the other side as quickly as safely possible. She would watch them looking for her.

And there was no way Mikhail was on this side of the planet if he wasn't looking for her. She was Number One on Petrovski's very own Most Wanted list.

The waterfront could wait.

"Why are we in here, Mikhail?" Dimitri picked a ball cap off the rack, tried it on and checked himself in the mirror. "You looking for a better knife?"

"I will see what is here. I am happy with what you provided, but maybe there is something better. I need to get some stuffy koalas, kangaroos. That sort of thing. I will be a dead man if I do not return with *something*."

"Then maybe we are in the wrong place."

Mikhail headed toward the back of the shop. "No, there are some here."

Terri stood in the arcade shadows. Mikhail would recognise her, of that she had no doubt. It had been six years, but the circumstances were such that she would never forget him, and she doubted he would ever forget her. A baseball cap and a pair of sunglasses wouldn't do the trick.

They knew she was in the city. She had no idea how they knew, but they knew. She'd take the game to them.

Mikhail stood at the checkout counter with a handful of stuffed animals. He placed them on the glass-topped counter and looked at the knives on display under glass. He pointed. "And that one. The knife for…" He looked at Dimitri. "The fish one."

"I thought you said… Never mind." Dimitri took out his wallet. "Get the filleting knife, please?" He handed over cash. The proprietor bagged the three stuffed animals and the knife and handed them to Dimitri, who handed them to Mikhail. "I'm not carrying this shit."

"Not a problem, mate." Mikhail grinned. "Why are we walking all the way? We have less than a week to find this bitch."

Terri watched Mikhail walk past the arcade with the associate. She heard Mikhail say they had less than a week to find the bitch. She waited a few seconds, stepped out onto George Street, and followed at a discrete distance. They knew she was only in town for a short time. This was worse than she thought. There was a leak. She shook her head. "Not a problem for now," she muttered.

The two Russians were about fifteen to twenty

metres ahead of her. Too far away to hear their conversation but close enough to see the interaction between them. While he was the smaller of the two, Mikhail was obviously the boss.

She upped her pace until she was close enough to overhear them.

"No, really, Dimitri. Why are we walking?" Mikhail reached into the plastic carry bag and extracted a long, slender box. He pushed the carry bag into his friend's hands. "Hold this."

He flipped open the end of the box, upended it, and slid a sheathed knife into his hand. He tossed the box on the sidewalk and unsheathed the knife.

Terri dipped and picked up the box. It was a fish filleting knife. Nine-inch steel blade, five-inch bone handle with a leather sheath. She swallowed. She tossed the box into a trash bin on the street and caught up to them again.

Dimitri was looking around, so Terri ducked her head.

"Mate, you've got to put that knife away. You're getting too much attention."

Mikhail tested the edge with the ball of his thumb. "Not much good for anything but stabbing right now, *mate*. I will need to sharpen." He dragged his thumb across the blade and slid it back into its sheath. He slipped the knife into his back pocket and took the bag back from Dimitri. "You did not tell me. Why all the walking? It is hot in this fucking country."

"This lady, she was walking down Martin Place. Looked in a hurry. There's a train station at the top of that pedestrian mall. She probably got off the train there."

"She would rent a car."

"No. She is in and out. She doesn't want anyone to know she's here. She's going to be using cash. Day tickets on trains, youth hostels, the kinds of places where you don't need a credit card or ID. Or at least where ID won't be scrutinised."

Terri shook her head. She slowed to a stop and let

them get further ahead of her. No chance of tourism now. She wasn't afraid of a fight, but it would be stupid to walk into one.

Especially against a psycho with better-than-average knife skills.

She ducked into a coffee shop and ordered a latte and a muffin. Two hours to kill and nowhere to go.

Dimitri checked the map on his phone. He pointed ahead and to the left. "Youth hostel across the street."

"These hostels, they are for the backpackers?"

"Yeah." He dodged traffic crossing the street. They stopped at the entrance. "I'll talk. Your accent is going to freak them out."

"I do not have an accent, mate."

"Yes, you do, comrade." Dimitri smiled and pushed open the front door. He walked past the front desk, ignoring the young man managing the facility who was scrambling to stop him. He stopped when he saw the menacing look on Mikhail's face.

Dimitri found the common room where half a dozen young backpackers puttered, charging phones, updating blogs and whatever else idealistic young international travellers do on downtime. He opened the picture of Terri on his phone, expanded it to fill the screen, and held it up in front of him. "Hey, all of you. $100 dollars, cash for *any*one who can tell me where and when they saw this woman."

A redheaded man with a scraggly rusty beard stepped forward and looked closer. "Why?"

"Why what?"

"Why are you trying to find her?"

Mikhail stepped forward beside Dimitri.

Dimitri held his hand out to stop him. "It's okay, Mikhail. I've got this. I am trying to find this young lady because we received a message from her stating she needed help, and then she dropped off the grid. We're concerned for her well-being."

"Who is she to you?"

Dimitri glanced at Mikhail and slightly shook his head. "She's our boss's daughter. She arrived here yesterday from Miami and planned on travelling through Australia. Last night, though, she sent a short text message saying she was in trouble. Her last phone location was here." He looked at each of the backpackers. "Anyone?"

Five of the six shook their head and returned to their puttering. The sixth, a tanned young woman from somewhere in South America, approached and held out her hand. "The phone, please."

She took it from Dimitri and looked at Terri's picture. Squinted and held the phone at arm's length. She shook her head and handed it back.

"You haven't seen her, either?" Dimitri locked his phone and slid it into his pocket. "You haven't seen her?"

"I *have* seen her. This morning. She left here about an hour ago. Didn't seem to be in distress at all. Didn't seem to be American. Seemed to have an

Irish accent."

Dimitri leaned forward. "And your name is?"

"None of your business." She hoisted a backpack onto her shoulder and strode out of the room.

"I can follow her and make her talk." Mikhail slid his hand into his pocket and grabbed the bone handle of the filleting knife. "It would be my pleasure."

"No, not necessary. The bitch was around here somewhere, and recently. We have a starting point. Let's get out of here before the kid up front calls the police."

Chapter Nine

"What's the deal with the laptop, Reg?"

Reg had parked the car at a meter on a cross street near George Street. They got out and stood on the sidewalk in front of the Apple Store.

Nick looked in the window. "We picking up a Mac? I don't mind Macs. But I think I can do a better job with a PC."

"You're not getting a Mac. The laptop will be delivered later today. In the meantime," he pointed at Nick's feet, "You'll be using those."

Nick shook his head. "Philip Marlowe to the rescue." He unlocked his phone and found Terri's picture. "Let's go."

"What's the plan? Lots of stores in the city. Not a

lot of time.”

“She’s in town for the week, right?”

Reg nodded. “Less, or so O’Shea thinks.”

“And we can’t find her on any air manifest, rental car agency to hotel. No credit card ”

“Correct.”

“So she’s staying under the radar. Cash only. Fine for taxis and trains, not so fine for accommodations. She’s probably staying at cheap motels or youth hostels. We start checking those.”

“Maybe you’re not an idiot after all.” Reg unlocked his phone and pulled up the map app. “Four hostels in the CBD. None of the motels around here would take a check-in without ID.”

“Hostels it is. Lead the way.” He pulled his T-shirt from his chest. “How far? It’s bloody hot.”

“Three and a half blocks. Too hot for you to run?”

Nick sighed. “Yeah, I’m in this for the long haul. Get me the laptop, and it’ll be a lot quicker. And cooler. We could sit by the pool and finish this. With a beer or two."

"Keep walking."

They were at a cross street, south of where they parked, still two and a half blocks from their destination. "Can't." Nick pointed at the lights. "Red light."

"Cross it."

"Let me cool off a bit. I've got no interest in a jaywalking ticket."

A couple of people pushed past them and crossed against the light.

Reg pointed. "Fuck's sake, mate. Follow them. No cops around."

Two men approached from the other direction. They didn't slow as they crossed the street against the light. The larger of the two shoulder-barged Reg, and Nick stepped out of the way of the smaller man who yelled, "*Dvigaysya, pridurok.*"

Nick turned and watched them walk away. "Dicks."

Reg pulled him back around. "Green light now. March."

"What the hell did that guy say?" Nick stepped onto the street and pulled up short to avoid getting hit broadside by a bike messenger. "More dicks."

"It was something Slavic. Doesn't matter. Keep walking."

"Keep your eyes out. She's around here somewhere." He glanced at Reg, who was paying attention to the map on his phone. "What do we do when we find her? Do you have a burlap bag on you that we can stuff her in? Duct tape her mouth?"

"Jesus. We want to talk to her."

"O'Shea wants more than that, Reggie. I'm sure of that."

Reg stopped him and got in his face. "We just want to talk to her. And so help me god, if you call me Reggie again, I'll rip your arms off and shove them up your arse."

Nick nodded. "Classy. Okay. Just talking to her.

Excellent. Are we there yet?"

"You're not married, are you?" Asked Reg.

"No. Why?"

"I can't think of anyone who would put up with your horseshit."

Nick chuckled. "Just the next block ahead. This is the closest hostel?"

Reg panned the zoomed map on his phone. "Yeah. There's another one on Clarence and one further down George."

"Only three. That's good."

"You being sarcastic?"

Nick glanced at Reg. "No. Serious. High probability that she's staying at a hostel. Only three to check gets us out of the heat all that much faster."

Lucy made herself comfortable on Davie's sofa. "How's it going?"

Davie was in his recliner, reclined. He tapped a couple of keys, and his laptop screen mirrored on his television. "It's going pretty good." He tapped a couple more keys, and a map of Sydney's CBD was displayed on the wall. A wave of over a hundred blue dots spread across the map. "All the CCTV cameras I could find and access."

"A lot of videos to troll through."

He tapped a key, and a picture of Nick popped up in the corner. "There are some good facial recognition APIs out there. Stuck Nick's face in the algorithm and," he tapped a key again, "we have this." A speckle of almost a dozen blue dots turned green. "Confirmed sightings over the past twenty-four hours.

Lucy was leaning forward now. "You can do this?"

"I did this."

"So, where is he?"

Davie hovered the mouse over successive green dots until he found one on George Street with the most current time. He backed up to the one with the next earliest time. "He's heading south on George Street."

"Show me."

He double-clicked the green dot, popping up a video window. It was from the entrance of a shop on George Street facing east, across the street. The video started as Nick and the big guy entered the frame from the left. They walked up to an intersection and stopped, the big guy looking at his phone.

"Yeah. That's him."

They watched Nick and the big guy talk for a few minutes, pedestrians pushing past them.

Lucy pointed at the screen. "Anything more current than this?"

Davie looked at the time stamp and shook his head. "This was five minutes ago. I'm still trawling through footage, but this is the most current."

She stood. "Okay. That's where we're going. We're only about ten minutes away. We'll start further south on George Street and hope to intercept him."

He closed his laptop and pushed himself out of the chair. "Then we better get moving."

Nick pushed open the hostel door and entered. A young man was sitting at the front desk. He looked up, and a wary look crossed his face. "You're not backpackers. What can I do for you?"

"My name is Nick Harding. I'm a private investigator looking for this woman," he held out his phone, "on behalf of her father."

The man looked at the phone, then at Reg. "Who's the big guy?"

Reg leaned on the counter. "I'm his bodyguard." He pointed at the phone. "You seen her?"

"Maybe. I see many people." He gestured with his thumb toward the back of the property. "Try the common room. You might get more info there."

"Thanks, mate." Nick tapped the countertop and

headed to the back.

He held up his phone as he entered. "Good morning."

Reg leaned close. "It's afternoon, mate."

"Good afternoon. I'm hoping you can help. I'm a private investigator. My name is Nick Harding. I'm looking for this woman on behalf of her father. Her name is Terri O'Shea, but she might be travelling under another name. Have any of you seen her?"

A young, blonde, tanned woman in cut-off jeans shorts and a bikini top walked up to Nick. "Why aren't the police involved if she's a missing person?"

"I would have to ask the father. I'm just doing what my client asked."

The blonde snorted. "Bullshit."

Nick shrugged. "It is what it is. Have you seen her?"

"Why in the hell should I tell you?"

"Good faith?" Nick watched her as she left. "Or not."

A redhead with a wispy rust-coloured beard sauntered up and took his ear pods out. "You working with the other guys?"

"Just us." Nick frowned. "What other guys?"

"So, no?"

"What's your name?"

"Ian." Ian crossed his arms and held Nick's gaze. "Weird."

"What? What's weird?"

Ian shook his head. "Two other guys showed up about half an hour ago. Asking the same question." He pulled the phone closer. "Same picture." He smiled. "They didn't tell us her name, but they were doing the same thing, holding up their phone like it was The Breakfast Club or something. Told us they were looking for her on behalf of her father. Some bullshit about her texting him that she was in trouble and then going off the grid."

Nick looked at Reg, then back at Ian. "What did they look like?"

"Big guy, a bit bigger than this unit, who did all he talking. And a little, pale, creepy, scary mother fucker who I wouldn't trust as far as I could spit."

"Shit." Nick looked at Reg. "Any idea about this?"

Reg looked away. "No."

Nick continued to stare at him for a few moments. "Bullshit." He turned back to Ian. "Did you see her?" He pulled his PI identification from his back pocket. "I'm really a private investigator."

Ian took the ID and examined it. He looked at Nick, then back at the ID. "Yeah, she was here. Left this morning. About an hour and a half ago. She didn't seem to be in any distress. Focussed, on a quest of some sort, but not distressed." He paused. "And a little bit older than the typical backpacker, if I'm honest."

"Thanks. Do you know which way she went?"

Ian handed the ID back. "Nope. Sorry. She exited and that's the last I saw of her."

"Thanks for your help. Reg, let's go."

They stood on the sidewalk outside the hostel.

"Are you thinking what I'm thinking?" asked Nick.

"I'm thinking my balls are sticking to my thigh, and I'm tired of running around in this fucking heat."

"Not even close. We ran into those two guys. The two Ian mentioned." Nick looked back up the street from whence they had just come. "Why are they looking for her?"

"Don't care." Reg headed back from where they came.

"I do. What's going on?"

Reg pointed. "If they're looking for her and they went that way, we're going the same way."

"What do you know about them?"

Reg glanced at him and kept walking.

Nick skipped ahead and got in front of him, blocking his progress. He faced him, arms crossed. "Spill it."

"Get walking."

He stood his ground. "Reg, mate, what do you know about two foreign, nasty-looking blokes looking for the same O'Shea we're looking for? Did the old man hire me as back up? He hired the other two first?"

Reg leaned down, face-to-face with Nick. "I don't know who they are. I don't know why they're looking for Terri. I have no who they are, and it has zero relevance to what we are doing." He sighed. "Look, *mate*, I don't like this either. They sounded Russian. Maybe Ukrainian. I'm not good enough with languages to differentiate. Terri is way under the radar. This is going to be a lot harder than I thought."

"You have *any* idea why she's in town?"

Reg scratched his jaw, grimaced and shook his head. "I've got some ideas, but I don't know for sure."

"So, like I said, spill."

He shook his head. "I'll talk to the old guy first.

Let's keep walking."

"No. No fucking way. We're going back to O'Shea and I'm waiting until I get the equipment I need."

Chapter Ten

"Jesus, mate. What's your hurry?" Reg lengthened his stride to keep pace with Nick. "It's too hot for this."

Nick stopped. Reg almost ran into the back of him. "Too hot? Yeah. It's too hot." He turned to face Reg. "This whole thing is bullshit. My hands are tied. I don't have the access I need, and I don't have my IT support. I usually have IT support." He took a breath and plucked his shirt from his sweating chest. "Truth is, I've never resolved a case without my IT support."

Reg turned him around and shoved him in the middle of his back. "March. You'll get your computer, but you're not getting your IT support.

She cute?”

Nick stumbled forward. He turned back again. “Look, Reg. You’re a big unit. I doubt I’d win a fair fight.” He shook his head. “But I don't fight fair if I’m in a fight. Shove me again and find out.”

Reg laughed. “Wouldn’t fight someone small like you. Imagine how embarrassed I’d be if you won.” He pointed south on George Street. “Walk.”

The sidewalk was crowded with mid-day pedestrian traffic. Nick weaved his way through, checking out gaps in the middle distance. He almost missed them.

He saw Lucy’s red hair first. She walked beside Davie, both heading his way. “Fuck.”

“What?”

“I need Davie’s help.” He kept his eyes on the approaching pair. They were half a block away and hadn’t seen him yet. “You ever met Davie?”

Reg shook his head. “No.”

Nick breathed a sigh of relief.

"But I've seen his picture. Why?"

"Fuck. Nothing. I need his hacking skills." He hoped telepathy worked. They were getting closer.

"Unlucky."

"Right." Nick slowed his walk, keeping his eyes drilled into Lucy's. He was a quarter of a block away when she finally caught his eyes. She opened her mouth, and he shook his head, then glanced at Reg. She paled and pulled Davie into a storefront. Nick smiled at the surprise on Davie's face and picked up the pace.

He glanced in the shop window as they passed. Davie was holding his phone against the shop window. *'Stop for lunch'* was displayed on the phone's screen. He subtly nodded and kept walking.

"Hey, Reg. Buy me lunch?"

"Thought you were in a hurry."

Nick grumbled. "There's a sandwich place up ahead. Buy me lunch."

Davie looked around the store Lucy had dragged him into. Thin lace bras and panties. Flimsy loungewear. "Women wear this stuff?"

Lucy grabbed him by the elbow. "Let's get out of here."

"That guy with Nick - he was the one who grabbed you?"

"He was." She shivered. "Not a pleasant guy. We need to hope Nick saw your message and stops somewhere around here."

"He saw it," said Davie. "He nodded. We can't just march up to him and hand him a phone. Not with Reg there."

"I have a plan." Lucy unlocked her phone and placed a call. "Bobby, I need you to meet us downtown." She looked around. "There's a Macca's by the Apple store. Meet us there as quickly as you can get here." She listened for a second. "Us. Davie and I. Hurry."

Nick and Reg were inside, in the air conditioning, sitting at a table near the back of a small cafe. Nick had managed to grab the seat facing the door. Reg had his back to it.

Nick had a schooner of beer. Reg had a diet cola with a slice of lime floating amongst the ice.

"Happy now? You're just delaying the inevitable."

Nick sipped his beer. Licked his lips and let out a satisfied sigh. "I was getting hangry, mate." He took another sip of beer and leaned back as a server placed a BLT in front of him. "You not getting anything? You really should get something. This looks delicious."

Reg took a long hard look at Nick's sandwich, then grabbed the server by the arm before he could leave. "I'll have one of those, too."

Nick smiled. He had to stay here as long as possible, as long as it took for Davie and Lucy to come up with something.

Davie picked the last pickle out of the Quarter Pounder box and dropped it on his caramel sundae.

"What in the hell is that?"

He smiled. "You should try it sometime, Lucy. It's not bad." He checked the time on his phone. "How long is your brother going to be?"

"He reliable. He should be here in about - he's just walked in." She stood and waved him over.

Bobby slid onto the table's bench beside his sister and across from Davie. "Why am I here? I'm supposed to be at work."

Davie dropped the pre-paid phone on the table. He scribbled an email address and password on a paper napkin and dropped it on the phone. "Our friend Nick is having lunch somewhere around here. We need to get this phone and that email information to him without his gorilla handler knowing."

"His - his what?"

Lucy held her hand well above her head, parallel

to the floor. "Giant. Named Reg. The guy who grabbed me that night. They're up the road a bit, I hope, and we need to get the phone and whatever Davie just wrote to Nick without Reg knowing. I can't do it because Reg has already seen me, and there's a better than even chance he's seen Davie."

Bobby's eyebrows threatened to crawl off the top of his head. "Give that phone to some guy I've never met, guarded by a gorilla, having lunch who knows where and not get caught? I got that right?"

Lucy handed him the napkin. "And this. Please and thank you."

"It's important?"

"Extremely, dear brother."

Bobby looked at his sister, then at Davie. "What's this guy look like?"

Lucy tapped a couple of commands on her phone. "In your inbox, brother."

Bobby wrapped the napkin around the phone, stood, and slid them into his pocket. "I'll be right back."

Davie saluted him with a spoonful of Carmel-covered ice cream topped with a slice of pickle. "Take your time. Don't rush."

Nick waited. He nursed his beer and looked at his BLT, a masterpiece of creation, the bacon perfectly crispy, the tomatoes perfectly ripe and sliced exactly the correct thickness, and the lettuce fresh like it was just plucked from the garden. All of this on toasted Turkish slathered with real mayonnaise and ground black pepper. His mouth watered. His stomach grumbled.

Loud enough, apparently, that Reg heard it. "Dig in. Don't wait for me."

Nick waved him away. "That wouldn't be polite. Yours will be along any time now." He glanced at the front door, expecting to see Lucy or Davie. He hoped he understood the message correctly.

The server returned with Reg's version of BLT,

looking just as good.

"Now, now I'll dig in. This looks fantastic." He waved for another beer and took a healthy bite from his sandwich. He nodded at Reg. He chewed a bit and talked around a mouthful of food. "Good, isn't it?"

He nibbled at the sandwich and nursed his second beer as long as he could get away with.

Reg had finished his sandwich and drink and sat back in his chair with his arms crossed. "What the hell is this, Harding? I thought you were in a hurry to get the laptop and get online to do whatever it was to find Terri."

Nick let out a long breath through pursed lips. "Okay. I'm finished. Not a fan of the heat."

"In the wrong bloody country, then." Reg left a fifty-dollar note on the table and stood. "Let's go."

"Okay." He tipped back the remainder of his beer and stood. "Lay on, MacDuff."

"What?"

"Just go."

Reg led the way out of the cafe. Nick felt the heat of the sun before he got to the door. "Christ." He stepped out of the cafe and was bumped by a vaguely familiar man.

"Sorry, mate." The man shoved something into his hand. "Lucy says hi," he whispered as he walked into the cafe.

Nick looked at the phone in his hand and the crumpled napkin. He slid the phone in the small of his back, held in place with his belt just as Reg turned. He pretended to wipe his mouth with the napkin and stuffed it in his pocket. "Let's go."

He took a couple of steps and immediately shoved his hands in his pockets, applying tension to his belt to keep the phone in place. It turned his walk into a waddle, but better than having the phone slip into the crack of his arse and eventually down the leg of his trousers.

They arrived at Reg's car, and Nick eased into his

seat. The phone dug into his back. He ignored it, willing Reg to drive faster.

As soon as they walked into the flat, Nick made a beeline to the bathroom. "Beer's going right through me. I'll be a minute."

He locked the door and retrieved the phone from the small of his back just before it slipped into his butt crack. He pressed the napkin flat on the counter. An email address from a popular hosting company and a password were written on it. Below them was the word 'draft'.

He checked the phone. Made sure to turn off the ringer. It was asking for a password. A six-digit number.

He looked at the password on the napkin and entered the first six letters as digits on a phone keypad. The phone unlocked. "Davie, you bloody genius," he muttered.

The phone had an email program. He opened it

and went to the drafts folder. There was an email with the subject line: 'Read me'

So he read it.

Nick, mate, what the hell is going on? Create draft messages here, and we can communicate. Let me know how I can help. Lucy has told me as much as she knows. It was her brother who gave you the phone. We might be using him again if we need to physically contact you.

Nick smiled. Davie the spy. He created a new email, entered Davie's email address, and tapped out a message:

No need to use the drafts folder, mate. Thanks for the phone. Your help is really appreciated. I'm supposed to be looking for Theresa (Terri) O'Shea. I'm holed up in old man O'Shea's apartment at the top of the building this phone is located at. I'm assuming you've been tracking this phone. O'Shea is a guy I chased back in my AFP days. Among other things, he launders money for the Russian mob. His daughter was the brains behind it. The old man wants a reconciliation with his daughter after three years of estrangement. O'Shea is not well. He's ballooned up like a bloody whale. By the way, a couple of Russians are also looking for her. Probably from his old client base.

Keep in touch. I'm going to need your hacking skills.

He pressed send. The day was starting to look up.

Davie's phone chimed. He dipped a fry in a small tub of ketchup as he read the email. He smiled. "We're connected. We should get back to my place. I'm his guy in a chair, and I need to get in my chair."

Chapter Eleven

Nick tucked the phone into his sock and pulled the leg of his trousers down over it. It wouldn't stay there long. He needed to get it to the desk he was working at without drawing attention.

He sauntered - no better word for it - from the bathroom to the sofa facing the balcony. An unopened box had been placed there, a major laptop manufacturer's logo plastered on the side facing up. "That was fast."

Reg grunted as he pulled the fridge open and extracted two beers. "If that isn't good enough for what you have to do, I'll throw you over the balcony myself."

Nick smiled as he unpacked. "I'm sure it'll be

fine." He tossed the packaging to one side and slid his hand over the sleek laptop. It was a dark metal grey, matte finish and felt solid. He removed the metal twist-ties from the power cord, extended it and shoved it into the mains plug on the wall. Stuck the business end into the small jack on the side of the laptop.

He felt the phone vibrate against his leg. "I'm going to set a desk up on the balcony. The weather's been beautiful." He looked around. "Monitors?"

"Two of them. Around here somewhere." Reg twisted the top off one of the beers. "If you need help setting them up, I'm not the guy to ask." He nodded toward the balcony. "Go ahead and set up out there. It'll make it easier for me when I have to toss you over." He handed a slip of paper to Nick. "Wi-Fi and password. Email hosts are blocked. Ports used for email are blocked. Have fun." He took his beer and left, heading toward the TV room.

Nick waited until the door closed behind Reg.

Waited another minute. He reached for the phone and remembered the camera in the corner of the ceiling. "Dammit." He brushed imaginary lint off his leg and stood.

He found the two monitors behind the sofa, still in their boxes. He left the cardboard packaging strewn across the lounge room, muscling the monitors to the glass-topped table on the balcony.

The table was situated so that the balcony railing was on his left and the sliding doors to the balcony were on his right. This setup allowed him to keep an eye on the interior of the premises and still enjoy the view. It also kept the content on his screens out of casual sight.

The phone was going to be difficult to hide. The tabletop was glass and had no drawers. He took a glance around. A security camera to his right surveyed most of the balcony. Removing the phone from his sock would be impossible.

It buzzed against his leg again. He fought the urge

to reach for it. He sat back in the chair and thought for a moment, drumming his fingers on the keyboard. "Shit."

Nick pushed back from the table and returned to the bathroom. He locked the door and turned on the sink faucet. Sat on the toilet lid and extracted the phone from his sock.

"Heard anything from him yet?" Lucy paced Davie's small apartment. "It's been ten minutes. Is he okay?"

Davie shrugged. He sat on the sofa with his laptop beside him, open to the email program. "Not a psychic. He can take care of himself." He refreshed his inbox and sat forward, pulling his laptop to his lap. What there was of it. "Speak of the devil."

Lucy leaned over the back of the sofa and read over his shoulder. *Eyes everywhere. Can only get to the phone in the loo. The laptop/router has email sites blocked. Mail ports are closed. Ideas are welcome.*

Davie tapped out a quick reply. *Get me the IP address of that network.*

He waited for a minute. His laptop chimed with an incoming mail: *61.302.186.101*

He smiled and sent a response back. *Check back in about two hours.*

"What are you going to do?"

"There isn't a Wi-Fi router on the planet I can't get into." He leaned sideways, dug his wallet out, and handed it to Lucy. "Could you order some pizza and whatever you want?"

Nick turned off the phone and slid it back into his sock. "Do your best, Davie."

"Who are you talking to?" Reg hammered on the door.

Nick pulled it open, smiled, and pushed past him. "The only smart person in this place." He dropped onto the sofa. "I'm a bit blocked. I need to give some thought to how I should proceed." He gestured toward the balcony. "With that hobbled machine."

Reg walked toward the sliding doors and stood there, arms crossed.

Nick reached down, faux-scratching his leg, and palmed the small phone. He sat back up and slid it between the seat cushions. "Where's the old man?"

Reg grunted and turned. "Resting. He's not feeling well." He leaned over Nick, getting in his face. "Finding his daughter would make him feel a lot better."

"Yeah, yeah." He shoved his hand deeper between the cushions, made sure the phone was well and truly out of sight, and then stood, forcing Reg to step back. "My beer is getting warm." He pointed to the balcony. "You going to let me by? I've got to set that thing up."

"They said it was set up at the shop."

Nick chuckled. "Basic stuff. I need more than basic stuff." He pulled the paper with the Wi-Fi information from his pocket. "Hope old man O'Shea paid for the high-speed package. I've got a lot to download before I'm ready."

Reg stood to one side. "Off you go."

Nick smiled as he walked onto the balcony. He took a sip of beer—it was still cold—and entered the Wi-Fi credentials. He navigated to a Microsoft Office Suite site and started downloading the largest applications on their site. He needed to make his machine look busy while Davie tunnelled in from the outside.

He opened another tab on the browser, navigated to the Australian government data site, and started downloading every dataset he could find — topological data, mining data, fisheries information — everything he could grab at the highest resolution possible. A couple of hours of downloads were queued up. Hopefully, that was more than enough time for Davie.

"I'm feeling kinda useless here." Lucy dropped a

pizza crust in the empty box and wiped her hands with a square of paper towel. "Anything at all I can do to help?"

Davie looked up from his screen. "Huh?"

"How close are you?"

"Whoever set up this router is good."

"So no joy?"

Davie looked up at her and smiled. "I said good. Not great. I'm almost there." Davie was sitting at his desk. His laptop was connected to two large monitors. He tapped a couple of more keys, and the monitor's display on the right split into four images from inside O'Shea's flat. The top left showed a view of the living room from the camera high on the wall. Top right was the camera on the balcony. They could see Nick at a table working on a laptop. The bottom left camera faced the entrance to the flat. Bottom right was a camera overlooking the pool on the roof.

"This is that O'Shea guy's place? Nice."

"Crime does pay," said Davie.

She pulled a chair over and sat beside him. "What kind of crime, exactly? Is Nick in danger?"

Davie shook his head. "Just money laundering, mostly. O'Shea is a genius at moving dirty money around, making it appear squeaky clean. Law enforcement agencies around the world have been trying to find him." He looked over to Lucy. "Including Nick. Almost eighteen months of his career in the Australian Federal Police were spent trying to track this guy's money flow. Personally, I think his frustration at not getting anywhere was one of the reasons that convinced him to quit."

"That makes no sense."

"I know." Davie tapped another couple of keys, and a mirror of Nick's screen appeared on the right-hand monitor. "What in the hell is he doing?"

Nick's had thirteen files consecutively downloading. He was going through the online App Store and grabbing every bloated, massive installation file he could find. "What's taking you so long, Davie?" He glanced at the camera on the wall and shook his head. "I thought you were better than this." He smiled and flipped the bird at the camera. "Hurry up, mate."

He searched for a file-sharing service. The Lord of the Rings movies should chew up some time.

Then his cursor stopped responding to his mouse commands. It moved to an applications folder and opened a blank word-processing document. Words appeared. *Patience, mate. Do you have headphones? Might get noisy. Turn down the volume if you don't.*

Nick looked at the screen, smiled, and muted the speakers. He held out a thumbs-up toward the balcony camera.

Good. Are you okay?

Nick held out his hand palm down and waggled it back and forth. So-so.

The screen changed again. The top left corner

now showed the security video from O'Shea's living room. Reg had entered the far side and was walking toward the balcony.

Another note appeared in the document. *Want us to look for Terri or the Russians?*

The cursor blinked in the document, waiting for Nick to type.

So he typed: *You look for the Russians. I'll look for Terri. Feed me video?*

Sure. Most camera credentials = Admin / Password. For real.

The document disappeared, and Nick's laptop was quartered with CCTV video from the Sydney CBD. It looked live. An icon at the top of the laptop looked like a map. He clicked it, and the four videos were replaced by a map of the Sydney CBD, a small camera icon wherever an accessible camera feed was available. He found an accessible camera on George Street and clicked it. He entered the requested credentials and hit OKAY.

The map was reduced to half of the screen, and the live camera feed took up the other half. He dragged the feed to one of the external monitors.

The sliding door to the balcony opened, and Reg stepped through. "Making progress?"

Nick nodded. "This is the feed from a camera near the Youth Hostel. Where we were this morning."

"Live, though. She's not there anymore."

Nick grabbed the mouse and scrubbed the video back eight hours. "Decent-sized buffer. I'll be able to track her, catching up to where she is now." He looked up at Reg. "Pull up a chair. I should find her in a couple of hours."

"Nah, mate. That's why you're here. I'll let the boss know you're finally up and running."

She had thirty minutes to get to her appointment at the bank. Unfortunately, the Russians were between her and her ultimate destination. And they were taking their time. She was still a safe distance behind them. The little creep hadn't seen her yet. They had stopped at a high-end store and were talking to the staff, showing them a picture. She assumed it was a picture of her, but she didn't know how old it was.

She pulled her hair back and twisted it on top of her head. Jammed the hat on top and put on a pair of sunglasses. But if they took more than half a glance, they'd make her.

As she walked passed the front of the shop, she saw the attendant look up from the picture she was being shown on the big guy's phone, catch a glance of her as she walked by.

"Shit." She increased her pace, running across George Street to the east side, ducking in front of the light rail tram. She ran north on George Street until she reached Martin Place. She took the sharp right turn onto the pedestrian mall.

She slowed to a stop. It was unbearably hot. Time was running out. Her appointment was a few blocks east, up the hill. She checked her watch. Twenty-five minutes to go. She could afford to walk.

Terri adjusted the bag on her shoulder and maintained a slow and steady pace. She crossed over to the north side of the pedestrian mall, moving into the shade. Her head was down, the brim of her cap covering her face.

The mall was packed. Voices came and went as people passed her, heading up the hill or coming down. It was a background din sitting under her thoughts.

Until she heard "*Vot ona*!" from somewhere ahead of her. The Russian language cut through the background noise. The urgent Russian of someone yelling, "There she is!". She lifted her head. Across the mall, up the hill at the next intersection, Mikhail and his giant friend were pointing at her.

Chapter Twelve

The camera at the entrance to the youth hostel provided a clear side-on view of everyone entering and leaving. It faced south, so those who left the hostel and headed north provided a clear, face-on image for about two seconds. Nick checked the timestamp on the footage and scrubbed back to before he had visited with Reg.

Then he let it play forward at 4X speed. People moving like characters out of a 1920s movie hustled past the camera and in and out of the hostel. He watched, waiting for her to leave.

He almost missed her.

She wore a hat and sunglasses and had a bag over her shoulder. She was dressed in a T-shirt and cut-off denims, barely recognisable as the woman O'Shea showed him from Martin Place.

He reduced the speed to normal and watched her exit, turn north, and glance at the camera. The corners of her mouth pulled down to a frown, and she walked off camera.

He noted the time and moved to the next camera, about half a block north on George Street.

It was going to be a long day. He tracked her through three additional cameras, slowly catching up to the current time when he noticed the two men he ran into at the lights, who had spoken something to him in a Slavic-sounding language.

He frowned and returned to the camera in front of the hostel.

He only had to scrub ahead ten minutes before he saw the Russians. They entered the hostel, there was a gap of a couple of minutes, and then they left.

The smaller one seemed to be more aggressive. It was the smaller one who yelled something at him before shoulder-barging him.

He followed them through the cameras and, by the third one, confirmed they were tracking Terri. He caught them outside a sports shop, the little one discarding the packing of a knife, examining the blade, and then slipping it into his back pocket.

"Shit."

He looked around, made sure nobody was watching and toggled to the Word document.

You still there?

There was a delay of a few seconds.

Yo. What's up?

Nick nodded and flashed a thumbs-up at the camera. *Can you focus your effort on finding Terri, with urgency? 2 Russians def following her. I'm going to track them. Ping as soon as you find her. Thx.*

Got it, boss.

Nick grimaced. He hated that term. He changed his thumbs up to a middle digit and glared at the security camera.

Davie laughed.

"What?"

"Nick seems to be okay. Hot focus on finding Terri," said Davie. "High priority."

Lucy frowned. "What have you been doing?"

"Looking for Terri." He cleared his throat. "But looking harder now."

"What's the urgency?" Lucy sat beside him and pulled her laptop out of her bag. "And how can I help?"

Davie slid her laptop closer and started typing commands. "A couple of Russians are looking for Terri, and Nick believes they are a threat. He's looking for them and wants us to look for her." He returned her laptop. "And you can help. Icons in green are accessible cameras."

"Nick is supposed to be a smart guy, right? I mean, he seems smart to me."

Davie nodded. "Smart enough."

"So why are we sitting here looking for someone on our laptops when she is, if she's still in the Sydney CBD, roughly ten klicks from here?"

Davie stopped typing and looked at her. "Let me finish this. Fifteen, twenty minutes, max."

"You've got a tablet that'll work for this?"

Davie chuckled. "Absolutely."

"Okay. Hurry. Twenty minutes, and I'm leaving without you if you're not ready."

Nick pushed back from the patio table and went looking for O'Shea.

He found him on the roof, carving very slow laps in his pool, barely staying afloat. Reg sat in a chair at the shallow end, holding a towel.

O'Shea saw him and switch from a crawl to a breaststroke. "Nicky. What brings you up here?"

Nick watched O'Shea slow to a pace that almost had his body vertical in the pool. He walked slowly alongside, keeping pace. "You need to answer a question."

"You need to ask it first. My telepathic abilities stopped working the day I married my late wife."

"She died?"

"May as well have. Is that why you're here and not spending every waking hour of your day looking for my daughter? My ex-wife?"

"Why would two Russians, one who looks and acts like a pure-blood psychopath and the other bigger than Reg, be looking for your daughter?"

O'Shea stopped swimming and almost sank. He dog-paddled to the edge and hung on, looking up at Nick. "Are you positive?"

"Don't answer questions with questions. It pisses me off. Why are they looking for her? Unhappy customers from the old days?"

O'Shea slowly hand-walked along the pool edge until the water was shallow enough to walk. He pushed through the water to the bathrobe Reg was holding. He shrugged it on, but left it open. "What did they look like?"

Nick shook his head. "You really need to switch to salads at least once or twice a week. There were two of them. One gorilla-sized, one like a psychopathic ferret. Likes knives." Nick shook his head. "No, I'm wrong. He *loves* his knives."

O'Shea dropped into a patio chair, severely testing its structural integrity. He closed his eyes and dropped his head, his hands fumbling with the edges of the robe.

Nick thought he'd passed out for a second until he lifted his head and sighed. "There's an outstanding beef with the Russians. Three years ago. I thought it was written off. A bad debt. Surprised Petrovski is still pissed." He shrugged. "I thought he was dead, truth be told."

"How much?"

O'Shea shook his head and waved him away. "Doesn't matter. Find Terri. That's your only priority."

"Really? I think a couple of Russians, one with a penchant for knives, would be of more interest to you."

O'Shea scowled and sat deeper in his chair. He crossed his arms. "Just find her and bring her to me, right?"

"The job is a lot more complicated now. I have to find your daughter while two people who apparently want to kill her are tracking her through the city. You need to tell me more."

"No, I don't. Find her and bring her to me."

"You're making this harder than it needs to be."

O'Shea sat in his patio chair, arms crossed, and glared at Nick.

"This is feeling less and less like a family reunion and more like bounty hunting."

O'Shea scowled and clenched his fists.

"Okay, okay," said Nick. He held up his hands in surrender. "I'll find her. If you ever feel like opening up, you know where to find me."

Terri was out of breath. And hot and sweaty. She was moving east through the city, ducking into shops as often as practical and watching pedestrian traffic for minutes at a time from the shadows of the shop fronts.

She pointedly ignored any shop staff who tried to move her along. One glance and they backed off.

She looked at the time on her phone and swore. "Mother*fuck*. I'm not going to get to the bank."

A sales associate sidled up to her with a pasted-on smile. "Is there anything at all I can help you with?"

Terri looked at him and shook her head. "I need you to point me at the back door. I have a vicious ex-husband on my tail, and you don't want the altercation to happen here."

The salesperson stammered. "I-I-I don't?"

Terri pursed her lips. "Oh, no. The blood splatter would take ages to clean up, wouldn't it? Where's that back door?"

Nick was on autopilot. He tracked the Russians in real-time now. Based on their action, they pursued Terri, moving fast and with a sense of purpose. He clicked ahead, skipping forward to a camera on the Russians' path. The camera was mounted on the front of a cafe. He saw a brief second of a woman running out of frame. He scrubbed the video for thirty seconds and watched Terri run past, glancing over her shoulder.

He got up from the table, ran to the balcony railing and looked over the edge. He looked right and saw two men coming, one tall, one short. Too far down to clearly identify, but also too much of a coincidence. "Shit."

He closed the laptop and ran into the living room. grabbing the phone from between the cushions, and bolted for the door..

He was in the lift, and the doors closed, before

Reg left the apartment.

Chapter Thirteen

Nick paused at the front door of the apartment building to take stock.

Traffic poured down the street, separating him from the cafe and his target. He trotted along the sidewalk, looking for a break, powering up the phone as he moved. He dodged vehicles as he dashed across the road. Called Davie when he landed on the other side, in front of the cafe.

"Nick?"

"Mate, I hope you're on your cameras right now." Nick kept his head on a swivel, looking for the Russians.

"We were just about to go mobile and track from the field."

"No time. I need to know exactly where she is now."

"Okay, okay. Hang on a sec."

"Don't have a sec, mate."

"A little testy, aren't we? I'm tracing Terri. Just found her." Davie chuckled over the phone. "Funny, she was in front of the cafe Lucy and I were at, right across from that building you're in."

"Not in that building right now. I'm in front of that same cafe. The Russians are close on her heels. I need you to get me to her before they do."

"Shit. Where are they?"

Nick looked around. No sign of them. "Not sure. The private hospital is just down the road. They probably turned the corner there. The thing is, I want you to get me to her. Quickly. You've been following her path. You should have a decent idea of which way she's going. Shortcut me there." He took the phone away from his head and glared at it. He yelled into it. "I can't run with this thing stuck to my head. Send me text messages."

Reg stood at the front entrance to the apartment building, fists clenching, eyes darting up and down the street. "That son of a bitch." His phone vibrated in his pocket. He checked, but he knew it would be O'Shea. "What?"

"How, in the hell, did you let this happen?"

"I'm going hunting."

"HOW?!!?"

"Shut up, old man." He terminated the call and shoved the phone into his back pocket. He dodged traffic as he crossed the street and mentally tossed a coin. Left or right? He turned left and set off at a half-jog.

Davie placed his phone on his desk. "We're staying here for now. You take the cameras toward Hyde Park, and I'll take the ones toward the Art Gallery." He handed her a slip of paper. "Use the messaging program and let Nick know what you see."

Lucy sat back on the sofa, cradling her laptop. She took the paper and entered the number into the messaging program. Sent a quick message so she'd have a record of the number: *Nicky, it's Lucy. Stay tuned.*

She minimised the messenger program and returned to the cameras. "This gets monotonous, fast, Davie." She arranged the images from the next four cameras in line and ran them at 4X speed. "I'm going cross-eyed."

Davie pinched the bridge of his nose and nodded. "I know. Never thought I'd miss being on the streets with him, in danger of getting slapped around."

"That happen much?"

Davie chuckled as he frowned. "His busted nose? A sort of regular occurrence. I was frequently in the way. Got a couple of smacks in myself, time to time." He nodded at her laptop. "Keep looking. Terri is in trouble."

Nick looked at Lucy's message and smiled. "The more, the merrier." He was running blind in the general direction he'd seen Terri go—Russians on her tail, Reg on his.

Ahead was Hyde Park, and to the right was The Domain. Two wide-open bucolic recreation parks with nowhere to hide. He doubted she'd go to either.

Unless she was double-bluffing.

He shook his head and continued straight. Hyde Park wasn't that large. There'd be a better chance of finding her if she was in there.

His phone vibrated in his pocket. A message from Davie. *Just saw her on the corner of Riley and Kennedy. Heading North. Russians are half a block behind her. You're half a block behind them.*

He tapped back a *Ta* and sprinted up Riley Street. Slowed as he got behind the Russians. He looked past them. Terri was a block ahead, oblivious to her followers, and making good time.

"Oi, you commie fucks," yelled Nick. "What the fuck are you doing stinking up my country?"

The small one slowed and grabbed the big one's arm. He turned and faced Nick. "What is this? Do I know you from somewhere?" His Russian accent was thick. "I think I have seen you somewhere before."

"What are you doing here?" Nick stood with his hands loosely by his side. "You should go back to your own country." He looked past them. Terri was out of sight. He backed into an alley.

"I am tourist in this beautiful country." The little guy had his hands out to his sides. "What is it to you?"

Nick took another half-step back. "I've been following you while you followed a young woman. What's your intent?"

The bigger guy took a step forward, clenching his fists. "Piss off, mate. None of your business."

"Ah," said Nick. "Local accent. You've been here

a long time. Still a hint of Russian, though." He nodded at the small one. "You his handler? What do you want with Terri?"

Mikhail deftly slipped the knife from his back pocket and snapped the blade open. "How do you know Terri? Where is she?"

The big guy grabbed the little guy's arm. "Mikhail. Not in the open like this." He looked around. "Put that away."

Mikhail grimaced. "Pussy fucking country." He looked at the big guy. "You would not survive a day in Moscow, Dimitri."

Nick clapped his hands together. "Great. Dimitri's right, Micky. Put the knife away, or the coppers will lock you up. Why are you following my friend?"

Mikhail took a step closer, backing Nick further into the narrow lane. "How. Do you know. That woman?"

"Like I said. A friend. Keeping an eye out for her.

Back it up, mate. Your breath stinks like old fish."

Mikhail looked around. The narrow lane took them out of sight of any passersby. He slowly raised the knife. "Should be okay here, no? No prying eyes? She is not your friend. I am not an idiot." He held the knife, blade pointing up. "Talk to me."

Dimitri stayed where he was, feet planted, arms crossed. He had a half smile on his face.

"Hey, Dimitri," said Nick. "You going to let your pet off his leash like this?"

"Oh, he's not my pet. No leash. You should talk while you can." It was a full smile now, and it wasn't pretty. "He'll take your tongue first."

Terri stepped into a shop doorway. She'd been trying to lure the Russians into the park, out in the open, where she could expose them and keep them occupied answering questions from the local police. Somehow.

But they'd stopped following her. And she needed

to know what the hell they were up to. If they were moving to cut her off, somehow. She opened the mapping app on her phone and oriented herself, slowly turning until she figured out her position.

They were between her and the bank if they were still behind her. Not good enough. She needed to draw them further away.

The last time she'd seen them was a couple of blocks back. They had been poor at tracking her, but she assumed their strengths weren't in the subtle arts. They were going to kill her. They weren't the best she'd run across in her life, but they were the vilest. She needed to get them out of the picture, or she couldn't finish what she needed to finish.

"Hey, Davie, come here." Lucy half-turned her laptop so he could see the screen. "Nick, right?"

"When is this?"

"About two minutes ago." She tapped the icon for the next camera on the path and sped the image to

4x. She waited a second, then jabbed her finger at the screen. "There."

Davie nodded. He leapfrogged to the next camera. He scrubbed the video up to the current time and didn't find him. "I don't have him. Do you?"

"Ah, shit."

Davie looked startled. He hadn't heard Lucy swear before. "What?"

Nick backed into a laneway, the Russians slowly walking in after him. "We need to help him."

Davie calculated the distance from them on his phone map. "Ten, maybe fifteen minutes to get there. It'll be too late by then." He stared at his phone, his brow furrowed in thought.

She smacked his arm and pointed at the screen. "Look at that guy. Maybe Nick'll be okay."

"I like my tongue." Nick held his hands up. "I'd prefer if you'd let me keep it."

Mikhail was running his thumb along the flat of

the blade. "I will work up to your tongue. Maybe you keep it if you tell me where the girl is before I get to it."

A large presence darkened the alleyway. Nick glanced past Mikhail and Dimitri to see Reg. He relaxed and smiled.

"Why are you smiling? I will start with your fingers. Your tongue, I will remove from below."

"I wouldn't recommend that, comrade," said Reg.

Dimitri and Mikhail both spun in their tracks. Mikhail pushed past Dimitri. "Who are you?"

"Take a walk, mate," said Reg. "Get out of here before you hurt yourself."

Mikhail held the knife loosely in his right hand. "Who. Are. You? What business is this of yours?" He brought the knife up in a slicing motion. "None. It is no business to you. Fuck off before I slice you up like fish."

Reg cracked his knuckles, his biceps flexing as a by-product. "You and your ugly friend leave right now, and I won't break both of your hands. You can't fight me with your knife in your mouth, can you?"

The small Russian stood still, looking at Reg in thought. "You're not his bodyguard. I would have seen you around him before. You were too far away. So you must be here because of the woman we were following."

Reg glanced at Nick, then back at the Russian. He said nothing.

"So if you are interested in the woman, I have to ask myself, why?"

Mikhail snapped his fingers. "I know you. You work for the old man, don't you?" A smile slowly formed on his face. "Yeah. You work for the old man." He flicked the knife open and closed, open and closed. Like a deadly metronome. "Take us to him."

The video on Davie's monitor showed Reg walking

up to the laneway, pausing just outside. The camera across from the laneway showed a good view of the activity inside. Nick was backing up, his hands in surrender, and the little Russian was slowly advancing on him.

"That's the guy who was in the car with Nick," said Lucy.

"He looks like he can handle himself. Is he just going to stand there, or is he planning on helping?"

Lucy grabbed her bag. "We're going. Hurry."

Davie tucked his tablet under his arm and followed her out of the flat. "He's paying my data charges for this." He struggled to keep up with her. "Slow down. I'm fat."

Chapter Fourteen

"So you blokes are looking for Terri?" Reg stood in front of the Russians, hands loosely at his sides. "How did you know she was in town?"

"Stop talking. Tell me where old man O'Shea is before I fillet you like a pike."

"I don't know pike. Barramundi would be my choice." Reg narrowed his eyes. "Nicky, lad, get the hell out of here. I'll handle these two. You get your arse back to the apartment."

Nick tried to skip past the group of over-testosterone-fuelled men, but Dimitri managed to grab him by the left arm and slam him against the wall. "You're going nowhere."

"I don't know who the fuck you are, but he's not

yours to beat up. That's my job. Let him go." Reg clenched a fist.

"What he said, Dimitri." Nick tried to pull his arm free. It was like it was in a vice. He suddenly realized (if a dawning realisation could be sudden) that he was about to be in a fight—a real, going-to-get-some-bones-broken fight. "You started this."

Nick pulled on his arm until Dimitri compensated by pulling back, then pushed, causing the Russian to stumble backwards. He pushed forward, swinging his right elbow toward the larger man's head.

He missed, over-rotated and fell at Dimitri's feet. He rolled out of the way as a boot heel came crashing down, just missing his head. He kept rolling until he smashed into a skip bin. It stunk of rotted food, stale beer, and last night's urine.

He pulled himself up, grimaced at the mess on his hands, and wiped them on his trousers. "You're lucky I missed."

Dimitri chuckled and stepped toward him before

he was knocked sideways by Mikhail, who was on the receiving end of a Reg roundhouse. The knife skittered across the laneway and under one of the skips.

Reg took a few quick steps forward and stood over Mikhail. "You didn't tell me. Why are you looking for her?"

Mikhail slowly stood and retrieved his knife. It was Reg and Nick facing off against Mikhail and Dimitri. Nick felt the odd one out. He was pretty sure he was the only one in the quartet who hadn't killed anyone yet. He faced Dimitri, the giant and Reg faced the scrawny, scrappy Mikhail. He nudged Reg. "I think we should swap."

Reg didn't take his eyes off Mikhail. "Trust me. You don't want this one."

"I sure as hell don't want the other one."

Dimitri snorted. "Tell us where Terri is, or you'll get the other one."

"How in the hell would—" Nick was cut off by a

jab in the ribs from Reg's elbow.

Dimitri's eyes narrowed. "So you don't know where she is either?" He crossed his arms. Nick took this as a good sign. He'd have a few more seconds to duck if the monster unleashed a punch in his direction.

"He didn't say that," said Reg.

"He almost said that. And if he almost said that," said Mikhail," that means maybe we work together to find her, no?"

The object of their search stood just outside the laneway, back against the wall, listening. Reg and the other guy could solve her problem for her.

Reg.

She hadn't seen him in years. And if Reg was here, so was her father. And her father being in the same city as her—well, that wasn't something she'd factored into her plans. It sounded like her father was looking for her, too.

Best case scenario, Reg and the nerd with him would take care of the Russians, and she'd get to her task and be gone before they knew it.

Worst case, they'd team up and work together to find her.

She shook her head. "They won't work together."

She squatted and peered around the corner. They weren't fighting. The stance seemed to be more relaxed than aggressive. "Shit. They're going to work together."

She ducked back out of sight, stood, and walked briskly to the bank.

Davie and Lucy ran up to the alley and stopped short. Reg and Nick faced off against the two Russians. There was no fighting.

Lucy leaned close to Davie. "Do we announce ourselves?"

Nick turned and frowned. "You two. What in the hell? Get out of here before you get hurt."

Davie squared his shoulders. "We're here to help."

Lucy stepped forward and hugged him. She slipped her hand down to his ass and patted it before disengaging.

Reg held a hand up to the Russians. "Give me a sec." He half turned, looking at Nick. "Who are these people?"

"Friends. They're leaving." More bystanders started to gather. Nick glanced back at the Russians, then back to Lucy and Davie. "This isn't safe. You need to head back to wherever you're calling home base. Seriously."

"I think we'll be okay," said Lucy. She nodded toward the Russians.

Mikhail had closed his knife and stowed it in his back pocket. He looked nervously at the growing crowd. He tapped Dimitri on the arm. "We go. We can do this later." A couple of policemen approached the back of the crowd. "We go now."

"Get fucked, lads." Reg watched them leave, waiting until they had turned the corner and were out of sight. "So, where did Terri go?"

"No idea. Lost her in the drama." Nick shook his head and pointed at Davie and Lucy. "You two get out of here, okay? And keep an eye out for the Russians."

Reg waited until they left, then grabbed Nick by the arm. "How in the hell did the Russians know you were here?"

"They didn't, at first. They were gaining on Terri and didn't look like they just wanted to have a beer with her. I caught their attention and let her get ahead. Slowed things down. Good thing that the crowd grew. I think that kept us both from getting injured."

"Injured? Killed. Jesus. Now we've lost Terri, and those two are on the loose. Mikhail is ruthless. He'll slit her throat as soon as look at her."

"How do you know them?"

Reg turned and walked. "Not important."

Nick skipped ahead and stopped him. "Like hell it isn't. The competition is pretty fierce. I want to know who I'm up against."

"It's enough to know that they are very dangerous." Reg held up his hands. "*How* I know is for discussion at a later time."

Nick looked at him for a long beat. "Then we better find her."

"We? You. And keep your friends out of it. We told you what would happen if the authorities found out O'Shea was in the country."

Nick glanced at the cops outside the crowd and walked away, Reg behind him. "If you were that concerned, you'd keep your voice down. Don't worry about Davie and Lucy. They're cool. I need to get back to the laptop and track Terri."

Reg grunted.

"And," said Nick, "the population of people in Australia who know O'Shea the elder is in the country is larger than you think."

Mikhail trotted ahead to the end of the block and looked around the corner.

"She's gone, mate," said Dimitri. "We need to start from scratch."

"We're running out of time. She's not here for long. Starting from scratch is not ideal." He looked at his watch, then up at the CCTV cameras on the corner of the building. He pointed at them. "Do we have somebody who knows how to access those cameras? We could search that way. Or have someone else search and, you know, tell us where to go."

"Possible. There's a guy." Dimitri nodded in thought. "I'll make some calls. We should head back."

"No. You call and arrange for this person to look at the cameras, and we get food. They can point us to where to look." He looked at his watch again. "We look for maybe all night. She has to sleep somewhere, right?"

Dimitri grumbled, dialled a phone number, and walked a few steps away.

Mikhail retraced their steps, making a mental note of the cameras. He returned to Dimitri as he was finishing his call. "Don't hang up."

"Hang on," he said to the phone. He put his hand over the mouthpiece. "What do you want?"

"There is a camera where we almost cut those fools. She was there. They can start looking there."

"Right." Dimitri glanced at where they came from and put the phone back to his ear. "When the kid gets into the cameras, start at the one we were in front of ten minutes ago." He gave him the intersection. "Look for the girl there who sneaks off when we get distracted, then call this number when you find her. Our visitor and I are getting some food."

He closed the call and pocketed the phone. "What do you want to eat?"

"I do not give a shit what we eat. How long will it be before we know where the girl is?"

"They're tracking down a kid who knows how to do this shit. It might be an hour or so."

Mikhail spat on the ground. "*Fignya.*"

"Not bullshit, friend. Come on. We need food."

Terri made it to the bank five minutes after it closed. "Oh, son of a bitch." She banged on the door with her fist and swore again. She turned her back and slumped against the door. Maybe this wasn't the right time to do this. She set her jaw and stood. "No." It was now, or she'd never get another chance.

There were no business hours posted on the building. It was by appointment only. She dug through her pack, extracted her contacts book, and called Nigel.

"Nigel speaking."

"I'm glad I got you, Nigel. This is," she closed her eyes in thought, "Grace Rawlson. I'm very sorry. I missed the appointment today. I got tied up in other matters."

"Grace *Rawlston?*"

"Yes. Rawlston." Terri shook her head at forgetting her cover name.

"I was surprised when you didn't show. I apologise, but I'm not at the bank right now. I'm about to go out for the evening."

"That's okay. Are you available tomorrow?"

"If you call me tomorrow after 9 am, I'm sure we can find a mutually agreeable time."

Terri smiled. "I'll talk to you then." She hung up the call and opened a mapping app. She'd be staying in a hotel tonight. The hostel experience had grown old.

Lucy opened the app on her phone that let her track her devices. Her AirTag was three blocks east and moving slowly. "He's heading back to O'Shea's apartment."

"Probably."

"No, Davie." She shoved her phone into his hands. "Definitely."

It took him a second to register what he was seeing. "Your tag?"

Lucy nodded, a satisfied smile on her face.

"When did you do that?"

"In the alley. When I hugged him. He's definitely heading back to that place. We should head in for the night."

Davie watched the tag move toward the building O'Shea lived in. "Yeah. Let's go. We'll pick this up in the morning."

"Except."

"What?"

"Those two guys Nick was about to fight in the alley. They're probably not going to stop looking for Terri."

"Yeah, well." Davie chewed the inside of his cheek. "I suppose we should at least find her and warn her about the Russians."

Reg held the door. "You're going to sit on the sofa, and you're going to wait until O'Shea is finished doing whatever he's doing, and then he's going to come down here and have a word with you."

Nick shook his head and continued walking to the balcony and his desk. "I've got to find Terri. And those Russians. They're going to kill her if they find her." He shrugged. "I'm assuming O'Shea wants her alive?"

Reg took a deep breath in through his nose and let it slowly out his mouth. "Jesus, you're an annoying son of a bitch. Stay out on the balcony, and don't go anywhere. And find her. This is important."

Chapter Fifteen

"I'm going to need food." Nick stepped onto the balcony. "I'm getting hungry."

Reg stopped his walk to the study. "I'll get the chef right on it, asshole. There's something in the fridge. You're on your own."

Nick sighed and backtracked to the kitchen. He yanked the fridge open, and a vial of insulin fell off a shelf on the door and onto the floor, bouncing across the hard tile. "Shit." He grabbed it before it rolled under the oven and checked it for cracks. "Damn. Strong glass." He placed the vial back beside the other three in the fridge and scanned for food.

He had a loaf of bread, sliced chicken, tomatoes,

lettuce and mayo on the island counter when Reg returned, O'Shea waddling along behind him.

"Did I hear a vial drop?"

Nick continued constructing the sandwich. "Yeah. Didn't break, though." He slathered mayo on the bread, then ground pepper.

"It bruises, you oaf. The insulin is a delicate solution. Which vial was it? Was it more than one? Do I have to buy all new ones?"

Nick leaned back and slowly opened the fridge door. He lifted out the vial he had dropped and held it up to the light. "Doesn't look bruised to me." He tossed it underhand to Reg. "Look bruised to you, Reggie?"

O'Shea grabbed the vial from Reg and walked it back to the fridge. "I swear to Christ." He replaced the vial and snagged a slice of chicken from Nick's half-made sandwich. "I am not impressed, Mr Harding."

Nick replaced the stolen chicken and added a

couple more slices. "Reg told me to help myself. I'll buy you more chicken tomorrow." He finished constructing the sandwich and cut it in half. "But I'm eating this now. I'm starving."

"Bring it over here." O'Shea wheezed as he sat on the recliner ninety degrees to the sofa. He motioned to Reg, who poured him a heavy whiskey. He sipped, sighed, and placed the glass on a coaster.

Nick put his sandwich and a beer bottle on the coffee table and sat on the sofa. He washed a mouthful of food down with a mouthful of beer. He suppressed a belch. "Okay, O'Shea. Why are you not impressed?"

"Where's my daughter?"

"We, Reg and I, were close today. Almost. Got interrupted by—"

"Tomorrow, O'Shea. We'll get her tomorrow."

"Interrupted by what?"

Reg glared at Nick and shook his head. "Nick got distracted by a young lady in a sundress, and your daughter got away from us."

Nick almost choked on his beer. "Hey!"

"Shut up, Nick. I'm talking."

O'Shea looked between them. "What the fuck is going on?"

"We almost had her today. Guaranteed we'll scoop her up tomorrow." Reg glared at Nick

The old man grunted and took another mouthful of whiskey. "I don't think you get the enormity of the situation, Mr Harding."

"Please, call me Nick." He smiled and toasted O'Shea with his bottle of beer.

"Shut up. Terri isn't going to hang around long. Once she is gone, it will be," he shook his head, "maybe never before I get this opportunity again." He rolled his shoulders and drank another mouthful. "Do you know what happens to you if she disappears before you find her?"

"You drink yourself to death?" Nick was onto the second half of his sandwich. He licked the mayo drippings off his fingers. "Come on. We'll find her. Reg and I have a good system going."

"What, you run out of the apartment, and he has to catch up to you?"

"Just a communications problem, boss. And Reg did catch up."

O'Shea finished his drink and put his glass down on the coaster harder than necessary. "Here is the deal. You are going to find her tomorrow and bring her to me." He held up a hand to stop Nick from interrupting. "Shut up, Harding. If you do not bring her to me tomorrow, I will ruin you financially. How would your clientele react to finding out you willingly *worked for* one of the world's most sought-after money launderers? Everybody will know. I'll make sure. And while I'm destroying you financially, Reg will put you in the hospital for at least a month. You'll probably be in a coma for part of that month." He pushed himself to his feet. "I'm not bullshitting. He'll tell you."

Nick watched the old Irishman slowly walk into his bedroom. "Huh. What the fuck was that? Is he okay?"

"He's not bullshitting. If he asks me to beat on you, I'll do it and enjoy it."

"Oh, mate. I thought we were pals." Nick finished his beer. "I'll leave this to you to clean up." He stood and stretched. "Why didn't you tell him about the Russians?"

"He's old. He has a bad heart. High blood pressure. Bad enough he knows they're in town. It wouldn't do him good to know they were that close. Better we find Terri and be done with it. Get back on your cameras. Find out where she is staying tonight. Find out which hostel she's picked out."

Mikhail finished the last of his kebab and wiped his mouth with the paper napkin. "This is good food. But enough waiting. Does your contact have access to these security cameras yet? We need to find out where the bitch is staying. And we need to find out where her father is. The ten million and the old man would be a nice bonus."

Dimitri redialled a number on his phone. "Just the girl for now." He put the phone to his head and walked away from the table.

Mikhail reached across the table and grabbed a couple of fries from his partner's plate. He ate them while he watched Dimitri put his Bluetooth EarPods in and open a mapping app on his phone.

He nodded as he approached the table. "That's great, kid."

Mikhail reached up, grabbed the earbud from his left ear, and stuck it in his own. "…two more blocks down George Street on your left."

"You have Mikhail on the line also, Geoff. When did she go there?"

"It was about twenty minutes ago."

"While we were eating?" Asked Mikhail.

"I-I don't know when you were eating."

"Da, da. What is this place she is staying?"

"I'd the Four Seasons Hotel. Right down by Circular Quay."

"You are sure she did not walk in the front door and out of the back door?" Mikhail looked at the map on Dimitri's phone and pointed toward the harbour. "That way?"

"I only saw her enter. I didn't see her leave. At least not yet."

The kid sounded to Mikhail like he was twelve. "Are you positive? I do not want to be wasting my time."

"I am. I am. Positive she is still in there."

"Thanks," said Dimitri. "We may need you tomorrow. Stay by your phone." He pocketed his phone and motioned for Mikhail to return his earbud. "Let's go get her."

The walk to the hotel took less than five minutes.

They entered the lobby and were stopped at the concierge stand. "Gentlemen, are you checking in?"

Dimitri plastered on his most winning smile. "No, sir. We are here to meet a friend."

"Is your friend a guest at the hotel?"

"Yes. A Miss Terri O'Shea."

The concierge typed a command on his terminal. "I'm sorry, sir. There is nobody checked into our hotel by that name. Are you sure she's here?"

Dimitri held up a finger. "One moment." He walked away and made a phone call.

"Geoff speaking."

"Kid, you positive the bitch is in the hotel?"

"Yeah."

"I mean really positive?"

"One hundred percent. Why?"

"We're here, and they don't have a record of her checking in."

There was a chuckle on the phone. "Doubt she'd check in under her own name. You tried the Rawlston name, right? I'm on a date, comrade. Talk to you later."

Dimitri returned to the concierge stand. "It's possible she checked in under a different name. Grace Rawlston." He smiled. "Her ex-husband is looking for her."

"Rawlston?"

"Well, I'm not sure. She mixes it up a lot. Did someone check in about an hour ago?"

"I'm sorry. We respect the confidentiality of our guests. I'm sorry. I can't help you."

Mikhail took a step forward and leaned on the concierge stand. "Tell us."

The concierge's smile tightened, and he pressed a button. Two large men in tightly fitting suits came through a door beside him and flanked him. "I'm going to ask you two gentlemen to leave politely. Now. If you can't find your way, my friends will help you."

Mikhail snarled. "We can take these pussies, Dimitri."

"No. They will have backup, and I'm sure the

local police have been called. We'll come back in the morning." He pushed Mikhail toward the entrance. "Let's go."

Davie scrubbed camera feeds until he found Terri walking down George Street toward the waterfront. He checked the time on the CCTV and looked at the time on his laptop. "Thirty-five minutes ago."

He watched her walk into the hotel. It was the Four Seasons. Way out of his price range. He sped up the feed until it caught up to the current time. She was still in there. He texted Lucy: *If you're up for it, Terri is staying at the Four Seasons at Circular Quay. I'll be at the coffee shop across the street tomorrow morning at 6.*

He did some electronic prodding and got into the hotel's computer. There was no check-in for Terri O'Shea, but there was a lone check-in thirty-three minutes ago for Grace Rawlston.

He sent a message to Nick's burner. *Terri is*

staying at the Four Seasons Hotel under the name Grace Rawlston. I'll be outside, in the coffee shop across the street, tomorrow morning at 6 am.

Nick's pocket vibrated. It took him by surprise. He'd forgotten about the burner. He stood and stretched, then walked to the balcony rail and leaned on it, taking in the view. He turned a full circle to make sure nobody was watching him. He took the phone from his pocket and flipped it open. He read Davie's message and smiled. He thumbed back a quick message. *Long black for me. And pancakes.*

He pocketed the phone and leaned on the railing. The air was warm, the view over the city was spectacular, and he had a full stomach. If it was any other situation, he'd be feeling content. He looked over his shoulder when he heard the sliding door open. He turned and leaned back. "Hey. You here to beat me up?"

Reg shook his head. "Maybe tomorrow. You

should be looking for her."

"I already found her." He pushed off the railing and closed the laptop. He tucked it under his arm and stood in front of Reg. He looked up at him. "Early morning tomorrow. You should get your beauty sleep." He went to step around Reg and was stopped by a meaty fist grabbing his upper arm.

"You'll want to give me more details, mate."

Nick pulled himself free. "She's at the Four Seasons. I'm going to pick her up in the morning."

"I can pick her up tonight."

Nick grimaced. "It's pretty late. You'll encounter hotel security, hurdles you don't want to hit this time of night in a hotel that is undoubtedly wired to the local cops."

Terri got out of the shower, feeling clean for the first time in days. The steam billowed out of the bathroom into the rest of the suite. An extravagance, but there weren't many options without a reservation.

An envelope had been slipped under the door. She peered through the peephole. The hallway was empty. There was a short note inside the envelope:

Miss Rawlston, two gentlemen were looking for you this evening, perhaps Russian by their accents. They asked for you by another name also. I can arrange for security to accompany you in the morning if required. Dial 1 on your phone to reach the Concierge Station.

"Thank you very much, Mr Concierge." She tossed the note on her bed and ordered room service and a 5 a.m. wake-up call.

Chapter Sixteen

Nick and Reg stepped off the Light Rail tram at Circular Quay. It was that time just after dawn when the air was cool, but held the threat of oppressive heat.

"Why so early?"

"Quit bitching, Reg. I'll buy you breakfast." Nick pointed across the street. "There."

Davie and Lucy stood as Nick approached the cafe. They were sitting at a table for four on an outside patio. Both of them had almost full cups of black coffee.

Nick stepped over the low railing, gave Davie a bro-hug, and reached for Lucy. Before he could hug her, she grabbed the sides of his face and kissed him.

A kiss long enough to let Nick know it meant something.

She came up for air and hugged him. "You okay?"

"I am, now." He pointed to his keeper. "This is Reg. My keeper. He doesn't want me to work with the two of you, but you know what?"

"Fuck him," said Lucy.

"I second that." Davie sat and pulled a chair out for Nick. "How are we doing this?"

Nick and Lucy sat. A server dropped two additional menus on the table.

Reg remained standing. "I don't like this."

Nick sighed. "Listen, mate, we wouldn't be here without them. They've been doing all the digging. Sit down and buy us breakfast. O'Shea pays you a motza. I'll have Eggs Bennie and a long black." He handed his menu to Reg. "So, Lucy, Davie. What's the plan?"

Davie pointed at the Four Seasons across the street. "She spent the night there. A big step up from the hostel."

"Do I want to know how you found that out?"

"Probably not," said Lucy. "Plausible deniability."

The server returned, took their menus and orders, and returned to the kitchen.

"Why so early, though?" Asked Reg. "I mean, Christ, this is early."

"Big guy's a wimp, Nick. How have you put up with it?" Davie laughed at the look on Reg's face.

The way the table was positioned, Lucy was facing the hotel, Nick was on her left, facing Circular Quay, Davie was across from Nick, looking south on George Street, and Reg was across from Lucy, his back to the hotel. He noticed Lucy's expression first.

"What's wrong?" Lucy's face had folded into a frown.

"That's them, isn't it?" She pointed to the two Russians on the other side of the street.

Nick and Davie looked where she was pointing.

Reg twisted in his seat. The Russians hadn't noticed them. They were standing near the entrance of the hotel, animatedly discussing something.

"How in the hell did they find out?" Davie started to stand, and Lucy stopped him with a hand on his arm. "What?"

"She's right, mate. Give it a bit. I doubt she's up yet. They're waiting like we are." Nick thought for a moment. "I'm going to give her a heads up."

Terri checked to ensure she had all her essential papers stowed in her pack. She didn't care about leaving any clothes behind. She was hitting the bank, performing the needed transactions, and getting on a flight. She'd bounce around Southeast Asia, Europe and South America for a few months before ending up at her place in Costa Rica. She took a deep breath and let it out slowly. She had enough to spend the rest of her life travelling. Anonymously.

She'd checked the lifts the previous night. She

could take them down to the parking garage below the hotel, and there was an exit out the back of the garage to the street behind the hotel.

She reached for the security latch on the hotel room door, and the hotel phone rang. She paused and looked at it. Debated whether she should answer, then thought of the note from the concierge the night before.

Okay. "Who's this?"

"Not important at the moment. You're Terri O'Shea. You checked in as Grace Rawlston. I'm telling you that so you know I'm not taking the piss. Two nasty-looking Russians are waiting downstairs for you. You should probably—"

"I know. I've got it handled." She paused. "Hey, are you that bloke with Reg? Tell my father to stop looking for me. And tell Reg to ease up on the 'roids. His nuts are going to shrink." She hung up and left the room.

Nick disconnected the call and placed his phone face down on the table. "She seems to have things well in hand." He smiled at Reg. "She recognised you and wants you to tell her father to piss off. And she's concerned about your nuts."

"Yeah, fuck her." Reg turned back to the table. Coffee had been delivered for Reg and Nick. Reg grabbed his cup and sat back, hard, in his chair. "We know where she is. We go get her and drag her back to the old man. Job done." He pointed at Nick. "And you are out of my fucking hair."

Lucy shook her head. "I don't see how you will get past those Russians to grab her."

Reg stood. "The food will be here when I get back. Maybe grab another chair for our guest." He vaulted over the railing. Nick looked at Davie and shrugged. His friend smiled and took off after Reg.

"You guys are on your own," said Lucy. "I'll call the police."

"And tell them what? Nothing's happened yet.

We might be able to reason with them," said Nick.

She shook her head. "I doubt it." She held up her phone. "I'll wait. But don't take long."

Nick checked for trams, then trotted across the street and joined Davie and Reg. "Where are they?"

"The lobby," said Davie. "Sitting facing the lifts."

"Let's do this, then." Nick pushed open the front door and marched across the lobby to the Russians. He sat on the sofa and leaned forward, elbows on his knees. "*Privet, rebyata.* You here for Terri?"

"Again, you," said Mikhail. He looked around the mostly empty lobby. "I bet I could kill you while you sit there, and nobody would notice for many hours."

Reg hopped over the back of the sofa they were sitting on and sat beside Mikhail. "I'll take that bet, comrade."

Davie eased onto the sofa beside Nick. "She knows you're waiting for her. She's not going to come out of that lift, champ. You're wasting your time."

Dimitri leaned forward. "You warned her?"

"Of course I did," said Nick. "Any decent person would. Are we going to have a problem?" He slowly stood.

Mikhail started to stand, and Reg clamped his hand on the little Russian's shoulder. "Sit, fucknuts."

Reg heard a *snick* and looked down at the blade pressing against his side. "Really?" He snapped his hand down and grabbed the little Russian by the wrist. "Where do you want me to stick this?"

Mikhail tried to wrench his left hand free, and when he was unsuccessful, he swung his right hand around and caught Reg just below the eye.

Reg kept his grip and stood, pulling Mikhail with him. "You little shit." He wrenched Mikhail forward with his right arm, keeping the knife clear, and followed through with a hard blow to the little guy's sternum.

Dimitri surged to his feet and squared up on Reg. Nick and Davie jumped in front of him and pushed him back, the sofa cushions hitting the back of his knees and dropping him on his ass. Nick looked at the security coming out of the door behind the concierge station and turned to Dimitri.

"Stay there. The security team looks a lot bigger than you. Bigger than Reg even."

The Russian sagged back on the sofa. Reg had Mikhail's knife hand controlled and was hitting him repeatedly with his weaker left hand when the police arrived.

Terri stood outside the front entrance, watching the commotion inside. She shook her head and turned and came face-to-face with Lucy. "Excuse me." She stepped to the left to get past her, and Lucy moved to block her progress.

"Terri, my name is Lucy. Wait, don't go."

"Are you with Reg, too? My father can piss off. I have no desire to see him. The fact that we are both in the same country at the same time is a horrible coincidence. I'm leaving this afternoon, and we will never be in the same place at the same time again."

"Your father isn't well. He wants to reconcile."

"Horseshit. He wants the ten million back. Tell him it's gone."

Lucy smiled. "That's a shopping trip I would have liked to be on."

Terri frowned. "It's not like that. I need to leave. Don't follow me. I hit hard." She adjusted her pack on her shoulder and headed south on George Street.

Terri upped her pace. The brawl would soon be over, and some of the combatants wouldn't be going in the paddy wagon. It depended on who told the better story to the local constabulary.

The bank opened at 10:00 am. She had to lie low and kill a bit over three hours.

Three blocks south was a fast food restaurant with an upstairs eating area. She stood in line with some early-riser backpackers and ordered the standard breakfast when she reached the front of the line. She took her food tray and sat at a corner table on the upper floor. She could see the entrance from where she sat. Nobody would be sneaking up on her.

As she sipped the bitter coffee, her phone rang. She placed her cup slowly on the table. Very few people knew this number. "Hello?"

"Miss Rawlston, this is Nigel. I trust this isn't too early for you."

"I'm having breakfast. What reason would you have to call me when we're going to see each other in a bit over two hours?"

"I'm afraid that's why I'm calling."

Terri closed her eyes and leaned her head back. "What now?"

"I've just received notification that auditors from the Australian National Audit Office will visit today. Surprise inspection. Given your circumstances, it would be wise for you to put off our appointment until tomorrow."

"Shit, Nigel. I did not want to hear that." She

picked up her coffee cup and put it back down. "How much of a risk are we talking about?"

"It is very hard to say. I'm a very risk-averse guy. You know we share no identifiable personal customer information with the local government. Our accounts are all numbered. That level of privacy is within the laws of the country. But I'm sure if you were to be present and the auditors were to become aware of the millions in cash in your safe deposit—"

"How would you know that?"

"I don't know the exact amount, but you are using two of our largest boxes. It's not for jewellery."

She nodded. "Go on."

"If the auditors knew about that, and the balance in your account and that you were here, there might be tax implications you could avoid by *not* being here."

She sighed. "The audit will be complete by tomorrow?"

"It will be," said Nigel. "It is a quarterly formality. I know the auditors. They'll be here all day, but they'll be finished today."

"My flight out of here is tomorrow afternoon. Can we meet early morning?"

Nigel let out a slow breath. "How much work are we going to do?"

"Transfers, deposits, the usual things people do in banks."

He sighed. "Would it put you out too much to shift out your flight by 24 hours? I would rather we weren't rushed."

She sipped her coffee. "I don't think that's necessary."

"It's up to you. But there is a lot of paperwork. Tomorrow morning at 9:30, then? I'll meet you at the door and let you in early."

"Thanks, Nigel I'll bring you a muffin." She hung up, took another sip of coffee and winced. She opened the airline app on her phone and checked flights for the next day. Only first class seats available. "Well, screw it. Better safe than sorry. I'll just have to keep my head down for another day."

Chapter Seventeen

"Stop hitting him, Reg."

"But it's so therapeutic."

Nick chuckled. "The cops just walked in."

Reg stopped, fist cocked. The hotel security stood by, watching, amused. One of them saw the police enter. "Okay, lads. Break it up."

Reg shoved Mikhail back onto the sofa and shook out his hand. "Thanks."

Nick pointed at Dimitri. "Stay sitting, mate."

The police took names and numbers, questioned the advisability of starting a fight in a high-end hotel lobby with dozens of security cameras, and told them not to leave town while they investigated.

Hotel security waited until the police left and then placed themselves between the combatants. They didn't say anything, just pointed.

Mikhail looked at Dimitri, who shook his head and nodded toward the hotel entrance.

"My weapon, I want it back. I like it."

One of the security team reached between the sofa cushions and retrieved the knife. "We'll keep this. Find another one."

Mikhail took a step toward them and was restrained by Dimitri. "Idiot. The cops will lock us up if they're called back here. Let it go."

"Davie, let's go. You're on your own, Reg," said Nick. "We'll catch up with these arseholes later."

"No." Mikhail jutted his chin. "We will catch up with you later."

Reg chuckled. "Sure thing, comrade." He looked at Nick. "I'll go with you. I want to talk with you and your friends." He pointed at Mikhail and Dimitri. "If I see you guys around, I'll drop you without warning."

He followed Nick and Davie out of the hotel. Nick turned left and headed toward the waterfront.

"Isn't your girlfriend still across the street?"

"You think I'm leading those apes to Lucy? Circuitous route."

"Ah, you're not as dumb as you look."

"Wish I could say the same."

They walked a couple of extra blocks and ended up around the corner from the hotel. Nick called Lucy.

"Nick, where are you guys? Saw the cops enter and then leave. And then you and Davie left with Reg and went off toward the ferries. Staff is looking at me like I'm just taking up space."

"There in a minute. Where'd the Russians go?"

"They left about a minute after you. Waited out front for a couple of minutes before a white van pulled up and picked them up."

"We are around the corner. We'll be there

shortly." Nick hung up, waited for a tram to move out of the way and trotted across the street.

Mikhail had the side door of the van open before the vehicle came to a complete stop at the office. As he stepped out, he spun and jabbed a fist into Dimitri's chest. "What in the hell are we doing back here? I need weapons, and I need to be back in that city."

Dimitri pushed the fist out of his way and continued walking into the clubhouse. "Watch your place, mate. Kon wants to talk to us." He looked back at Mikhail, still standing by the van, and motioned for him to follow. "You might be big shit where you come from, but you're just another cog in the machine here. Don't piss off Kon."

Mikhail narrowed his eyes. "Did you call me shit?"

"You need to improve your idiomatic English."

"I'm an idiot?"

"For fuck sake, hurry up."

Kon waved at them to sit in the chairs across from his desk as he leaned back. He looked at the end of his cigar, tapped off the cold ash, and flashed up his lighter. "You're a fuck-up, Mikhail. I don't like that."

The wiry Russian placed his hands on the arms of his chair and tried to stand but was stopped by Dimitri's hand on his shoulder.

Mikhail tried to pull his shoulder away. "Get off me. You call me shit and an idiot, and this fat man calls me a fuck-up. Someone should be bleeding right now."

Kon held the flame to his cigar and puffed it to life. He exhaled a mouthful of smoke. "Listen, Mikhail, and listen very carefully. You are a visitor here. My relationship with the authorities in this country gives me a bit of leeway regarding the lads in my employ misbehaving, but," he leaned forward and held his thumb and forefinger very close together, "a very little bit of leeway. If those boys had found your knife at the hotel, you'd be in a cell right now, and I'd be in a heap of shit."

"You are lecturing me? We would have completed this exercise in the alley if this *mudak* had not stopped me."

Dimitri clenched his fists and looked at Mikhail. "*Mudak*?"

"Boys, settle down." Kon tapped the ash off his cigar. "Your boss is on the way. He'll land shortly." He chuckled. "He is not going to be pleased with your run-in with the police, and if you haven't found the girl by the time he lands, he will share that displeasure very personally with you."

"Why would you tell him about the police?"

"I haven't yet. He's still in the air."

"When does he land?

"Fucking soon. I'm not a travel agent. There's a man at the airport to pick him up and bring him here. You both will stay to give him a status update."

Mikhail shifted in his seat. "But I should be—"

"Shut up. Work out your story."

"So you two are helping Nick? I told him to keep it on the down low." Reg settled into the chair opposite Davie.

"He doesn't listen very well." Davie nervously scratched his arm. "But he asks, we help."

"Very loyal." He handed the menu back to the server. "I'm not staying for food." He pointed across the street. "It's no coincidence the Russians were over there. Terri is staying at the hotel. So, well done tracking her down. I doubt very much that she'll stay there after the bullshit in the lobby." He tapped the table. "Find her again. You're good at this. And try to stay ahead of the Russians. That little one scares me."

He stood and looked at his watch. "Nick, you're still with me."

Chapter Eighteen

The flight from LA approached Sydney from the north, along the coast. Petrovski looked out the right side First Class window at Sydney in the early morning light. The Sydney Harbour Bridge, the Sydney Opera House, all nestled in the great expanse of the city. Somewhere in that sprawling mess was the key to his missing ten million dollars and bitch who stole it.

He was travelling under his own name. Maintaining a clean persona meant acting like it.

He slid the immigration arrival card into his passport on a clean page and retrieved his carry-on from the overhead compartment. The shiny metal hook that he preferred to use as a prosthetic stayed home. He was wearing a ceramic hand. It looked obviously fake. The gap between the fake thumb and the fake forefinger was perfect for securely jamming his passport.

Immigration was seamless, and customs waved him through without checking his carry-on. He walked through the security mini-maze and into the arrivals hall. A chauffeur in full livery stood holding a cardboard sign with 'Petrovski' in bold type. He nodded at the man, who turned and led him to a black SUV.

Petrovski tossed his carry-on into the back seat, opened the driver's door, saw the steering wheel, and smiled. "I think this is your seat."

"Don't worry about it," said the driver. "It happens more often than you think. You'll get used to it. My name is Devi, by the way."

Petrovski chuckled, walked around the front of the truck, and awkwardly hopped into the front passenger seat. "I imagine so." He pulled the door closed and buckled his belt. "How long is the—" He looked at the driver, who was staring at his face. "You'll get used to it."

"Uhm, what happened?"

"To…?"

The driver pointed at his face. "Hey, if I'm out of line, just let me know."

"Very forward here."

"First time?"

"In Australia? Yes." He cleared his throat. "You're not out of line. It's a natural question. I was in a fire in The Everglades. It was a decade ago. I forget I look like this." He held up his prosthetic hand. "Lost this, too. I don't forget that too often."

The driver tapped a credit card at the exit and waited for the boom to lift. "Half an hour."

Petrovski nodded. "Thanks."

"Does it hurt?"

"Hasn't for almost a decade. The first year was a test. Now it lets people know I'm not to be trifled with."

The driver grunted and smiled. Petrovski enjoyed the silence for a moment, then remembered the phone in his inside suit pocket. Two messages arrived shortly after he turned it on.

The first was from Martin: *Hey, thought you'd like to know. The woman has moved her flight out by 24 hours. Maybe she wants to get some surfing in.*

The second was from his local contact: *A driver will pick you up. When you get here, we will arrange accommodations for you.*

The driver moved off the highway and onto surface streets into a suburban neighbourhood. He pulled the car up to a chain-link gate, nodded to the man behind it, and waited while it slowly rolled open.

"Not much security."

"This is a social club. We hide among the sheep." He pulled the car into the parking area behind a low, flat building and led him in. It was a community hall of some sort.

Petrovski nodded with approval. Very under the radar.

The driver led him to an interior door, gave it a short knock and opened it, ushering Petrovski in.

It was a plain office. Cheap wood panelling covered three walls, rendered brick the fourth, on the right, with a louvred window cracked open. Kon sat behind a desk facing the door. He had a lot of mileage on him. An unlit cigar jutted out of the corner of his mouth as he worked on a laptop.

He looked up as the door opened. "You've arrived. Good flight?"

"Mr Petrovski, this is Konstantin. He is your host for the duration."

Konstantin perched his cigar on the edge of an ashtray. "Call me Kon." He stood and extended his hand. Then blanched when he saw Petrovski's prosthetic. "Oh, shit. Sorry, mate. I forgot."

"Not a problem." Petrovski grabbed the

outstretched hand with his left hand, shook it, and then sat. "Happens more often than you think."

The driver smiled and sat beside him.

"So I'll be staying here?"

Kon laughed and sat. "Oh, hell no. I messaged you, right? I've got a flat for you downtown. You're only here for a couple of days, right? The place I've set up is nice. Serviced apartment in the CBD. Devi will be your driver while you're here."

Petrovski nodded. "Thanks. I need to talk to Mikhail and debrief him. How can I reach him?"

Kon nodded and leaned back in his chair. "He's out back with Dimitri. They were in the city very early this morning. The woman you're looking for is staying at the Four Seasons hotel on the waterfront. They were going to intercept her."

Petrovski leaned forward. "So they have her? It's after 10:00 am."

Kon shook his head. "The hotel security was too thick." He held up his hands. "Mikhail and Dimitri could have taken them, but the risk of getting picked up by the police was too great."

Petrovski narrowed his eyes and sat back. "So you don't have police in your pocket?"

Kon waggled his hand. "To a certain extent, yes. But there would be nothing the police could do if your angry little protégé left a lake of blood in the lobby. They backed off."

"I need them in here. Now."

Kon picked up his mobile phone and dialled.

"What are you doing?"

"Calling them."

Petrovski reached across the desk, grabbed Kon's mobile, and terminated the call. "Maybe not now. We talk in the van. I need to be taken to that hotel right now." He looked at the driver. "Bring the truck to the front. Grab Mikhail and Dimitri and wait for me outside. I need to speak to Kon in private for a minute."

He waited until the door closed behind the driver.

"I need a gun."

"Oh, mate, you sure about that? Look, I can get you a weapon taken from the evidence locker of one of the police stations, but the penalty for being caught with it is pretty prohibitive."

Petrovski held out his good hand. "I'll be careful."

Kon looked at him for a moment, shook his head and pulled open his middle desk drawer. He placed a .22 calibre Smith and Wesson pistol on his desk, with three magazines and a case of shells. "This won't come back to me if you're apprehended with it. Understand?"

Petrovski pulled the box of shells closer and deftly opened it one-handed. He spilled the shells on the desk and filled the magazines one-handed, ten shells per. "Understood, but I'm not sure you understand that if anything happens to me, there will be repercussions." He smiled, the scars on the right side of his face turning it into a grotesque sneer. "But I won't get caught."

He stood. He slid two of the magazines into his suit pockets, one in each so they wouldn't rattle. He slid the other magazine into the grip of the pistol. He placed the pistol under his belt in the small of his back. "I'll catch up with you about that serviced apartment later."

"Where in the hell did she go? Your guy on the cameras, he is looking, right?" Mikhail paced the boardwalk at Circular Quay. The van had dropped Petrovski, his driver, Mikhail and Dimitri near Central Station half an hour previous. They had been walking non-stop since. "I am wasting my time, and my boss is here."

"Yeah, and he's looking just like we are. Stop pacing, for god's sake." Dimitri looked at his watch. "It will be another 30 minutes before we get a location. We should have something to eat." He pointed to a small cafe. "My treat."

Mikhail looked over his shoulder. "Are you

crazy? Petrovski will skin me."

"Have you had anything to eat today so far?"

"No."

"And where is your boss?"

"Also looking. I don't know exactly. Could be just around the corner." He shook his head. "I've never seen him as quiet as he was in the van." He swallowed. "Made me nervous."

Dimitri shook his head. "You're soft. Get over there and grab a table. I'll let Kon know we're grabbing a quick coffee."

Mikhail grabbed a table on the outside patio, near the railing, and took the seat facing the waterfront. Dimitri sat across from him. He was scanning the menu when the server appeared, asking for their coffee order.

"Flat white for me. What about you, Mikhail?"

The diminutive Russian stood. "Nothing. Come on. We have to go."

"What?" Dimitri stood and turned. He saw the

disfigured man walking with Devi. "You'll have to tell me what happened to his face one day."

Mikhail wagged his finger in Dimitri's face. "Oh, no. You can't ask him that. He'll kill you."

Dimitri's eyes grew big, and Mikhail couldn't help laughing. He hopped over the railing and waved at Petrovski. "Over here."

Petrovski and Devi altered their path and they met near one of the Ferry wharves. "Quit waving your hands about, Mikhail. We're trying to keep a low profile. Why are you sitting on your ass instead of looking for Terri?"

Dimitri glanced at Petrovski's hands and held out his left. "How are you enjoying Australia so far?"

Petrovski scowled at him.

"Right. Okay, I have a person scouring CCTV footage looking for Terri. His name is Geoff. We know she was in the Four Seasons Hotel last night and is not there now. Mikhail and I were at the hotel by 6 am this morning, and she'd left by then." He held his arms out wide. "This is a large city. Rather than chase our tails, my contact will let us know as soon as he's tracked her down."

Petrovski looked at him for a full minute, his expression not changing. He sniffed and nodded. "Makes sense. I could use some food." He nodded toward the cafe Mikhail and Dimitri had just left. "That place will do."

The server returned with menus. "You've decided to eat after all?"

Petrovski glared at him, and he shut up, took their coffee orders and retreated.

"So tell me why it's taken over four hours for this contact of yours to find her?"

"It has not been that long since we asked," said Mikhail. "We had an experience with the local police this morning."

Petrovski scowled. "I heard. You're lucky you're not in their systems right now."

"Yes, fortunately," said Dimitri. "There was a small argument in the hotel while we tried to find Terri. It's been sorted."

"With whom?"

Dimitri looked at Mikhail, who shrugged. "A couple of other people are also looking for Terri."

"Who?" barked Petrovski. He glared at Dimitri. "You didn't tell me this earlier."

Dimitri recoiled. "Just some guys. Looking for Terri. She probably pissed many people off."

"Would you know how to find them again?"

Mikhail shrugged. "Geoff is looking for Terri. We could ask him to look for these guys, but maybe it is smarter to look for Terri. We find Terri; they will find us."

Petrovski nodded. "Makes sense." He looked at the time on his phone. "How long until we know where she is?"

"I think we have time for food."

He nodded again and picked up the menu. "So

bring me up to date. Leave out nothing."

Nick sat sideways on the park bench. His arm was across its back, his hand close to Reg's shoulder. He tapped it. "The four of them are getting breakfast."

Reg twisted on the bench to look.

"Don't be so bloody obvious," said Nick. "A bit of subtlety."

Reg narrowed his eyes. "Four? Who are the other two?"

"Who knows? One of them has burn scars all over his face. Looks like a fake hand."

Reg craned his large neck and shifted in his seat until he faced Nick. He slowly shifted his gaze to his left until he could see the foursome at the cafe. He frowned. "You have no idea who he is?"

Nick shook his head. He held up his phone and took a couple of casual pictures of the group. "I'll see what I can find out."

"Back to the computer, then. As nice as it is out

here, we've got to find Terri." He nodded toward the cafe. "Before they do."

Chapter Nineteen

Terri watched Nick and Reg watch the cafe. She couldn't see the cafe from her vantage point, but they were obviously watching the two Russians they'd had an altercation with. The two Russians who tried tracking her down the night before.

She had to kill a day until she could get to the bank. A day avoiding being tagged by the Russians. She knew why they were looking for her. A distant figure from a distant crime. Keeping out of their way wouldn't be a huge problem.

But she could get some help.

Approaching Nick and Reg had to wait. If they could see the Russians, the Russians could see them. But they couldn't sit on that bench, in the sun, all day.

She put her hair up under a hat and put on a pair of oversized sunglasses. The patio cafe opposite George Street from the Circular Quay boardwalk was sparsely populated. She ordered a latte and a blueberry scone and sat back with her International Herald Tribune and its crossword puzzle.

It took her longer to complete the crossword than normal. She had to alternate her attention between the puzzle and Nick.

She'd made it about halfway through when Nick and Reg stood from their bench and started walking toward her. She waited until they were close and dropped her newspaper by their feet. Nick retrieved it from the ground and placed it on her table. Reg was half a dozen steps ahead of him.

"Thanks, Nick," she whispered. She slid a piece of paper with her phone number into his hand. "Call me as soon as you can."

Nick pocketed the paper and caught up to Reg.

"Hey, big guy, how serious is the old fart about finding his daughter?"

Reg looked at him like he was an idiot. "Very serious."

Nick nodded. "Okay. So, how about we follow the Russians, and when they find Terri, we find Terri."

"Knowing them, we'll find her dead." He shook his head. "No, we find her and keep an eye on our backs. They'll be using us." He stepped onto a Light Rail car. "So get on your computer and track her from early this morning."

"Fair call. Seems to be the best bet." He sat across from Reg on the LRT. "Or maybe we go sit at the airport and nab her there. She's supposed to be flying out today."

"I thought you were smart. The Federal cops swarm all over that place. No, we find her before she leaves the city." He tapped the face of his watch. "And you better hop to it."

Nick leaned back in his seat in thought. He knew

where she was. Something was off with this. He'd never been contacted by the person he was searching for. They were usually on the run. The last thing they wanted to do was talk to him.

This was different.

O'Shea met them at the door when they returned. "You find her yet?"

"It's been an interesting morning, old man," said Reg. We definitely have competition. Terri was at the Four Seasons. I expect she checked out and slipped out the back. Nicky will track her through CCTV, and, what do you think, Nick? We'll have her located within the hour?"

Nick waggled his hand and sat on the sofa. "Maybe two." He leaned his head back and closed his eyes, as if in thought. "Would you know when her flight is?"

O'Shea mumbled something as he sat on the coffee table across from Nick. He leaned forward, his elbows on his knees. "What are you doing?"

"Thinking." Nick opened one eye and looked at O'Shea. "I'll teach you how someday. When is she leaving? According to Reg, we need to find her before she gets to the airport."

"I'm told it's an afternoon flight, but I don't know the reliability of that data." He kicked Nick on the foot. "Get yer fookin' arse in gear and find my daughter. We're running out of time."

Nick palmed the mobile phone stuffed between the cushions and slowly stood, sliding it into his trouser pocket. "Absolutely. Don't give yourself a heart attack."

He pulled the sliding door open and stepped onto the partially covered balcony. He tapped the spacebar on his laptop and woke it up. "I'll let you know as soon as I find something."

Reg stood behind him, looking over his shoulder. Nick spun his chair around. "Hey, big guy. I do abso-fucking-lutely nothing with you looking over my shoulder. I know the time constraints, and I know the urgency. Back. The fuck. Off."

Reg chuckled. "I'll be watching TV in there. Anything - *any*thing - shows up, and you grab me, right?"

"Absolutely. Piss off."

Reg grunted in assent as he left the balcony. Nick waited until he heard the patio door close before he pulled the phone out of one pocket and the slip of paper with Terri's number out of the other. He glanced quickly at the door to ensure it was closed and placed his earbuds in. He dialled the number and held the phone on his lap, out of sight.

"Is this Nick?"

"Is this Terri?"

"Thanks for calling. Why did my father hire you to look for me?"

"You're quick. How did you figure that out?"

"Reg. My father hired him three years ago in New Zealand. If I see Reg, I assume the old fart is around somewhere. Why did he hire you?"

Nick chuckled. "Your memory isn't that good after all. I chased him seven or eight years ago, I was with the AFP back then. Your turn. Why are you in Sydney?"

There was a pause on the line, and she chuckled. "I thought your name was familiar. I'm in Sydney because I've got some funds to move around."

"You don't need to be here to do that."

"You'd be surprised."

"And you're leaving later today?"

There was a brief hesitation before she answered. "Tell my father I've got no interest in seeing him, okay?"

"You should probably know that a couple of Russians are also looking for you."

"Was that you who called me this morning?"

Nick smiled to himself. "Why are they looking for you?"

"You'd have to ask them. Thank you, really, for

warning me. Saved me a spot of trouble. I owe you."

"I'll take you up on that." There was an extended silence on the line. "Are you still there, Terri?"

"I am. Look, I have a proposal for you. I have no desire to mix it up with the Russians. I know the kind of things they do. Intimately familiar. I'll help you track them down, and you get rid of them for me, okay?"

Nick chuckled. "Right. And you're out of here before I get the mediation between you and your father set up." He listened to silence. "You still there?"

"I'm leaving today."

"No you're not. You planned on leaving today, but you've put it off for at least 24 hours, maybe longer. Why are you here?"

"I told you. Banking."

"Most of which can be done from a computer in Botswana." He stood and walked to the railing. "Must be physical. Bonds? Metals? Piles of currency?"

Terri sighed. "You're good at what you do, Nick. I'm not hurting anybody. I know you've got some eye-in-the-sky thing going on. No way you could have tracked me down as quickly as you did otherwise. Keep an eye out for me, okay?"

"Why don't you come and meet your father, bury all your hatchets, and stay at his place until your flight? It's safe here."

"You're at his place? He has a place here?" she exhaled. "How did I not know that?"

"Think about it. You've got my number." Nick ended the call and returned to his laptop.

Reg slid open the patio door and stood over him. "You don't need to hide the mobile anymore. I know you have it. You were just talking to your friends, right? Davie and what's-her-name, Lucy. We need to find Terri before she leaves." He looked at his watch. "I really don't want to do this at the airport. We've got maybe three hours."

Nick glanced at the camera to his right and held up the phone. "I'll call them back now. Impress upon them the urgency." He stood and walked to the railing. "Feel free to eavesdrop if you want, but it will be boring tech talk."

"I'm good. The old man wants me for something. Keep me across everything that's going on."

Nick turned his back on Reg and called Davie. "Where are you?"

"Just getting back to the pad. Where are you?"

"I'm on the balcony. Patch the CCTV through as soon as, okay?" He looked over his shoulder. Made sure Reg was gone. "Our brief has changed a bit."

Davie launched the viewer program and selected cameras near the Four Seasons. "I reckon Terri left the hotel out the back way, early."

"No," said Nick. "Look for the Russians."

"Look out for them, sure. Scary arseholes."

"No, look for them. I don't need to look for Terri

anymore."

"I'm pretty sure that was the brief. What changed?"

"I've got her phone number. I was just talking to her. She's the lesser evil. We need to keep the Russians off her back until she gets on a flight out of the country."

"You've - you've got her phone number?"

"We've talked, yes. Do you have the streams up yet?"

Davie tapped a couple of keys and sat back. "You should be getting them now."

"I am. Thanks. I'm going to take control."

"All yours, mate. Call me if you need any help."

Nick hung up and selected cameras near the Four Seasons. He couldn't access the cameras on the hotel property due to their security, so he grabbed the one from the front of a convenience store across the street from the back of the hotel, the front of a pizzeria and state security videos from the Circular Quay train station. He scrubbed them back to when he bumped into Terri at the front of the hotel and let them all run forward, in a grid, at double speed.

It was an art, keeping an eye on six simultaneous screens, filtering out the meaningless stuff while capturing the important. The top left vision was Terri at her outside table, sipping her coffee and working on her crossword puzzle. He wouldn't have recognised her if he didn't know it was her.

The middle-bottom vision was the Russians at the cafe. Mikhail and Dimitri and the other two who joined. The older, scarred guy looked like he was in charge. The characters looked like something out of the Keystone Kops, with jerky motion adding comic value to the display.

The scarred guy stood first, wiped his mouth and dropped the napkin on the table. Nick glanced at Terri's screen. She'd left the table.

"Shit." He added cameras facing south on George

Street, adjusted the time window and found her about a block and a half south. He checked the time codes. He was about five minutes behind live. He scrubbed them both to the end of the reel, getting them all current. Terri was stopped, looking in a shopfront window on the east side of the street.

Two of the Russians—Mikhail and Dimitri—were less than half a block from her and gaining. He grabbed his phone and called.

He watched her react to it ringing and pull it out of her back pocket. "Nick?"

"They're maybe a hundred metres behind you. Get out of sight. Your disguise isn't that good."

Terri started to turn.

"No, don't. You'll be too obvious. Ten more metres down the street and turn left into an arcade."

"Thanks. I owe you."

He watched her drop the phone into her pocket and take long, purposeful strides away from the camera, then turn left. The Russians were a few seconds behind her. They got to the arcade, Mikhail looked left into the Arcade, and they both broke into a run.

"Oh, shit."

Chapter Twenty

Dan MacCready came into the Joint Task Force office in Miami yawning, a takeaway cup of coffee in each hand. "James, where are the donuts? We've been at it for over twelve hours. I need a sugar hit. Any luck on the travel vouchers?"

"Fuck the donuts. Get over here." He was in front of a terminal, rows of data reflecting Petrovski's recent phone calls.

"Putting aside the blasphemy you just uttered, here's your coffee. You wake up on the wrong side of the bed this morning?" Mac rolled a chair alongside his partner.

James jabbed his finger on the screen. "He was offline for almost 24 hours. But he's back."

Mac took a sip of his coffee and winced. "The Feds must have something in their budget for a coffee machine." He squinted at the monitor. "So he's back. So what?"

James jabbed his finger at the monitor again. "He's back, but he's not back. About four hours ago his phone registered on an Australian network. He's been pinging off their towers ever since."

Mac put his coffee aside. "Sydney?"

James nodded. "The airport. But after that, we don't know where these towers are. We need to get tower locations."

Mac nodded. "I'll contact the carrier over there and get the geo-locations. You talk to the overlords. If this doesn't get us tickets to Oz, nothing will."

It took two hours and half a dozen phone calls to Australia before Mac had the site information from the mobile phone carrier. He grabbed one of the younger techs and handed him a thumb drive with the data files. "Plot the sites for me and the phone data on this. There will be two different numbers. See how quickly they met up with each other. How fast can you get these to me?"

"Twenty minutes, Mac."

"Thanks. Find me. I'll be with the kid trying to get tickets to Oz."

"Lucky bastard."

Mac chuckled as he headed off in search of James.

"Keith, this is an opportunity like we've never had before and probably won't get again."

Keith, James' superior, looked over the top of his reading glasses. "I'm not convinced."

Mac opened his mouth to respond and stopped when James shook his hand to shush him.

"What do I need to tell you to convince you?" James leaned forward, his hands on his boss's desk.

"Why now? What's different about him being in Australia that would justify the thousands of dollars it will take to get the two of you there for what will appear as not much more than a boondoggle to those above me?"

"We would never go on a boondoggle," said Mac. "It's a hellish long flight, we'll only be there a couple of days, and we'll be jet-lagged the entire time."

"I got this Mac. Thanks," said James. "Why now? Petrovski will be out of his element. We know he will be there to meet a money launderer he hasn't used in three years. We are also looking for her."

"Who?" Keith took off his glasses and leaned back.

"Teresa O'Shea. We have info that she is in Sydney, and will be for a week, or less, to close out some financial dealings. Dealings that are related, we believe, to Petrovski's business. He'll be focused on her, and there is no doubt he will fuck up."

Keith was nodding now. "Who will be your liaison in Australia? AFP, not local cops."

"I'm making some calls. We've worked with

them before. Someone will meet us at the airport.”

Keith considered this for a few seconds, nodding. “Yeah. Okay. Makes sense. Talk to travel and get your tickets and accommodations sorted.”

“Business Class, right?” said Mac.

Keith barked out a laugh. “Cheapest economy seats you can get. And maybe a tent in the park instead of a hotel room."

Chapter Twenty-One

Terri's mouse act in the cat-and-mouse game with the Russians was tiring. If Nick weren't in her ear, she would have been tagged at least half a dozen times.

It was nearing the end of the day. She circled back to the Four Seasons and waited by the shops across the street. She was patient. She sent a message to Nick. *Any sign of them?*

She waited for a couple of minutes and got a response. *They went into that hotel you stayed in last night. About ten minutes ago. Is that you across the street?*

She looked around until she saw the camera and gave it a short wave. Her phone rang.

"You shouldn't hang around there. They're going to find you, and that little shit with the knife isn't pleasant."

"Thanks. I know." Terri looked around. "I need to find somewhere else to spend the night. And it's getting late." Her shoulders slumped. "And it's likely they've got someone checking hotel bookings and will find out where I am tonight."

There was silence on the phone for almost a minute.

"Are you still there, Nick?"

"I am. Can you find a hidden corner inside the cafe beside you?"

Terri took a few steps into the entrance. It was half full. The corners away from the window were pretty dark. "Yeah, I think so. Why?"

"Hide in a corner, grab some food and give me thirty minutes."

"Why?"

"Trust me." The call terminated.

"Right. Like I have a choice right now." She stepped into the cafe and headed to a back corner. She was intercepted by a server.

"Table for one?"

Terri pointed to the back corner. "Yeah. That one."

The server tried steering her toward the front. "We have a couple of lovely seats by the windows."

"No. That back corner." She evaded the server's hand and placed her bag on one of the chairs. "Can you get me a beer? Whatever low carb you have on tap."

The server raised one of his eyebrows and placed the menu on the table. "Pint or Schooner?"

"I don't know what a schooner is."

"Smaller than a pint."

Terri nodded. "Definitely a pint."

"Coming up."

She nodded in thanks and took a quick look at the menu. Now that she was sitting and smelling the food in the kitchen, her stomach started rumbling.

The pint of beer arrived at her table just as she had made a decision. "Chicken Parm and beer-battered wedges, please."

The server smiled and took the proffered menu. "Done."

Terri sipped the beer and leaned back in her chair. Her view out the window faced right angles to the hotel, out toward the cruise ship dock at Circular Quay. For the first time in a couple of days, she started feeling relaxed.

She took a tentative sip of the beer, never her favourite drink. But it was hot out, and the brew was refreshing. She followed the sip with a larger mouthful and got her phone out. *I don't know what your plans are, but this was a good idea. I'm starving.* She checked the spelling, then pressed *Send*.

She put her phone down and took another mouthful of beer. She watched the tourists outside the window, walking along the boardwalk, taking pictures in front of the buskers. She needed to relax. She needed to find a place to hide that nobody would think of looking.

The beer and the heat was sapping her energy. She needed sleep. And food.

The server arrived with a massive plate, a slab of chicken parmigiana sitting half on top of a bed of crispy potato wedges.

"Thanks," she smiled and grabbed a wedge, dipped it in the sour cream, then the sweet chilli and popped it in her mouth. It was delicious.

She was cutting into the slab of chicken when her bag was lifted off the chair opposite and Lucy took its place.

"Don't let me stop you. It looks good."

Terri smiled while she chewed. Lucy waited. "It is good. Are you Nick's plan?" She smiled at the slight blush.

"I'm not sure exactly what plan you're referring

to. But for tonight, we're going to have dinner here, and you'll spend the night on my sofa." She looked over her shoulder at the bar. "I should have ordered that. It looks good."

Terri was slicing through the chicken like a milling machine. "What did you get?"

"Fish and chips. Hard to screw that up, though by the looks of what you're demolishing, I've got nothing to worry about."

Terri took another drink and wiped her mouth. "What about the pricks across the street?"

"Davie and Nick are keeping an eye on the place. They'll let us know if they leave, or if they haven't, they'll guide us safely to my car."

"Handy having an eye in the sky."

The server placed a plate as large as Terri's in front of Lucy, a massive piece of deep-fried, battered fish on a bed of chips. Two slices of lemon, a small packet of vinegar and a single sprig of parsley adorned the rest of the plate. "Could I get some tartar sauce?”

The server nodded and disappeared.

“So, Lucy, what’s the deal between you, Nick, and Davie?”

Lucy shook her head. “I’m eating while this is hot. We can talk later.”

Terri smiled at the blush creeping up Lucy’s neck. “Fair enough. Later.”

The plates were empty, Terri’s second beer was gone, and Lucy was looking at her watch. “We should get going.”

Terri stood and stretched. “Any word on the slugs across the street?”

“Let’s find out.” Lucy handed an AirPod to Terri and placed its mate in her ear. “My ears are clean. Don’t worry.”

“Sure thing.” Terri slid the earpiece in and raised her eyebrows. “Well?”

“Hang on.” She called Davie.

"Hey, Luce."

"It's Lucy."

Terri smiled.

"Hey, Lucy. Finished eating?"

"Yeah. And I've got Terri on the phone, too. We're about to leave and need a status up on the," she looked at Terri. "What did you call them?"

"Slugs."

"The slugs across the street. They still there?"

"Hi, Terri. My name is Davie. I'm Nick's guy in a chair. I've had eyes on all ways in and out of that hotel since you went in the cafe. They haven't left."

Terri shook her head. "That you know of. Do you have the ability to look at a couple of blocks around this location to see if they are on the street?"

"Absolutely. Give me a minute. This is weird, by the way. Your voice is in my left ear, and Lucy's is in my right ear. Sharing AirPods?"

Terri sat back down. She pushed her plate out of the way and leaned her elbows on the table. "How long is this going to take?"

"Minutes. Shit."

"What?" Ask Lucy. "Shit, what?"

"They just came out of the front of the hotel. They're crossing the street. Heading your way. Go through the kitchen and exit the back way. Take a right in the alley once you get out."

Terri slowly pushed back from the table.

"Come on, you two. You've got to move. They're almost at the front door."

"You fucking with us, Davie?"

"I'm not, Terri. Move it."

Lucy grabbed Terri by the arm and pushed past the cashier. "He doesn't fuck around, Terri." They dodged past startled staff.

"This door is alarmed," said Terri.

Lucy laughed. "As am I." She hit the bar across the width of the door and they spilled into the laneway behind the restaurant.

"Okay, I see you. Turn right. They just came in

the front door of that place. Your car is half a block away."

"I know where my car is, Davie."

"Of course you do."

"I hope to meet you to thank you one day." Terri pulled the AirPod out and handed it back to Lucy. "Your car? Where are we going now?"

Dimitri stepped over the café's patio railing and pushed into the café, Mikhail tight behind him.

"Gentlemen, table for two?"

"No," said Mikhail. "Two women were in here. One had red hair, and one was blonde. We are looking for them."

The server involuntarily glanced at the table Terri and Lucy had just left. "That's not a very specific description. I don't recall anyone like that here."

Mikhail pointed at the table the server had glanced at. "They were sitting there. I did not see them leave. Did they go out back way?"

"Is that a Russian accent? I've been meaning to learn Russian. It's a cool language."

Mikhail stepped closer. "Punk. Did they go out the back?"

The server held his hands up in surrender as he backed up. "Sorry, guys, I don't know what you're talking about."

Dimitri pushed him out of the way, and he and Mikhail ran through the kitchen and out the back door.

Dimitri pointed to the end of the alley. "I think they just went around that corner."

"Call that Geoff guy and get them on camera." Mikhail took his knife from his back pocket and flicked it open. "Talk while you run."

"Jesus, they're right behind us. Lucy, take off. You don't need to be involved in this."

"And miss all this fun?" They ducked right down an intersecting lane, and Lucy pulled Terri behind a dumpster. She held her finger over her lips. Her phone buzzed just as the Russians ran past. She muffled it with her clothes, waited until the two had made it about half a block down the lane, then pulled Terri up and backtracked their path.

They ran.

The phone buzzed again, and Lucy put in her AirPods. "You see that, Davie?"

"Buy a lottery ticket."

"That wasn't luck, champ. That was skill. Where are they?"

Terri held out her hand, and Lucy dropped one of her AirPods in her palm.

"They kept going. I think they're lost. What are your plans?

"Calling it a night," said Lucy

"You don't want to double back and take those two out?" Terri had a small smile on her face.

"No, that's fine." She took two right turns and ended up half a block from her car. "Are they still lost?"

"I think they've given up. You're clear."

"Thanks, Davie. We'll talk tomorrow, okay?" She hung up and stowed the AirPods.

"Davie seems competent. Are you two…?" She let the question trail off.

"Oh, god no. He's Nick's best friend. Nick and I," she hesitated. "I think Nick and I are becoming a thing." She unlocked her car with the key fob. "But enough about me. I have a million questions for you."

Terri got in the car and waited until Lucy started it. "I'm sure. I might have two, maybe three answers." She fastened her seatbelt and smiled at Lucy. "But fire away."

"The obvious, girl. Why in the hell is your father so intent on tracking you down? And follow up, why are you so intent on not meeting him?"

Terri let out a slow breath. "Coming in with the hard one-two, aren't you?" She settled in her seat.

"How long is this drive?"

Lucy glanced at her. "I suspect not long enough."

"Well, it's a long story, and not one I'm comfortable talking about. It's a personal, family story. Sorry."

"I'm not going to pry into personal stuff." She glanced at her passenger again. "You know that your father is literally keeping Nick captive while he looks for you, right? He could hand you over now, and be free. Get paid. But instead he and Davie are tracking the Russians for you until you leave town tomorrow."

"Captive? Bullshit."

"Not BS. He was taken to your father's place. The big guy, Reg, is basically his minder. He tried to slip out a couple of times, and Reg made sure he wouldn't try again."

Terri shook her head. "That doesn't make sense. He could have called the police and been 'released' the same day."

"I had to slip him a phone. When they grabbed him from the beach they took the SIM out of his phone."

"They grabbed him from the beach?"

Lucy nodded. "We were winding up a rather nice date. Walking along the surf under the moonlight." She sighed. "Our first real date, actually."

"Oh, Jesus. I'm sorry."

"It was your father, not you. No worries. I'm still confused, though. What time is your flight tomorrow?"

"What will happen to Nick if he doesn't turn me over?"

"Worst case, he doesn't get paid, I expect." Lucy parked outside her apartment building and tossed the local parking permit on her dash. "Your flight? What time. I need to know how drunk we're going to get tonight."

"Not too drunk. I have an appointment in the morning. The flight is at three. I should be at the airport by 1:30 at the latest."

"What appointment?"

"A million questions, is it?"

"A million and one. I will drive you so you don't get made by the arseholes following you. I'm going to need to know where you're going."

Terri named a small personal bank. "On Martin's Place."

"I haven't been in a bank branch in years. You can't do this online? Even signing documents can be done online now. Had to, during the pandemic."

"Some things you need to do in person."

"Well, you've got a reason."

"Yeah," said Terri under her breath. "Ten million of them."

Chapter Twenty-Two

Davie called Lucy as soon as he got up. "She stayed with you last night?"

"Terri? Yeah. We were trying to decide what to do for breakfast."

"The cafe across from O'Shea's place. I think she should know where her father is."

Lucy laughed. "We can do that. Are you buying?"

"Why not? How soon can you two be there?"

"Fifteen minutes, max."

Dave glanced at the time on his microwave and added an hour. "About the same. Grab a table outside if you get there before me."

Nick woke in O'Shea's apartment, determined it

would be the last time he used it. He quickly shaved and showered, and stormed into the living area.

"O'Shea! Reg! Where the hell are you?"

Reg stumbled out of his bedroom in boxers, a thickening layer of fat masking his muscular physique. "Shut up, you prat. Why are you making so much noise?"

"This arrangement is over. I'll continue doing what you requested, but I'm not doing it here."

"Like hell you're not," growled O'Shea as he padded out of his bedroom, hair tousled and bathrobe loosely tied around his gut. "The rules haven't changed." He grimaced. "Ow. Look, kid, my daughter is leaving the country today, and you're doing a piss-poor job finding her. You and Reg will be hitting the streets. Get your techie friend to be the eyes. That seems to work. And find her."

Nick frowned. He slowly shook his head. "You're losing, old man. This is my last day doing this. Whatever the outcome, I'm gone before dinner."

"You don't find her, and you don't get a cent."

"I try to maintain a professional outlook on all my jobs. Even those really mundane ones. But you're really, really trying my patience. Limit what I can do *and* get pissed when I don't succeed? Get fucked. I'm having breakfast at the cafe across the street." He pointed at Reg. "You stay here. I'll be back in an hour."

Reg cleared his throat. "If you're not, I'll find you and break your legs."

Nick barked a laugh. "Right." And he walked out the door.

He nodded at the security guard at the front door, exited and stepped left, leaning against the wall. He gave Reg ten minutes to follow him. He leaned his head back against the concrete wall, the sun shining on his face. He closed his eyes and soaked up the early-morning warmth. This was one of the strangest jobs he'd ever taken. He grunted and shook his head. He didn't take the job. The job took him.

He checked his watch. Seven minutes. If Reg were coming, he'd be in the lift now, on his way down. He'd have company for breakfast if he showed. Not much he could do about that. Not ideal, though.

He'd make Reg pay. And he'd get steak and eggs, with sautéed onion and capsicum.

Ten minutes passed, and Reg hadn't appeared. He yawned and crossed the street, dodging taxis. He stepped over the railing around the patio and sat at a table for two. He took the menu from between the salt and pepper shakers.

"You're not going to sit with us?"

Nick lifted his head and smiled. He turned to his right and saw Davie, Lucy and Terri sitting on the patio, closer to the cafe's interior. "Shit. You guys should move inside." He looked out on the street. "Deep inside." They stood and grabbed their menus. Nick pointed to a table in the far recesses of the cafe. "Over there."

Davie sat across from Lucy, and Nick sat beside her. He leaned over and they had a long kiss. Terri, across from Nick, smiled.

Lucy exhaled, a full blush on her cheeks. "I missed you."

"We need a do-over on that date."

Lucy nodded and placed her napkin on her lap. "You don't have a minder?"

Nick looked toward the street. "Surprisingly. Half expected him to chase me out the door." He looked at the empty places at the table. "Have you ordered yet?"

"We just got here."

On cue, the server arrived, took their coffee and food orders and departed.

"Steak and eggs?"

Nick smiled. "I promised myself." He looked across the table at Terri. "Your father would have kittens if he knew I was having breakfast with you. Why is he so insistent on mediating with you?"

Terri almost choked on her coffee. "Mediation is not what he wants." She dabbed her mouth with her napkin. "Not at all."

"So why is he so hell-bent on me finding you and bringing him back to him?"

Terri rubbed her forehead. "You all have been very helpful this past twenty-four hours, and I'd love to tell you what's behind all this, but, really, for your safety, I shouldn't."

There was a second of silence, and then Lucy, Davie and Nick all started talking at once. Nick tapped his knife on his water glass. "Hang on, everybody. Don't pile on. Terri, the danger isn't a concern. Danger is my—"

"Shut up, Nick. You sound like an idiot," said Lucy. She smiled and patted his hand. "Terri, why are the Russians tracking you?"

She shook her head. "Same reason. I have to stay below the radar until the flight leaves Australian airspace. You shouldn't get involved."

"Don't play hard to get," said Nick. "We're already involved." He glanced at the building again. "I hope Reg doesn't pop out for a coffee." He took a settling breath and composed his thoughts. "You and your father have been laundering money for at least a decade. As you know, he and I butted heads back when I was in the AFP."

Terri had a half smile. "He may have mentioned you once or twice."

"So this has something to do with money laundering. A fallout between your father, you and some Russians. It's not rocket surgery. Of the three, you're the least offensive, so we'll help you get to the airport, and I'll tell your father that he was mistaken, that it wasn't you he saw on TV."

She frowned. "I was on TV?"

"You walked behind a reporter in Martin's Place the day you arrived. He saw you cross the frame. Pure luck."

"Jesus. *Bad* luck. All this because he saw me?"

Nick shook his head. "The Russians caught on to you some other way. No idea how."

Davie scratched the back of his head. "Same way we did, I expect. They're not stupid." He paused. "I think I know how to hobble them, though.

The conversation paused as the server brought their breakfasts.

Terri broke the silence. "How?"

"A trap." Davie sliced through his poached egg on Turkish. "Two of us lie in wait," he nodded toward Nick, "while you lead them into the said trap, and we, you know, take them out."

The other three at the table stared at him for a minute.

"I can't tell if you're serious or not," said Terri. "You can't be serious."

"Why not? We'll have the element of surprise."

"Look, Davie, I don't know you. But I know enough by looking at you that there's no way you could hold your own against these guys. The two at the hotel, plus I have no idea how many others are on the hunt. These guys have killed people before."

"She's right," said Nick. "And there's more of them than us now. I expect there'll be even more before you leave. It's not an entirely bad idea, though."

"We're getting reinforcements?"

"Of a sort." He looked at Davie. "Our cop friends might be interested in helping out."

Davie looked at Nick like he was crazy. "Seriously?"

"And they can bring along the feds." Nick tapped the table. "But once they're gone we still have to deal with the original job."

"Me?" Asked Terri.

"Yeah." Nick nodded toward the front of the cafe. "Your father is across the street and forty-some floors up. He really wants to bury the hatchet."

Terri shook her head. "No, he doesn't. And I'm not meeting him."

"Okay. A problem for later. Right now, we need to assume that the Russians are looking for you and won't give up until they do. I need to get back in front of the CCTV, and you three need to lead them to where the police are." He opened a map on his phone. "I'm thinking Circular Quay. It's not far from here, and we can get the police there quickly."

He closed the map and placed a call. He stood from the table while it rang. "You guys figure out a plan. I'll get the cops."

He walked from the table. "Detective Sergeant Wallace, please. Tell him Nick Harding is calling."

Petrovski threw his coffee cup against the wall of Kon's office. "I do not give a flying fuck how severe the gun laws are in this country. Everyone going out is armed. How many men do you have?"

Kon swallowed and quickly motioned for someone to clean up the mess. "Fifteen by this afternoon. Eight now." He swallowed. "Technically, guns are not a problem. I can get them." He held his hands up as Petrovski opened his mouth to yell something. "I have enough for the eight on hand. I'll need to acquire more for the others."

Mikhail twirled his knife. "No need for a gun for me. I prefer cutting."

Kon nodded. "Yes, yes. No gun for you. Fewer for me to get."

Petrovski shook his head and took a sip of his espresso. "Where is she?"

"She didn't stay at the hotel last night. I've had eyes on all four sides," said Kon.

"I fucking didn't ask where she wasn't. The last time we saw her, she was with a girl, but we lost them in the city."

"My guy is scouring the cameras. We know she hasn't left the country. She needs to complete whatever she came here to do, so we'll find her. I suggest heading into the CBD, and we'll let you know where to look once you get there."

Petrovski looked at his watch. "How long?"

Kon shrugged. "Fifteen, twenty minutes, depending on the traffic."

"*Fignya!*" He looked for another cup to throw. "We're leaving now. Do you have a van to take the men with us?" He glowered. "You have a van, no?"

"Yeah, yeah. It'll be out front in a minute. I'll drive. There's room in the back for ten."

"I want the eight coming in with me in here, right now, with their firearms."

Mikhail held up his hand. "I am one of the eight. I will not need a gun."

Petrovski closed his eyes for a second, taking a deep breath. "Yes, we know. The seven. Now. Guns." He waited until Kon had them assembled.

He looked at the group. Young, most in their early twenties, but hard. All with serious looks on their faces. "You've all used guns before?"

They all nodded.

He looked at Kon. "They're untraceable?"

"Every one of them."

He looked at the men again. "You prefer knives?"

A spattering of "*Da*s" filtered through the scowls.

"Tough shit. You won't get close enough to cut. As soon as you see her, she needs to be finished." He looked at Kon. "You've sent them all her picture?"

Kon nodded. "A good one from yesterday. They all have it."

"No mistakes, then. As soon as you see her, kill her, drop the gun and walk away. Go to ground. Don't come back here for a few weeks."

Chapter Twenty-Three

"Okay," said Nick. He pocketed his phone as he approached the table. He looked at his watch. "We need to shepherd the nasties into Anderson Reserve. The cops balked at Circular Quay. Too many civilians. Wallace is setting it up with the North Sydney LAC. The police will have the Reserve staked out. Got to give them some time to set up. Then you, Terri, act as bait and lure them in."

Davie frowned. He opened the mapping app on his phone. "That's across the bridge. North Sydney."

"Hence the coordination with the North Sydney local area control.

"No, no, no," said Terri. "I need to be at the bank in two hours and at the airport immediately after. I can't help."

Nick dropped back in his seat, his breakfast forgotten. He looked at Lucy, then back at Terri. "I give up. I just - just give up." He slumped back in his chair. "You're just as bad as your father. You know they'll find you wherever you go, right? They found you here. I don't think you expected that."

Terri leaned her head in her hands. "I can't miss this bank appointment. I can't."

"You need to decide."

Davie kicked Nick's chair leg. "You're about to be busted."

He looked over his shoulder. Reg was crossing the street. "Shit. Terri, get out of here. Take the back way. Let Lucy know what you're going to do. Lucy, if we're going to the park, let me know as soon as possible." He trotted to the front of the cafe and exited just as Reg finished navigating the traffic and reached the curb.

"What's taking you so long?"

"Guy's gotta eat, Reg. Back to the cameras."

Davie watched Reg and Nick talk as they walked north. Terri was still in her chair. "Why didn't you leave?"

She sat there, quiet, thinking. She looked at Lucy. "Will this work?"

She shrugged. "I don't think Nick has ever attempted to trap vindictive Russians in a small park. He does seem to make things work out in the end, though. Push your bank appointment and fly out another day. It's better to finish this. Get those guys off your back." She held up her hands. "I don't want to know why they're intent on killing you. I really don't. Let's end this, okay?"

She sighed and nodded. "I have to make some calls." She stepped away from the table with her phone to her head.

Davie watched her walk and talk. "Well, Luce, this is going to be fun. How do we get the Russians to follow us to Anderson Park?"

"It's Lucy. They're monitoring cameras, just like we are. They have to be. We stay undercover as much as we can until we get to," she looked around, trying to get her bearings, "Town Hall station, I expect. Then we make sure we're really visible on the platform just before the train arrives and then when we get off at Milsons Point. We should be ahead of them by then, enough to get to the park before they do."

Davie shook his head. "We stay under cover until Milsons point. Safer."

"Fair enough. It's about a ten-minute walk to Anderson from there."

"Then what?" Asked Davie.

"Wing it."

Terri returned to the table. "So how are we going to do this?"

"Get on your phone and tell your partner to track her.

He's good at that, right?"

Nick looked up at Reg. "Yeah. Sure. It's what he's best at." He smiled at Reg and dialled.

"Nick, mate, you free from the ape yet?"

"Thank goodness you're awake, Davie. Get your laptop fired up. We have a task."

"He's with you? Terri agreed to the thing. She's moved her appointments out. We'll take the train to Milsons Point and draw them out there."

"How long before you get your laptop up, then?" Nick glanced at Reg.

"Ah, okay. So how about I send you text messages slowly leading you to the park?"

"Fifteen minutes? That's good. Let me know what you see as soon as you see it." He pocketed his phone. "Davie is on the job, Reg. I suggest we head toward the CBD. Davie will text me updates."

"Is your phone off silent?"

"I'm not a moron, Reg."

"This is," Petrovski looked up at the Sydney Tower Eye, "a big city. Your man on the cameras has his hands full."

Kon nodded. "Geoff is good. Been looking since before we left. Starting at the hotels around here."

"She was at a hostel before, right? Have him check those, too."

Kon saw a parking spot and pulled the van over. "Good thinking, boss, except she stayed at the Four Seasons last time we tracked her, and I don't think she will give up those creature comforts again." He turned off the van's ignition. "The search software uses facial recognition to search for her, anyway. So the start point is arbitrary. If she's on the street, we'll find her."

Petrovski looked at his watch. "How long does it take to get to the airport?"

"From here? Twenty, twenty-five minutes."

"Train or car?"

"About the same. Train is easier at the other end,

though. No parking."

Petrovski scowled. "She doesn't have a car. She wouldn't have to park." He stopped Kon from removing the keys from the ignition. "You will, though. Take two and head to the departure area. If you see her, hold her and call me." He looked at the small army in the back of the van. "The rest of you spread out and be ready. Keep your eyes open." He opened the van door. "Mikhail, pair up with a local."

Mikhail slid open the side door of the van. "Yes, boss. Today is a good day."

Petrovski grabbed one of the locals. "You're with me. Take me where she stayed last night."

"I don't know where she stayed."

"The Four Seasons. That's around here, I assume?"

The young man looked at Petrovski, glancing, then turning his eyes away from the burn scars. "I'll check." He fumbled his phone out of his pocket and opened a map app. He nervously swallowed. "Yeah, it's about a fifteen-minute walk. But I don't think she stayed there last night. We checked it out very carefully."

"It's the last place we know where she was. It's as good a starting point as any." Petrovski held out his prosthetic hand. "Lead the way."

"Sure. Sure." He glanced at the hand. "This way."

"I frighten you?" The Russian held up his hand and gently touched the scars on his face. "What's your name?"

"Tommy Stojanovic."

"Ah. Serbian?"

Tommy nodded. "My parents moved here when I was very young." He glanced at Petrovski. "I've heard stories about…" He trailed off. "About your face. The burns. They're true?"

"How would I know stories you have heard?" He smiled. "Don't be shy. I don't know any shy Serbs."

They stopped at a red light. Tommy watched traffic for a couple of seconds while he thought.

"Okay. The story is that you were caught in a fire in that swampy area of Florida and had to fight off crocs to get out. That's how you got the burns on your face and lost your hand."

A tram passed in front of them, and the light turned green. "Close enough." He stepped over the trolly tracks and looked to his right, following it. "We could have taken that, right?"

Tommy half shrugged and leaned closer to Petrovski. "We could have, but they're crowded, and I have a gun." He pointed up George Street. "That's the hotel, at the end of the street."

"So keep your eyes open. Remind yourself what she looks like."

Tommy checked the picture on his phone. "Yeah, yeah. I've been staring at this since Kon sent it. I'll know her if I see her."

"Okay. Let's head to the hotel and keep our eyes peeled."

Terri wore a floppy sun hat over a curly brunette wig. She wore massive sunglasses and walked arm-in-arm with Lucy into Town Hall Station.

"You know where we're going, right?"

Lucy steered her to a ticket machine. "I'll buy it. I don't know if they're monitoring electronic transactions." She handed Terri the single-use ticket and pointed her to the platform.

"How many stops?"

"A couple. Five or six minutes. Don't bother sitting down." She put her earpiece in. "Davie, how's it looking?"

"The little guy is with someone new. They're around the Town Hall station. I spotted a van stop near the Needle and drop off half a dozen guys, including the skinny one and a dude with horrific facial scars."

"If skinny is at Town Hall, where's the other guy?"

Davie let out a slow breath. "Just missed him. He

was about two minutes behind the two of you when you popped into the station."

"Did he follow us in?"

"No. He and his guide kept going. Toward The Four Seasons."

Lucy chuckled. "Good. Thanks. Ping us if anything comes up." She hung up, made sure her phone wasn't on silent and leaned against the upright pole.

"News?"

"We're clear for now. The scary guy was at Town Hall station and a couple of others were right behind us when we entered the station, but they kept going toward the Four Seasons."

Terri scratched under the back of the wig. "Close. Close doesn't count. How long do I have to wear this piece of crap wig? Where did you find it?"

The train emerged from the tunnel and started crossing the Harbour Bridge. "I'm not sure if they can access the cameras at the station, but in case they can, remove the wig and the hat at the station. Look around. Make sure the cameras get a clear shot.

They stood side by side, looking out the train door window at the traffic on the bridge and the tops of the sails on the Sydney Opera House.

"You've lived here all your life?"

Lucy looked at Terri. "I have."

"It's a beautiful city."

"You're looking at it with fresh eyes. It's got its charms, but it hasn't surprised me in years."

The train slowed to a stop at Milsons Point Station, and the doors slid open. Terri stepped out of the carriage and pulled off her hat and wig. She shook her hair free and scrubbed her scalp. "That was terrible." She stuffed the wig into the trash bin, folded the hat, and tucked it under her arm. "Where's the park?"

Nick's phone vibrated. He checked the message and suppressed a smile. "Reg, Davie says he just saw

Terri at Milsons Point."

He frowned. "North Sydney? What in the hell is she doing there?" He looked around. "Where's the nearest train station? Your friend is going to update us on where she's going?"

"Lot of questions there, Reg. Answers, in reverse order. He will as long as she passes in front of cameras, Circular Quay is just ahead, and I have no idea why she's in North Sydney. Circular Quay is no good, though. We'd have to backtrack and change trains at Wynyard. Uber is faster."

"Taxi is faster than that." Reg stepped in front of an empty cab and flagged it down. "Milsons Point. Fastest route."

Nick slid into the back seat to the far side and waited for Reg to get in the front seat. As soon as the front passenger door closed, he got out of the back seat, slammed the door shut and slapped the top of the cab in the universal signal of "Go". He chuckled when he saw Reg turn in the front seat, register that

Nick wasn't in the car, and motion frantically for the driver to stop.

By then, Nick had already flagged down another taxi. He jumped in the front seat. "Anderson Reserve. North Sydney."

Tommy's and Petrovski's phones both vibrated at the same time.

"Where is this Milsons Point?" Petrovski read from his phone. "Is it close to here? Can we walk?"

"Nah, mate. We're going to have to grab a cab." Another message came in. "See this? She was disguised. Wore a curly wig and a floppy hat. Took it off as soon as she got to the station, so she knows we're looking for her."

Petrovski nodded. "She took it off. She must think she's safe there. Where is there?"

"North Sydney. Other side of the harbour." He pointed at the hotel. "Cab rank, there. We'll be at the station in ten minutes."

"We need updates on her travel. Where's she going?"

"As long as she passes near security cameras, Geoff can track her. We'll know where she is."

Chapter Twenty-Four

"I'm nervous about this, Lucy. How confident are we that this is going to work?"

"We? Honey, I have no idea. The cops that Nick called better be in the park because you can bet the Russians will be close behind us." She tilted her head. "*Are* very close behind us."

"That's encouraging. Do you know the names of the police we are meeting?"

Lucy scrolled through her messages. "There's a Detective Chang, local PD and two Federal Police." She smiled. "Jackson and Johnson."

"This is becoming a Bruce Willis movie." They passed a row of townhouses. "Not many businesses around here. Will Davie be able to track us?"

"Doorbell cameras every few houses. Piece of cake for Davie."

They reached a set of stairs leading down to the park, about halfway down the west side. There were a couple of people in a cricket batting cage, but other than that, the park was vacant. "Chang, Johnson and Jackson are very good at hiding. Where should we set up to meet the Russians once they get here?" Terri walked down the steps and put her hat back on. "The sun is hot here. Let's get this over with."

The park was a small, narrow triangle, bounded on the two long sides by busy roads and on the short side, on the south, by a small marina. A high rock wall stretched along the west side, and trees lined the east side.

"I can see why they picked this place," said Terri. "It's pretty isolated." They walked slowly toward the marina end of the park. The two guys in the cricket cage stopped their activity and watched.

Lucy angled toward a park bench that looked out

over the water. A retiree polished brass rails on a decent-sized sailboat moored at the dock. She sat and called Nick.

"Are you there?"

"We are," said Lucy. "How far away are you? And is the big guy still with you?"

"I'm a few minutes away. Managed to get a Reg divorce. He's going to be pissed whenever he catches up with me. He only knows you were at Milsons Point. No clue about the park. Have you met up with Johnson and Jackson yet?"

"Haven't seen anyone here who looks like cops."

"That would defeat the purpose. They're there. And the local cop, Detective Chang, should be there, too."

"Hang on a second." Lucy scanned the park. The retiree on the sailboat was paying close attention to them. The two men in the cricket cage were fit, young and had very federal police haircuts. "Okay. They're here. Didn't notice them at first, but if you look, they stick out like sore thumbs."

"I'm just outside the park. See you in a couple of minutes."

"Great. We're on a bench watching the local cop polish his brass." She waved at Detective Chang.

"Is that a euphemism?"

Lucy chuckled. "Where are the Russians?"

"Davie just pinged me that at least three cabs are heading this way. Six men."

She looked at Chang. "Six? We'll be outnumbered."

Nick appeared from behind them. "Skootch over." He closed his phone and sat on the bench beside Lucy. "That's Chang?"

Lucy stowed her phone and pointed over her shoulder at the cricket cage. "J&J are taking batting practice."

"Them I know. Saw them on the way in. We've only got a couple of minutes. All the cops need to do is grab them for threatening you, Terri. And they're going to want to talk to you after." He raised his eyebrows. "I didn't tell them much. Just that you were in town on business and that, for some reason, the Russians were threatening you. The Feds have been looking for a way in with these guys for a while. They were glad to pile on."

"I'm so glad we could help," said Terri. "You can't imagine. Are we just going to sit here like staked lambs for the slaughter?"

"With our backs to the advancing lions. I get your point. We should at least move so we can see them coming. We should stroll along the waterfront."

Petrovski and Tommy exited the taxi on the east side of the park. A stand of trees blocked their view of the park. He leaned down, resting his plastic hand on the roof of the cab. "Hang on here for a minute."

Petrovski held out his hand for Tommy's phone. "Show me this place on a map." He looked at the layout as two other taxis arrived. Mikhail and

Dimitri got out of one, and two locals got out of the other. He slowly handed the phone back to Tommy and turned to Mikhail. "My friend. Good to see you. Go with the locals and bring Terri back to me alive." He looked at the other locals. "I know. I said shoot and go, but I've changed my mind. This place is isolated enough to take the risk. I don't want her dead. I need to ask her a couple of questions. I will call Kon and have the van brought here."

"You are staying here?" asked Mikhail.

Petrovski held up his prosthetic hand. "I'm afraid I'm not much use in a physical confrontation. I'll arrange transportation."

He watched Mikhail lead the four locals across the narrow bridge from the street, bridging a storm drain channel into the park. Something didn't feel right. The layout had limited options to get in or out of the park. Terri appearing, full face on a camera after days of eluding her searchers also didn't feel right.

He hopped back in the backseat of the cab. "Can you take me to the far side of the park?" He leaned forward and pointed to the road above the tree line. "Over there."

"Your dime, mate."

Nick watched as Mikhail led the other four across the bridge into the park. The wiry Russian looked around, the spotted Terri. He was singularly focused on her face. He pointed, and something glinted in his hand. He yelled something in Russian, and they surged forward.

"What are the cops waiting for, Christmas?" asked Terri, looking around.

Nick stepped toward them when the Russian he had seen earlier travelling with the wiry one pulled a gun and shot. The sharp crack echoed as Lucy grabbed her arm and screamed.

Mikhail spun and lashed out at Dimitri with his knife, cutting his face. "Alive, you fucking moron!"

Nick turned his back on the Russians and blocked their view of Lucy. She was holding her upper arm. Blood covered her arm and hand. "Are you okay?"

"Oh, Jesus, Jesus, this hurts. I don't feel good."

Chang rushed off the boat, and Jackson and Johnson ran out of the cricket cage, sidearms drawn.

Mikhail swung his knife wildly at Chang and received a bullet in his chest for his troubles. There was a lot of yelling that Nick barely noticed. He ushered Lucy to the park bench and gently moved her hand out of the way. "You got shot."

"Bloody good detective." She smiled through clenched teeth. "That's going to leave a mark." She looked past him at the growing crowd in the park. "How did they get an ambulance in here?"

Petrovski watched Mikhail get shot in the chest by the Chinese man he assumed to be law enforcement. The young Russian writhed on the grass for a few seconds, then lay still. "Ah, shit." He unlocked his phone and made a call. "Kon, don't come to the park. It's a shit show. There's a parking area under the Milsons Point station. I'll be there in about ten minutes. Pick me up there."

"What about the others?"

"Dead or in custody."

"You good?"

Petrovski sighed. "It's an unfortunate setback. Ten minutes. Be there, okay?" He hung up and flipped up his collar. He tucked his prosthetic hand into his pocket and started walking, trusting his memory to get him to his destination. "Fuck, fuck, fuck."

Paramedics had already loaded Mikhail into the back of the ambulance and were treating Dimitri's facial cut. A crime scene technician's van was parked near the water, and technicians were bagging the knife and the Russian's firearms.

Chang wandered over to the bench and sat beside

Lucy. "You okay?"

"Detective Change, I assume?" Nick was holding a cloth on Lucy's arm. "You think the medical folks could have a look at Lucy's arm?"

Chang waved one of the medics over. He moved out of the way as the medic squatted beside the bench.

"We triaged you down the list behind a probably dead Russian and another with an impressive slash across his face." The paramedic took the cloth off Lucy's arm and gently examined it. "Hi there. My name is Cheryl. What have we got here?" She flipped open the top of her medic's bag. She started cleaning the wound. "This might sting, but not as much as getting shot."

She gently moved Lucy's arm and looked closer at the wound. "Through and through. There's a bullet out there the techs will have to find."

She poured antiseptic into the wound and bandaged it. "There's a good chance a decent plastic surgeon can make sure there are no scars if you get to it quickly. There's no broken bone, so I don't think a sling is necessary." She handed Lucy a packet with two large white pills. "Panadol with codeine."

"No codeine, okay?"

Cheryl took the packet back and handed her another one and a bottle of water. "Okay." She stowed her med pack and returned to the ambulance.

Chang sat on the bench. "So what went on here?"

Nick looked at the Russians being loaded into a police van. "Thought you'd know more than me. Terri has been on the receiving end of threats from some Russians. I called Warren in Sydney, who called you and Jackson and Johnson, who I know from my AFP days, to set a trap for them. It went a little sideways."

"Yeah, but the good guys won in the end." He glanced at Lucy. "Mostly."

"Thanks," said Lucy. "This has been a hell of a day."

"So," Chang looked around. "Where is Terri?"

Lucy jumped to her feet, swayed, then reached out her hand and balanced herself on the back of the bench. "Did she get shot?"

"No," said Chang. "It's just you, the big guy with the face cut and the injured guy I shot. I saw her here earlier. You sneak her out?"

"Jesus." Nick checked with Lucy. "You okay?"

"Yeah. Go."

Nick called Davie. "Hey, mate. You got eyes on us?"

"Not within the park, but I gather from the influx of visitors that things went to plan?"

"Close enough. Did you see Terri leave?"

"I didn't know she did. Which way did she go?"

Nick paced along the waterfront. "No idea. I was focussing on Lucy getting patched up. I didn't notice her go."

"Hang on. Is Lucy okay?"

"A flesh wound. A stray bullet that I think was

meant for Terri. She's been patched up. Look, I've got to take her to the hospital for a more thorough examination of her arm. Scour the streets for me, will you? Terri's out there somewhere."

"I'll ping you when I find her."

"Thanks, mate."

Lucy was talking with Chang. He caught her eye and raised his eyebrows. *Everything okay?*

She nodded, and he pointed to the Feds and held up his hand to her, fingers splayed. *Five minutes.*

She turned back to Chang, and Nick approached Jackson and Johnson. They had just finished talking to the big guy with the patched-up face.

"Boys. Thanks for being here. This turned into a bit of a shit show."

"Your girl okay?"

"Yeah. Thanks. You guys find out anything from these guys?"

The two feds were in shorts and baggy T-shirts. Jackson was taller by a couple of inches, both noticeably taller than Nick.

Jackson smiled. "How's civilian life treating you?"

"I've had some interesting days. This one goes on the list. Anything?"

"Not much. We need to talk to Terri O'Shea. She seems to have slipped away. You have anything to do with that?"

Nick laughed. "If you find her, let me know, okay? What did the Russians say?"

"Sweet fuck all. We'll put some pressure on them back at the office. The dead one was a recent arrival. Came from Miami. He's got a long sheet."

"It's not getting any longer. Miami? Seems a bit out of his way."

"And," said Johnson, "we were expecting to see his boss. A guy named Vladimir Petrovski. Scarred face, fake hand. Also from Miami and very, very pissed off at the O'Sheas." He crossed his arms. "You haven't seen the old guy around, have you?"

"Why is Petrovski so pissed at the O'Sheas?" The best way to avoid answering an awkward question was by asking another related question.

"So you've seen him? If you're holding out where he is, we could charge you with obstruction."

Nick clapped him on the arm and laughed. "If I see him, I'll tell him you're looking for him. I've got to get Lucy to the hospital. I'll pop by the office and give you my statement tomorrow, okay?"

"Don't make us chase you, Nicky."

Nick turned away and called Davie. "Any luck?"

"Nick, she headed south out of the park toward Neutral Bay Wharf and caught a ferry to Circular Quay. I can't access the cameras on the ferries."

"Find out for me everything you can about Vladimir Petrovski, okay? That's the scarred guy we've seen in some of the feeds. The Feds are very serious about him. I'll be at North Shore Hospital with Lucy."

Chapter Twenty-Five

"Hey, sorry about this." Nick nervously took her arm as they left the emergency room.

Lucy gently removed his helping hand. "I'm good, Nick. Scars are cool, right? And it doesn't even hurt anymore."

"They gave you good drugs. Good thing you're not driving. I'll get a cab."

"No need." Reg stepped out from behind a pillar at the entrance. "I'll give you a lift."

Lucy chuckled as she shook her head. "*De ja vu*, buddy. Where are your friends?"

He looked puzzled.

"I think she's talking about the guys who helped you grab me at the beach," said Nick. "You didn't bring them?"

"Don't need them today. I'm going to give you a ride back to the old man's place - both of you - and we will chat there. I heard stories I don't really like, and I want you to clarify some things."

"What do you want to be clarified, Reg?"

"I parked on the street. I don't want you to repeat yourself, so you can do your clarifying in front of O'Shea."

Nick shrugged. "Whatever. Hope you're not driving that little piece of crap car."

He pushed a button on his key fob, and the park lights blinked on a black Chrysler C300. Nick heard the solid clunk of unlocking doors. "Got the big piece of crap. I was expecting to pick up three or four of you." He held open the back door for Lucy. "When we get there, you'll have to explain where Terri went."

Lucy slid into the car, and Reg closed the door behind her. Nick got in the other side and looked at her, eyebrows raised. *So what do we tell him?*

She narrowed her eyes, flicked a glance toward the front of the car, then Nick, then frowned and shook her head. *Not a fucking thing.*

Nick nodded.

Reg looked in the rear-view mirror at his passengers. "Where's your friend?"

"Who, Davie?"

"You have more than one friend?"

"I," Nick stopped when Lucy tapped his arm and shook her head. "I don't know. I haven't seen him since this morning." He smiled at her and settled back in the car for the twenty-minute drive.

Petrovski slammed his good fist on the dash of the van. "This would not have happened in Miami."

Kon looked over at him while wending his way through city traffic. "You're not in Miami, mate. What exactly happened?"

"The cops knew we were coming. They were

lying in wait. Mikhail is dead, Dimitri is cut up. All of them are arrested." He took a deep breath. "They won't talk, right? They better not talk."

"Nah, the boys are all good. Dimitri will be okay. He'll like the scar. What do you want to do next?"

Petrovski sat in silence for a minute. "How many men can you pull together right now?" He punched the dashboard again. "Right fucking now."

"Three or four." He swerved to avoid a jaywalking pedestrian. "Right fucking now."

"Then park somewhere and get them. And your tech guy, what's-his-name Geoff, needs to start looking for the guy behind this."

"What guy?"

"He'll know who I'm talking about."

Reg shepherded Nick and Lucy onto the parking garage lift and pressed the top floor button. He followed them off the lift, unlocked the front door and ushered them into the flat. "Old man. We're here.”

O'Shea shuffled out of his room into the living area, dressed in a T-shirt straining across his gut and very large basketball shorts. He stopped when he saw Nick and Lucy. "That's not my daughter. Jaysus, Reg. You're fooking incompetent. Young lady, whoever you are, get out of my house."

"She's not going anywhere, O'Shea. She works with Nick. They had Terri. Had her since this morning, as near as I can figure. Somehow they managed to let her go after, or maybe during, a dust-up with some local Russians."

O'Shea took slow steps toward Nick and Lucy. "Are you fucking kidding me? I hired you to find my daughter and bring her to me. And you," finger jab to Nick's chest, "let," finger jab, "her," jab, "go?"

Nick held up his hands. "Old man, as much as I'd like nothing more than pop you in the neck right now, and take my chances with Reg, Terri disappeared during the, what did he call it? The dust-up. Do you have any idea why a flock of Russians are trying to do your daughter harm?"

He tried to jab one more time, and Nick batted his hand away. O'Shea shook out the sting. "You really need to find her. Now."

The three young men Kon was able to round up in *right fucking now* time sat in the van, chests stuck out, muscles flexed, trying to look hard. Kon sat in the driver's seat, and Petrovski sat sideways in the front passenger seat. "Call him. Put it on speaker."

Kon dialled a number, put it on speaker and held the phone out so everyone could hear.

"Hey, boss. What's up?"

"Do you still have eyes on the cameras?"

"I could. It would take less than a minute. Still looking for that girl?"

"Yes," said Kon. "Same as before."

Petrovski leaned close to the phone. "No. Not the same as before. Not the girl. I need to find the guy who was looking for her. A detective, I think."

There was a slight hesitation on the line. "Boss?"

"You heard him," said Kon. "He's the big boss."

"Oh, shit. Okay. So, um, what guy, exactly?"

"He was with Terri and another girl this morning when the team showed up at the park, and the police ambushed them. I saw him talking to the police. He appeared to be in charge."

"Got it," said the techie. "If we find him, we find the girl."

"The girl can wait. This guy, this FUCK, he set up the ambush that killed Mikhail. He effectively killed Mikhail." Petrovski scratched the back of his head. "Can you do what you do remotely?"

"Like not in the office, out there with you?"

Petrovski narrowed his eyes. "What else would I mean? Yes. Out here with us."

"I need a tablet."

"There is one on my desk," said Kon. "I'll send you our location. Grab the tablet and get a taxi to us as fast as possible." Kon dropped the call and tossed the phone on the centre console. "What benefit is there having him with us?"

"You're questioning me?"

Kon grimaced. "Look, mate, he has far more resources at his desk than in the field. Coming out here to make you feel better reduces his effectiveness."

"I don't think so. I need him to be aware of the urgency directly from me. In my presence." He touched his scarred face with his prosthetic hand. "I want him motivated."

"You want him shit scared, you mean. Well, the faster this gets done, the faster you can fuck off back to Miami."

"Where is he coming from? How long?"

"Maybe ten, fifteen minutes."

"Tell him to go directly to the park. We're starting where I last saw him."

Kon sent a message from his phone and started

the van. "We'll head back there, then."

"I'll need one of these guys to go in first and make sure the police have left."

"Obviously. Turn around and put your seatbelt on. We don't want to get pulled over."

The van lurched forward as Petrovski struggled to fasten his seatbelt. Kon yanked the van around a traffic circle and pointed back toward the park. "Kurraba Road side?"

"What do you mean?"

"The park's a big triangle. Water on the short end, Kurraba Road on the east, and Clark Road on the west."

"Whichever side the small canal is on. There's parking."

"Kurraba. Five minutes."

"When we get there," Petrovski twisted in his chair and pointed at one of the men in the back, "you go into the park and make sure there are no more police hanging around. We'll wait in the van for the guy with the tablet."

"My name is Peter."

"Whatever."

Kon's phone buzzed. He took a glance at the screen. "Geoff and the tablet are only five minutes away. Apparently, he has a motorbike."

"He's going to be travelling with us. He'll have to fetch his bike later."

Kon pulled into a parking spot along the curb on the canal side of the park. Petrovski motioned for someone to check the park.

Peter opened the sliding door, stretched as he stepped on to the sidewalk and crossed the small footbridge into the park.

Petrovski adjusted his prosthetic hand as he watched. The stump, halfway down his forearm, needed to be attended to. It had been too long. This trip has been too long. He should have been on a flight back to Miami yesterday.

Peter stepped through the trees and spoke to

Petrovski through the front window "It's empty, except for a dad and his son in the batting cage."

"I hate baseball."

"Cricket, mate. Not much baseball here."

Petrovski grunted and got out of the van. "Mikhail was shot in this park an hour ago. I'm surprised there isn't still a police presence. I am extremely suspicious that there are no police here. In fact, I don't believe there *are* no police here. This place is still under surveillance."

"I swear. There's nobody there."

"Look at me, you fucking punk. I trust my survival skills over your eyes. LOOK AT ME. Does my face look like the face of a man who doesn't know how to survive?" He took a heavy breath. "Kon, where is that fucking tablet?"

The sound of a motorcycle grew louder, then stopped just outside the van. Petrovski moved to the back of the van and slid open the door.

A young man, 15 kg too heavy and with a wispy

beard and long stringy hair, was putting his helmet on the back of his bike. A laptop case was slung over his shoulder. He looked up when the door opened. "Hey, I made good time. Hit every light." He fumbled with the zipper on the bag and pulled out the tablet. "What am I looking for?"

"Not out here." Petrovski motioned for him to get in the van. He looked at his watch. "A man and a woman, maybe two women, entered this park about an hour ago and ended up at the bench near the water. I want you to identify that man and find out where I can find him."

"That all?"

"Was that sarcasm? I'm not in a great mood right now, young man. How long is this going to take?"

"It really depends." Geoff opened an app and replicated the screen at his office. "On a lot of things."

Petrovski looked at him, eyebrows raised.

"Right," said Geoff. "*What* things. If the person

you're looking for has any kind of social media presence where they use their own photo it shouldn't take more than an hour."

"You'll do it faster."

Geoff looked up at the menacing, scarred face and swallowed. "I will do it faster."

Chapter Twenty-Six

Nick sent a message to Davie. *You at your machines?*

I am. What's up?

Where's Terri? She knows you're looking now, so it won't be easy. Nick tossed his phone on the desk and tapped the spacebar on his laptop, waking it up.

Lucy stood behind him, her hands on his shoulders. "She's going to go way underground after today."

Nick nodded. "It's not going to be as easy as it was." He turned and looked into the lounge room. O'Shea was slouched on the sofa, looking deflated.

"What about the other guys? The Russians?"

"The old guy is paying the bill, we'll find his

daughter for him. Fingers crossed she stays ahead of the Russians." His phone buzzed. A message from Davie. *The crazy lady is back at The Four Seasons. I'll keep an eye on the doors for the Commie bastards.*

Nick laughed and sat back in his chair. He reached back with his left hand and took Lucy's right. He held up the phone and showed her the message from Davie.

"So we're finished?"

"You'd think. But she's there, and we're here. I'll reach out to her and see if she'll make the trip. If I were her, though, I'd stay out of sight until she absolutely had to expose herself. We're looking for the Russians now. " Nick looked at O'Shea on the sofa again. "Don't let him know, though, okay?" He grabbed his phone and sent a message to Davie. *Thanks. Send me the same feed as before, okay? I'm looking for the Russians now.*

Kon paced alongside the van smoking a cigar. "Geoff. What's taking so long?"

"I haven't found him yet, but I know who he is."

"It's about time," said Petrovski. "Show us how you got there. And then we figure out here he is." He moved from the front passenger seat back to the bench seat in the back of the van. He slid to the side, behind the driver's seat and patted the middle of the bench. "Sit here and walk us through it."

Kon got in the van, and they sandwiched Geoff in the middle. He looked nervously at Petrovski and then at Kon and tapped the screen.

"Okay. The guy we're looking for got out of a taxi right around here. His face isn't clear, and once he's in the park, he's too far away from any cameras to identify clearly."

"So that's it?"

"No, Kon. I had the taxi number. The cars all have internal cameras. I got a good shot of his face from inside the cab." He tapped the tablet, and the screen filled with a headshot of Nick's face. "I did a reverse image search and discovered Nick Harding and his little detective agency."

"Nick Harding? Why is a PI involved?" Petrovski tugged at his goatee. "Any idea where he is now?"

"Hang on. I've got more. I ran back that taxi, like reversed it to where he got in." Geoff pulled up a map of the city. He panned and zoomed to an intersection. "He grabbed it here, so I checked cameras in the area for the hour before he got in, and I found this footage."

He tapped the screen again and showed footage of Nick on the café patio, then joining the others and moving inside.

Petrovski leaned over and tapped the screen. "Back it up and freeze it with the four people."

Geoff complied and handed the tablet to Petrovski.

The Russian placed the tablet on his lap and used his good hand to zoom in. He pointed at the screen.

"That's Terri." He handed the tablet back. "Who is the other woman? And the guy who looks something like you, who is he?"

"I've got a better shot of the guy. He doesn't look exactly like me."

"Same vibe," said Kon.

Geoff scowled at him and image searched, conscious of both Kon and Petrovski watching him. Intently. "Hang on. I'm going as fast as I can."

"I said nothing." Petrovski loosened the straps holding his prosthetic hand and partial limb to his half-length forearm. He eased the forearm and hand off and leaned forward and placed in on the passenger's seat. He pulled the protective sock off his stub and grimaced at the sight of the raw flesh.

Geoff looked at the stub and the prosthetic. "You know you can get really good prosthetics now, right? Taps into the nerves on your arm. You can pick things up, open bottles, just like a real hand."

Petrovski flipped open the cap of a tube of lotion

and squirted some on what was left of his forearm. "Have you found out who he is yet?"

"Just sayin', mate." Geoff returned to his tablet. "He works with Nick Harding, sometimes. His name is David Sangster. He's head of cyber security at a large bank, so he knows his way around computers."

Kon tapped messages out on his phone. "The three others have spread out. One is walking across the bridge to Circular Quay. The other two are quartering North Sydney." He pocketed his phone. "More will join up in Sydney. We should have people within five minutes of wherever we find these guys."

"Are you any good at this, Geoff? Maybe we should find this David person and get him to track down his friend."

Geoff chuckled.

"Why are you laughing? I was serious. Find Mr Sangster."

Davie was locked into his task. Eight video windows across two monitors were advancing at 2X the normal rate. He wasn't looking directly at any of the videos. He was 'watching' all of them, looking for the guy with the scarred face and fake hand.

He'd been looking for almost an hour when he thought to check the images from around the park. He tracked Nick getting out of the park and entering. He scrubbed the video forward a few minutes and saw three taxis arrive. The scarred Russian was in the first. He got out, leaned on the taxi, directed his troops into the park, then got back in the taxi and left.

"Coward."

Davie tracked the taxi to the other side of the park where the Russian got out of the taxi. He tapped the cab on the roof, and it slowly drove away. He watched the activity in the park. After a few minutes, he made a phone call, flipped the collar up on his shirt and started walking.

Nick, the Russian watched you while the shit was

going down in the park.

He stared at his phone until he got a response. *Not surprised. Where is he now?*

Still looking. He slid the phone to one side and continued searching. The number of available cameras in suburban North Sydney was disappointingly low, but he managed to hit and miss his trip back to the Milsons Point station. He disappeared under the highway, into a parking area and a couple of minutes later a white panel van left. He watched the video outside the parking area for another two minutes until he was sure the Russian was in the van. He scrubbed back until he saw the van leaving the parking area and froze the image. He took a screenshot and sent it to Nick, then checked the registered owner of the van.

He quickly sent Nick a message: *Scarface got in a van registered to Konstantin Antonov. The registered address is in the Bankstown area.*

"I want to go home."

Nick looked at Lucy, who was sitting in a lounge chair next to him. "Yeah, I'm sorry. This isn't how we should be getting to know each other."

She shook her head. "It's not that. I've got things to do. Frankly, this is trial by fire. If we get through this, we're good for anything, right?"

Nick chuckled. "Fair enough." He stood and stretched. "Reg, O'Shea, where the hell are you?"

Reg poked his head around the corner from the gym. "What now?"

"Lucy is going home. She has a life. Needs to get some personal things done."

"Have you found the girl yet?"

Lucy stood and crossed her arms. Her eyebrows rose high on her forehead. "The girl? You mean your boss's daughter, Teresa, right? *The girl?*"

"Yes. Terri. Have you found her yet?"

Lucy glanced at Nick. "Well—"

"We're not looking for her. I've got a pretty good

idea where she is, and she's not going anywhere."

"What in the hell are you talking about?"

Nick took a step back from his advance. He smiled. "Relax, big guy. She's not going anywhere. We've got a bigger problem."

"The Russians aren't a threat."

"You're absolutely wrong about that." Lucy pulled the sleeve up and showed him the bandage. "This isn't nothing."

Reg pointed at it. "If I'd been there, it wouldn't have happened."

"If I hadn't given you the slip, she'd have been there with Terri, and they'd both be dead. So back the fuck off and take Lucy home and let me find these fucking Russians so I can get rid of them."

"I'm not—"

"You picked us up at the hospital. You're taking her home." Nick took Lucy's hand. "When you can, get Davie up to speed, okay? I'll be finished here tonight."

Davie's phone rang out to voicemail before he noticed it. He was buried in videos, looking for a specific white van in a sea of white vans. It was like everybody was delivering something today. He picked up his phone. A missed call from Lucy. "Shit."

He called her back.

"Davie, any luck so far?"

"Good evening to you, too, Lucy. You okay?"

"Yeah, it was just a flesh wound." She laughed. "Jesus. Listen to me. Does Nick affect everybody this way?"

"I'm afraid so. I haven't been shot yet, though. You've got one on me."

"Lucky me. The Russians?"

"I'm looking for a white van in apparently a city full of paedo-vans. I had no idea there were so many out there." His stomach rumbled as he leaned back in his chair.

"I heard that. Are you hungry?"

"Always."

"Want me to bring something over? I need to catch you up on what happened in the park."

Davie shook his head. He stood and stretched. "No, I need to get out of here. Kebab place is just down the road. Meet you there?"

The white van had moved from the park to the upper deck of a shopping centre parking structure. Kon found a spot on the roof as far from the complex entrance as possible.

Petrovski turned in his seat and watched Geoff for a moment before interrupting him. "Are you *any* further ahead?"

The tech geek didn't respond for a couple of seconds. Petrovski cleared his throat, and Geoff looked up. "What? Oh yeah. I know where this Sangster guy lives."

Petrovski's left eyebrow raised. He didn't have a

right eyebrow. "You do? How far away from here?"

Geoff opened the map app on his phone and entered the address. "With this traffic, seven minutes' drive."

"Give Kon the address. Let's go."

Chapter Twenty-Seven

Davie kicked the chair opposite to him, moving it out for Lucy. "How's your arm?"

"I'll live." She sat and pulled out the single sheet, laminated piece of paper that served as a menu. "What's good here?"

Davie grimaced. "It's all relative, okay? The fish and chips aren't bad. The chips are a little soggy. Look, doesn't matter what you get, there'll be a place that makes it better, somewhere. But this place is the closest." He leaned forward and rested his elbows on the table, his fingers interlaced. "You should get out of town."

Lucy slowly and firmly placed the menu on the table. She mimicked Davie's position. Their faces were centimetres apart. "Why in the hell would I do that?"

He blushed and sat back. "It's just, you know, those Russians are out looking for Terri, and they've seen you with her."

She smiled and also sat back. "They seemed to be a bit angry, yes. But what makes you think they also don't know you're involved? Are *you* going to leave town?"

Davie shook his head.

She leaned forward again. "Is it because I'm," she leaned slightly closer and whispered, "a *woman?*" She laughed at the look on his face.

"What?"

"I'm not going anywhere, Davie. And I'm hungry. Do they come to the table, or do I have to go to the counter?"

"To the counter. My treat. What are you having?"

"I don't know yet. You?"

Davie patted his stomach. "I've been eating too

much. The chicken Caesar wrap doesn't look too bad."

Lucy stuck the menu between the pepper and salt mills. "Sounds good. I'll have the same. And a bottle of water."

He tapped the table and stood. "Be right back."

Davie was third in line. He took out his phone and sent Nick a message: *Eating with Lucy. She's tougher than I thought she was. You may have met your match.*

He watched the little blue dots bounce until the reply: *Every day is more interesting than the last. Enjoy. Then get back to work.*

Davie chuckled and stepped up to the counter. "Two chicken Caesar wraps, a bottle of water and an orange juice. Large." He tapped the card reader with his credit card, turned, and leaned on the counter while the food was prepared. The cafe was open-air. A residual from the pandemic. More outside seating than inside, and it was a beautiful afternoon.

"Here you go."

Davie turned and took the two wraps and drinks with thanks.

He spotted a white van on the far side of the street and shook his head. "I'm seeing them everywhere." He handed Lucy her wrap and drink and sat down.

"Seeing what?"

"White vans. Everywhere." He peeled the wrapper from his food and stopped its progress to his mouth when that same white van pulled a U-turn across traffic. "Shit."

Lucy turned to look at what Davie was looking at and jumped to her feet as the van skidded to a stop in front of the cafe.

Davie stood and motioned Lucy toward the interior of the cafe. "Get in there."

"You've got to stop doing that."

The side door slid open, and two healthy-looking men stepped out. One of them pointed at Davie. "You. Get in the van."

"I've got other plans this evening. Thanks anyway." Davie crossed his arms and nodded for Lucy to leave.

The passenger's door opened, and Petrovski slid out. "Get in the van before I tell them to put you in the van."

"What the hell, man? You're looking for someone else. Not me."

"And I think you know where she is."

Davie shrugged, eyes on Petrovski's scars. "I can't help what you think. What in the hell happened to your face?"

Kon got out of the driver's side of the van and looked to Petrovski for guidance.

"Come with us, and maybe, between beatings, I'll tell you." Petrovski nodded at the two to grab Davie.

Lucy jumped in front of one of them, and Kon shoved her, hard. She hit the table and fell, her head bouncing on the sidewalk. She groaned and rolled to her side before stopping.

Davie pushed the table out of the way and kneeled on the sidewalk beside her. "Lucy. Lucy, are you okay?"

She was unresponsive. Davie reached for her wrist to check for a pulse when his arms were grabbed, and he was dragged to his feet. One of the two slugged him in the gut, and they threw him into the back of the van.

Petrovski got back in the front seat. Davie struggled to regain his breath. He heard the Russian in the front seat say, "Back to the office."

"Where's Reg?" O'Shea's mood was getting worse.

Nick shrugged. "He dropped Lucy off at her place about an hour ago. Probably getting a drink somewhere."

"Well, I need my fucking insulin, and I don't want to get up. Grab the vial from the fridge and a needle from the drawer below the silverware."

"I'm trying to find your daughter. Kinda busy."

O'Shea scowled. "I'm tired and my legs hurt. You can get the vial and sticks or give me CPR and mouth-to-mouth in half an hour when I pass out." He shrugged. "It's your choice."

Nick sighed and got up from his working area. "I'm not jabbing you."

"Grab the little black pack beside the needles."

"Sure. What is it?"

"The glucose monitor. I need to know how much to jab myself with." He smiled. "Too little, and I eventually go into ketosis and die. Too much, and my blood sugar plummets, I'm out in about five minutes and dead in fifteen if nobody intercedes. Grab it for me."

The vial was in the fridge door. He grabbed it, a syringe and the black pouch.

He underhanded them, one at a time, to O'Shea, the pouch first. O'Shea fumbled with the pouch but grabbed the vial and the packaged needle like he had practice.

"Thanks." He opened the pack and pricked his finger. He checked a drop of blood and waited for the monitor to beep.

Nick watched him draw insulin into the syringe, open his robe, and stab himself in the gut. He smiled at Nick while he depressed the plunger. "Uncomfortable?"

"Not as uncomfortable as stabbing myself in the gut. You good now? I won't have to, you know, revive you or anything?"

"I'm good."

Nick shook his head and returned to his laptop. "Whatever you pay him, you don't pay Reg enough."

The door opened, and Reg walked in. "What he said. I like what he said."

O'Shea capped the used needle and tossed it in a trash bin by the sofa. "Where the hell you been?"

"Dropped Lucy off and grabbed a drink in the pub down the road. Panicking?"

O'Shea waved him away and turned to Nick. "You find the Russians yet?"

"Davie mentioned that white vans were everywhere, and he wasn't wrong. Working from their last known location, I've been trying to track them, but every time there's a break in video coverage I end up following the wrong van. It's a long, iterative process. A process that Davie is much, much better at."

"Why isn't he helping you?" O'Shea pushed himself to his feet. "I thought he was the expert in this."

"He's having dinner right now, I suspect. Speaking of which, I'm hungry. Is someone ordering pizza? Chinese?"

"Find him, and get him on this, dammit," said Reg. "We need to get the Russians out of the picture."

O'Shea stood. "I'm drawing a bath. I'm not feeling well."

Reg nodded and turned to Nick. "Find him, mate."

Nick stared at him while he dialled his phone. It went to Davie's voicemail. He tried again. Voicemail again. "He's not answering."

"Keep trying."

"He was catching up with Lucy." He frowned for a second and called her number. It rang four times and went to her voicemail. "Shit."

Nick returned to his laptop and searched for a camera close to Davie's apartment. He scrubbed the video back an hour and saw him leaving on foot. He tracked him to the mediocre cafe a block away, where he sat and waited. He sped up the video. Lucy showed up a couple of minutes later and sat across from them. Nick slowed the video to normal speed and checked the timestamp. "They were there fifteen minutes ago. Probably still eating."

"Then they should be answering their phones then, right?"

There was a knock on the door. Reg held up a

finger. "We'll come back to this." He checked the screen beside the door and took a step back. "Well."

He opened the door, and Terri walked in. "Where's me arsehole pa?"

Chapter Twenty-Eight

She looked up at Reg. "Fuck, you've gotten bigger."

She nodded at Nick. "Hello. Where's the old man?"

Nick noticed her Irish accent was stronger.

"Why are you here?" Reg had a look on his face that Nick couldn't interpret. Something between anger and sympathy.

"To see my father. Where is he?"

"You know some bad people are out there trying to find you?" Reg crossed his arms. "You're walking around on the street like nothing's happening?"

"I'm alive, aren't I? Where is he?"

"In the tub," said Nick. "He's fine. I'd let him soak. I don't think I could stomach seeing him in the tub. Naked."

Terri grimaced. "Fair point. I'll wait. Where's the whiskey?"

"Did you notice anybody following you?"

"I'm not an idiot, big guy."

"The whiskey is in the bar. Where whiskey lives."

She smiled, tossed her floppy hat on the sofa and sauntered to the bar. "Have you been holding Nick hostage again?"

"He's looking for the Russians who are after you."

"They're not all Russian." Terri poured a heavy two fingers of whiskey into a crystal glass and took a large mouthful. "I heard one of them in the park. Sounded Serbian." She shrugged. "But allies, though, right?" She emptied the glass, licked her lips, and refilled it. "You found them yet, Nicky?"

"Is that my daughter?" O'Shea waddled out of the bathroom, cinching his robe over his gut. "Where the fuck is my money, girl?"

"It's been three years."

"Over three million a year. Where is it?"

Terri stared daggers at her father and sat on the sofa. "It's not your money."

He perched on the edge of the chair at right angles to the sofa. "Young lady, it certainly isn't yours. Where in the hell is it?"

"That was human trafficking money. *Sex-*trafficking. We swore we'd never get involved in that, and you jumped on it like a pig on a corncob. There was no way in hell that money was going back to that slimy piece of shite. Not a single punt."

O'Shea sighed and slid back on the chair. "Daughter dearest, you and I have been hiding from Russians because of that stunt. I don't have many years left." He slapped his stomach. "I may not have *any* years left at the rate I'm going. I'm tired of hiding." He leaned forward. "Have you spent it all?"

"I haven't spent a cent. It's sitting in a safe deposit box, and I've been trying to get to it for most of the week. How did the Russians know I was here?"

"Probably the same way we did," said Nick. "That brief—"

"That's what you said, but I don't believe it. I have the worst luck." Terri ran her fingers through her hair and looked at her feet. "Damn."

"I've got a couple of people looking for the Russian ringleader as we speak, Terri." Nick smiled. "We'll have them rounded up in no time."

Terri looked up at him from the sofa. She placed her drink on a coaster. "Lucy and Davie? How are they doing?"

"Fine. You disappeared pretty quickly."

Terri grimaced. "Sorry. Had to disappear. It was getting too close for comfort. I heard a gun go off as I was leaving. Nobody important hurt, I hope."

Nick stared at her for a second. "Nah. All good. Is someone ordering food? I'm hungry and need to get back to finding a white van."

Davie was on his back on the van floor behind the

seats.

A young, muscled kid crouched over him. "You're going to tell us where she is," he said.

"Who? Your mother? I haven't seen her since last night." Davie squeezed his eyes shut and tensed his muscles in anticipation of the hit. After a few seconds, when none came, he opened his eyes, and the kid ploughed his fist into Davie's face. He just managed to turn his head, avoiding a straight-on nose shot.

"You don't talk about a person's mother like that. It's not cool."

Davie wiggled his lower jaw back and forth. "Not bad. To be honest, I was expecting a bit more."

"It's cramped quarters in here."

Davie nodded. "That makes sense. What's your name?"

"Andy. Andrej. Call me Andy."

"What's the end game, Andy?"

"We're taking you to a quiet place where the

quarters aren't as cramped to ask you some questions. The boss is pissed that his boy was killed and the others were arrested. He wants some information he thinks you might have."

"Including where the O'Shea girl is?" Davie shifted his hands toward his back pocket, slowly.

Andy nodded. "That is the main thing. Plus, where someone named Nick is. And there's something about money, but I didn't catch all of that conversation."

"Sure, sure. Who is the boss?"

Andy looked toward the front of the van, and Davie took out his phone and rolled over on his stomach. He opened his messaging app and sent his location to Nick.

"Hey. What are you doing? Give me that." Andy grabbed at his arms.

Davie locked the phone and slid it under the seats. "Hey, mate, back off. What are you doing?" He wrestled an arm free and rolled to his side. "I'm getting carsick, down on the floor like this."

"Don't barf in the van, or I'll really have to kick the shit out of you."

Davie groaned and sat up. "You're going to anyway. How far away are we?"

"You'll know when we get there."

Nick's phone vibrated with an incoming message. "Hang on. This is Davie." He opened the message. It was a pinned map. And it was much farther west than he expected him to be. "What the hell?" He sat at his computer and tracked Davie's phone. It was heading northwest, toward Parramatta. He tracked Lucy's. It was at the cafe a block from Davie's flat.

Terri had gotten up from the sofa and was standing behind him. "What's happening?"

"I don't know." He called Lucy's mobile and put it on speaker. It went directly to voicemail. He hung up and called Davie's phone on speaker.

It rang three times before it was answered.

"Davie, where in the hell are you going?"

"Nick, go get Lucy. She's—" The sound of the phone clattering against something preceded some indecipherable yelling, then a loud rushing noise followed by silence.

He called back. It went directly to voicemail.

"What was that?" Terri walked back to the sofa and sat. "What's going on?"

Nick ignored her. He called Lucy's number again. Nothing. "Shit, shit, shit." He changed screens and went back to the cameras near the cafe.

Andy was breathing heavily and Davie was sitting in the back seat with his hands tied behind his back.

"Dumb move," said Andy.

Davie rubbed his bleeding ear against his shoulder. "That phone was new, you prick. I'm going to bleed out."

"It's a scratch, you pussy. And nothing compared to—"

"Yeah, yeah. Nothing compared to what you're going to do. How much farther?" He cleared his throat and spat blood-filled phlegm on the van's carpet. "I think you broke my nose."

Andy shook his head. "You did that to yourself. Banged it against the whatever it's called, the seat leg when you tried to avoid my punch the first time. And the boss isn't going to be pleased about that." He pointed at the mess on the floor. "Might make you clean it up."

"Let's save some time. I don't know where Terri is. I don't know why you're looking for her. The last I heard, she was leaving the country this morning, so you're all probably shit out of luck." He groaned as Andy punched him in the gut.

The video on Nick's laptop was grainy and in black and white, befitting a cheap CCTV camera. The police tape flapping in the light breeze was unmistakable. "Oh, this isn't good." He looked at the time stamp on the video and the time on his laptop and scrubbed the video back at double speed. A crowd appeared in reverse. An ambulance backed into the frame. A para got out of the passenger seat and opened the back. She pulled a gurney out of the back and put Lucy on the sidewalk.

"Jesus. Jesus." He grabbed his phone off the table. "Terri, you want to help?"

She put her drink down. "Sure. Why not?"

"Call the local hospitals and see if Lucy Simpson has been brought in."

Terri launched off the sofa and returned to her position behind Nick. "Wow. Was that your girl?"

He shrugged. "Maybe. What in the hell is going on?" He scrubbed the video back five more minutes and let it play forward at normal speed.

Davie had just returned to the cafe table with a couple of drunks and wraps. He sat and pointed off camera at something. He stood abruptly and Lucy turned and stood too.

The front half of a white van came in from the right of the frame and stopped. Sunlight reflected off the windscreen, obscuring the view of the people in the front seat. The sliding door opened, and two young men got out. The front passenger door opened and Petrovski got out. Then the driver.

Lucy stepped forward and the driver pushed her to one side. Nick watched as she stumbled against the table and fell, hitting her head on the sidewalk.

He watched the video as Davie squatted beside her. Davie was grabbed by the arms and yanked into the van. Nick heard Terri's sharp intake of breath.

"I'm sure he'll be okay. It's Lucy I'm worried about." The scarred guy got back into the van and it drove away. There was no angle on the rego.

"Fucking hell. Your mate is in serious trouble. Back it up to before that butt-ugly arsehole got back in the front seat. Get me a good face-on shot." She looked over her shoulder at her father. "Pa, did you know he was in town? Come here."

Nick moved the video back to where the face was best visible. He blew it up to fill the screen. It was grainy, but recognisable.

"Oh, jaysus, jaysus jaysus. It is him." Terri covered her mouth with her hands. "How?"

"Who is it?"

O'Shea shuffled to beside his daughter. "It's him. Well, this is bad."

"For Christ's sake, tell me what the hell is going on," said Nick. He jabbed a finger at his laptop screen. "Who is that, and why are you both shitting yourself?"

"Makes sense he'd be here, though, right, pa? They must have called him. Man, his fingers reach everywhere."

Nick slammed his laptop shut and stood. "Talk. Now."

O'Shea wobbled back to the sofa.

"You should get a drink, Nicky." Terri took the seat beside the sofa. "Reg, nobody gets in that door, yeah?"

Nick grabbed his laptop off the desk and sat on a second upholstered chair. He mirrored the laptop and projected the picture on the large television. "Who in the hell is this and why are you acting like it's Freddy Kruger?"

Terri looked over her shoulder at the TV, then adjusted herself in the chair. "That's Vladimir Petrovski. Runs the Russian mob in South Florida."

"So why in the hell is he here, and why did he throw Davie in the back of his van?"

Terri looked at her father, then sighed and shook her head. "I took ten million of his dollars. We, my father and I, were pretty good at laundering illicitly acquired money."

"Better than most. I never did manage to catch you. You just took his money? You really don't look that stupid."

O'Shea barked a laugh. "Dumbest fucking thing she's ever done."

"It was sex trafficking money, pa. We agreed. You shouldn't have told him we'd launder it."

Nick held his hands up in frustration. "Cut to the chase. How is this guy any worse than any other? I'll call the cops, and we'll let them wrap them up."

"Petrovski is one of the most vicious people I've ever encountered," said O'Shea, "and I've encountered a very wide spectrum of evil. Your friend is not going to fare well. The Russian wants to know two things. Where my daughter is, and where his money is."

"How long ago did you take it?"

"It was three years ago," said Terri.

"And you haven't spent it?"

"I'm in Sydney to clean it and send it to half a dozen NGOs that combat human trafficking.

"You had to come here to do that? I thought all you guys did this stuff online, in some estate in a non-extradition country, working your magic over a super-fast internet line."

"It's mostly hard currency in a couple of large safe deposit boxes in a small private bank. I've been trying to get there for the past three days."

"Any chance Davie knows this?" Nick paced, his hands on his head.

"None."

"But they think he does, and they'll keep cutting him until he tells them," said O'Shea.

"Shit. I need to find Lucy, and I need to find Davie. I need to find both of them now."

Chapter Twenty-Nine

Nick put his headphones in and dialled as he made his way to the door. "I'm done here, O'Shea. You and your daughter are in the same place. Sort your shit out, or don't. Couldn't care less. Keep the laptop. You paid for it."

He got to the door, and Reg was blocking it, his arms crossed. "Who said you could leave?"

The phone was answered. "Johnson speaking."

"Hang on a second mate." Nick looked up at Reg. "Piss off." He tried to push the big guy out of the way and didn't budge him. "Fucking, move."

Reg looked at O'Shea who nodded. "Let him go."

"Is this Harding?"

Nick nodded as he pushed past Reg. "It is. I'm

going to send you a location in a sec. A colleague was grabbed by Petrovski about thirty minutes ago, stuffed into a white van, rego unknown. I last tracked them heading northwest before his phone was disabled. Sounded like it was thrown out of the van." He pushed the call button at the lift. "Ring me at this number with updates, okay? I've got to see a guy about a thing."

He stepped into the lift, opened a mapping app, found the café, and sent the location to Johnson. Then he panned until he found the closest hospital.

James stood and stretched. The "Fasten Seatbelt" sign went out with a chime, and MacCready pushed himself to his feet and gathered his belongings from the overhead.

"What time is it?"

MacCready grunted. "I think a better question is what day is it." He turned on his phone. "Huh. It's tomorrow. And we might have missed dinner."

"Feels like breakfast time."

"Feels like it."

James waited for MacCready to get in front of him. "Think we can get through the line faster than the normies?"

"We flew coach. We are the normies."

James tapped his shoulder and pointed to the front of the aircraft. "Maybe not." A uniformed officer was talking to the lead flight attendant, who checked his manifest, then looked up and caught James' eye.

He pointed and picked up the intercom. "Please take your seats, except for Mr MacCready and Mr James. We have an emergency that requires their immediate presence."

Mac looked over his shoulder. "You arrange this?"

"No. Something's up."

Nick ran into the A&E entrance of the hospital and leaned on the triage nurse's counter. "Lucy Simpson.

Did she just come in here?"

She looked over her glasses at him and typed something into her machine. "Simpson. Lucy. She's in treatment."

"Great. Thanks. Where do I go?"

"You family?"

"No."

"Family only."

Nick hesitated a second. "I'm–I'm her fiancé. She was mugged."

She looked at him got a long second, then nodded toward the doors. "I'll buzz you in."

"Thanks again." He pushed on the door twice, looked back at the nurse, who shook her head before pressing the buzzer. The door opened inward, and he jogged in, scanning beds until he found her. "Lucy."

An intern was cleaning a wound on the back of her head. He grabbed her head as she tried to turn it toward Nick. "Hold still. I'm not finished."

"Ouch. You've ruined my hair. Nick, they took

Davie."

He took her hand. "I know. I've called the feds. How are you?"

"Screaming headache, and Mario the Butcher has completely ruined my hair."

Mario smiled. "I'm going to jab your skull with a local so that I can give you some stitches. Three, maybe. Maybe four."

"Will the local make my headache go away?"

"Unlikely. We've got paracetamol for that. Someone is looking at your scans to make sure your skull wasn't cracked. You'll probably have to stay overnight for observation."

"I can't." She squeezed Nick's hand, and he winced. She was strong. "I've got things to do."

"You should listen to Mario. This is the kind of thing he knows more about than us."

"Don't fridge me, Nick." She released his hand and tugged at her sleeve. "I can't stay here. Luigi here stitches me up and I'm walking out."

Mario stepped around to the foot of the bed. "It's Mario. Luigi is my brother. You might have a cracked skull. We'll know in about an hour. And even if the scan comes back negative, I'd strongly recommend you let us keep an eye on you. You've had a pretty nasty blow to your head. There might be small brain bleeds we're not yet aware of."

"Your bedside manner leaves a lot to be desired," said Lucy. "One star from me. Would not recommend." She took Nick's hand again. "You know where I'll be. I don't have my mobile. Write down your number, and I'll call you when I know what room I'm in. You go get Davie."

"And if anything abnormal shows up in your girlfriend's brain, I'll call you," said Mario.

Nick stifled a laugh and handed Lucy and Mario each a business card. "She's a redhead. I'll be surprised if you *don't* call."

James and MacCready were escorted through airport

security, immigration and customs in record time. The uniform brought them to Jackson and Johnson, standing against their car, waiting.

James stuck out his hand and smiled. "Jackson. Long time."

"What are you up to these days, James? You don't get a tan like that in Jersey."

"I've been in Miami for almost a decade now. Keep up. MacCready is Miami PD special liaison with the FBI on organised crime. Petrovski's here looking for the O'Sheas. Vladimir Petrovski. Russian thug with global tentacles."

Johnson shook Mac's hand, then James'. "We know. Got a call from a guy, Nick Harding, about it. One of his colleagues was picked up by Petrovski. We've got a team tracking him, Petrovski, now."

"What's Harding up to? I understand he left the AFP five or six years ago."

"Six. Resigned. I think he was burnt out, but he said he was bored. He runs a small Private

Investigator shop and seems to get his face stuck in all the wrong places."

"How'd he get involved in this?"

Jackson shrugged. "He has a talent. He called Johnson about an hour ago. Said his friend, David Sangster, was grabbed by Petrovski, and he tracked them northwest." He pushed a button on his key fob and the boot popped open. "Drop your luggage in and we'll catch up with the team in the field."

"Need food," said Mac. "I've had nothing but airline food for the past 24 hours, and my stomach thinks it wants pancakes and bacon."

"You're going to have to do with sandwiches and water. I've got cheese or chicken." He tossed a sandwich to each of them and handed them bottles of water."

"And we need to check into the hotel."

"Already handled."

"Thanks," said James. "How did you track them down so fast?"

"We're not country bumpkins, mate." Johnson shrugged. "We know the rough area. Making a plan."

Nick crossed the street to the taxi rank and grabbed one to Davie's flat. He pressed all the buzzers at the front door and pulled it when some overly naive resident buzzed it open. He ran up the two flights of stairs and reached inside the garbage chute across the hall from his apartment. He felt around until he found the magnetic key holder attached to the inside top lip.

Davie's laptop was still set up in surveillance mode. He had a nice setup, befitting an IT guy working from home for a few years. He checked for other cameras around the cafe and found one facing down the sidewalk. He scrubbed back a couple of hours until the van pulled up. He froze the image and wrote down the registration number.

"That's familiar." He scrabbled around the papers

on Davie's desk and found the rego written on a piece with Konstantin's name and the company the van was registered to. "Davie, you beauty." He pulled up a map and plotted the route to the address in Blacktown, and compared it to the last location he'd tracked Davie's phone.

Not even close.

He searched the business registry for other companies owned by Konstantin Antonov or where he was a director of the business. Most of them were spread throughout the west and southwest of the city, but two were in the northwest. One was in a small shopping centre in Castle Hill. "Too many people around that."

The other was a go-kart track in Windsor. Lots of space around it. The main office was in the centre of a large field.

Getting in and out was going to be a challenge.

An hour's drive. Maybe less at this time of day. Nick checked the time. It would be almost midnight by the time he got there.

Johnson pulled into the driveway half a kilometre from the go-kart track. "We've set up in here."

Mac hopped out of the back seat. The house was on a hill. Clouds covered the moon, and the streetlight was a couple of hundred metres from the house. "You guys own this?"

"Lease. We're not in the property business."

"What the hell?" James leaned his hands on the roof of the car and stretched. "You have enough shit happening out here you can justify a house?"

"Bikies, mostly. This will be the first time for Russians."

"Petrovski's around here?"

"We've tracked him to a go-kart facility just down the hill." Jackson led them into the house. It was an older two-story house. The front porch was enclosed and was a makeshift cloakroom. No coats were hanging there tonight. At almost midnight, it was still in the high 20s C.

A living room and dining room extended down the right-hand side of the house. In what would normally be the living room, a steel table was bolted to the floor, and a railing for securing prisoners' handcuffs was welded to the top.

Stairs to the upper level went straight up the left side of the house, with a landing and a right turn five steps from the top.

Straight down the hall was the kitchen. Johnson pointed to it as he hit the stairs. "Coffee is that way."

Jackson and James followed him. Mac went to the kitchen. "James, black?"

"Thanks."

Mac flipped open the cupboards until he found cups. Generic white porcelain ones stacked two high. A pod coffee machine sat on the counter. He made two mugs of coffee, double pods each and walked carefully up the stairs.

The first bedroom on the left was an electronic

observation room. Monitors lined the wall. One was segmented into four separate video streams from external surveillance cameras.

James, Johnson and Jackson were looking at a thermal view of the go-kart facility, so only Mac noticed the car coming up the driveway.

"You expecting someone?" Mac pointed at the surveillance video with his cup. "They seem pretty comfortable."

Jackson unholstered his sidearm. "You two stay here." Johnson followed.

"Fun and games, already," said James. He took the mug from Mac. "I need this. Thanks."

"Plenty more downstairs." Mac sipped coffee and kept his eyes on the monitor. Jackson and Johnson entered view with their sidearms extended. There was no audio, but Mac could guess what was being yelled. Two hands extended from the driver's side window and opened the door. A tall man about 35 got out of the car with his hands extended to his side.

Johnson shook his head, and he and Jackson holstered their weapons. They walked back toward the house, arguing with each other, the third man close behind.

Mac waited in a chair, sipping his coffee, listening to their feet come up the stairs. Johnson entered first, then Jackson, then the third man. James smiled when he entered.

"MacCready, James," said Jackson. "I'd like to introduce you to Nick Harding."

James was already standing. "We've met, but it's been years."

Chapter Thirty

"You have *got* to be shitting me." Davie's legs were cable tie-wrapped to the legs of a plastic lawn chair; his arms were similarly attached to the chair's arms. The chair was placed in the middle of the indoor racetrack portion of the go-kart facility. He bounced and tugged in the chair, moving it around in a small circle until he could see Andy. "This is like a really bad movie, man. Except the lights are on, and it's too hot in here. Can you open some doors and let a breeze through? I'm getting all sweaty."

Andy looked at his watch. "Save your breath, mate. We're a good distance from anybody. The heat confuses any thermal imaging. In case a hostage rescue team shows up." He laughed. "Not that anyone will find you alive." He flicked open a knife, and folded it closed. Flipped it open again. Closed it. "You'll be dead tomorrow." He looked at his watch. "Later today."

"Not much of a host. What are we waiting for?" He tugged at his restraints again, turning further around in the circle. He could now see the main power switchboard, the power source for the building. It was beside a closed roller door. He smiled at Andy. "Where's the big guy? The scarred psycho? I bet he could take me with one hand tied behind his back."

"He's only got-"

"I fucking know, you halfwit. How long am I going to be strapped to this chair?"

Andy lunged at him, a fist cocked over his head. Davie ducked, expecting the blow, but Andy pulled his punch. "Christ, you're annoying."

"Say that to my face," muttered Davie.

"What was that?"

Davie repeated it, even quieter, looking down at his feet.

Andy leaned over him, hands on Davie's forearms. "What did you say, punk?"

Davie placed his feet firmly on the floor and lunged upward, the top of his head connecting sharply with Andy's chin. He heard the crack of Andy's teeth smashing together and felt blood spraying on his neck.

Andy was heavy. Deadweight draped over Davie's shoulder. He pushed himself over sideways. Andy wheezed as Davie and the chair landed on his ribs.

The plastic tie-wraps on his wrists limited Davie's range of motion. He squirmed around until he felt the knife in Andy's pocket.

He finessed it out of the pocket, and it fell on the floor. More jigging around until he got it. "What the hell am I going to do now?" He looked at the folding knife. It took two hands to open. Unless you were a practised knife user, which he wasn't. He took a breath, wedged his thumb into the notch in the blade and tried to force it open. It took a couple of minutes and a busted thumbnail before success. He cut the straps off his wrists and legs and stood, rubbing the top of his head.

"What's the hold-up?" Nick pointed to the go-cart facility on the large wall monitor. "Davie's in there. Petrovski's in there. Kon Antonov is in there. Why are we sitting on our thumbs?"

"And probably a dozen young, armed men in there. There's a team on the way, and we need to get closer to get a feel for who is where." Johnson frowned. "You knew about this house?"

"I'm surprised you still have it."

"You were a desk jockey, chasing money around the globe."

Nick chuckled. "This place was an open secret.

Figured there'd be more beer in the fridge, though."

They were back upstairs in the surveillance room. Footage from a small drone with a thermal camera filled a large monitor. It showed the main building as a single, large heat source. Lights on the outside of the building were marginally "warmer".

Three bodies stood outside the structure, loosely arranged. They appeared as blobs of light. It wasn't possible to discern their features.

"Heat's on in there, right?" Asked Nick. "We're having a heat wave and they've got the heat on."

"Probably. Masking it so we have no way of knowing how many are in there. Three outside, plus unknown inside. We're going to have to sneak somebody down there to get a better look."

"Can you turn off the thermal and get a look at the building?" Nick crossed his arms and stood closer to the monitor.

"Easy as," said Jackson. He tapped a key and the glowing green changed to visual light. The exterior of the building was mostly dark, except for a lit window in a door beside the main rolling door and some outside lights above the rolling door. Three men were standing in the light.

"Petrovski," said James, pointing at the monitor. "I don't know the other two. He travelled here after he sent one of his thugs. Wiry little fuck called Mikhail Sidorov."

"We got Siderov," said Johnson.

"Is he talking?"

"To his dead relatives, maybe. A local cop plugged him centre mass. Died in the ambo."

"I was there," said Nick. "Nasty little prick."

"That's right," said Johnson. How's the girl?"

Nick continued staring at the monitor for a few seconds before it registered that he was being asked. "Lucy? Yeah, she's fine. A little achy, but she's okay. Overnight in the hospital for observation."

"For a flesh wound?"

"No, no, no. She got knocked down and cracked

her head. A few scalp stitches and a headache. She didn't want to stay overnight, but I don't think she has much of a choice."

James pointed at the security monitor. One of the videos showed a car slowing, then a woman getting out of the back seat and walking up the drive. "Does anybody know her?"

Nick squinted at the small but increasingly larger figure and shook his head. "I guess she's not staying overnight."

"How'd she find this place?"

"Relax, Jackson. She found me, not the house." He took the stairs down to the front door two at a time and trotted down the driveway until they met.

"Hey, Nicky. You okay?"

"You're sneaky. How did you find me?"

"My brother. He pinged your mobile." She held a finger to her lips. "Don't tell anybody."

Nick chuckled. "How's your head?"

She turned around and showed him the shaved

and patched-up spot. "I'll live."

Nick looked at it with the light from his phone. "Sorry about your hair."

"Hair grows." She nodded at the house, and the men standing on the front porch. "What's this place, who are they, and where's Davie?"

"Come on in. I'll introduce you."

Davie dripped with sweat. He was pretty sure less than half of it was due to the heat. He gave Andy a safety kick in the head. He didn't want him interfering with whatever he was going to do. In addition to himself, there were four in the van when they arrived at the go-kart track. Andy was on the ground, blood oozing out of his face and probably not at risk of drowning. He'd be useless for weeks.

Outside was the scarred one—Petrovski, Kon and another Andy-equivalent.

He could take Kon. The Andy twin scared him, and Petrovski terrified him. And it confused the hell out of him that they hadn't started in on him yet. Andy and his thug brother would make him squeal in Mandarin within five minutes. And he didn't know Mandarin.

A back way out didn't look like an option. The only two doors were the roller door and a standard door, both the same size. The power switchboard was on the wall between them. He crept to the switchboard, stepping over tyres on the side of the track, and quietly eased the power panel door open. It held a bank of large circuit breakers and three large cylindrical fuses across the top. A plan started to form.

Davie removed his shoelaces and tied them together, carefully looped one end around the three fuses, and tied it off. He hoped the couple of metres head start would be enough. He got on the far side of the standard door. It opened toward him, away from the roller door adjacent to it. He could hear them talking outside. He only had one way to get on the other side of them.

He moved a couple of boxes out of the way between where he would be when they came in and the door. It would dark. Pitch-black dark.

"We can't have civilians in here. Jesus. This is supposed to be a secure location." Jackson paced the kitchen.

"I'm also a civilian," said Nick.

"And you shouldn't be here. You two have to leave. I've got to get upstairs with the rest of my team to construct a clever plan to grab some baddies and liberate your buddy."

"Which is why we should be—"

Nick was interrupted by heavy boots on the stairs.

"Jackson, get up here. Something is happening."

Nick nodded at Lucy to follow him up to the surveillance room. "What's going on?"

"All the lights just went out. The place is cooling off fast. Someone pulled the power." James looked at Johnson. "Has your team shown up?"

"No. Ten minutes out."

Vision from the drone showed the interior of the building cooling. There was a prone blob of temperature on the floor, three blobs running into the building, and one blob squatted against the wall. As soon as the three were well into the building, the one by the wall stood and ran out the door with a ponderous, lumpy running gait.

Nick pointed. "Davie." He grabbed Johnson by the arm. "I need your keys."

"We're all going." He pointed at Nick and Lucy. "Including you two, but you stay in the truck."

Davie's feet were killing him. He was in his socks. The laces idea turned out to be not as bright as he'd hoped. His shoes came off after the first few steps, and the road was filled with gravel and potholes, and god knows what else.

His chest ached. His lungs were on fire. His legs

felt too heavy to lift. But he couldn't stop running. He couldn't even slow down to check if he was being followed. He had to get around the corner that was two hundred metres ahead and closer to civilisation before he even dared think about slowing.

Halfway to the corner, he saw headlights coming up the road. "Shit." He dove to his left, aiming for the bush and falling short. He groaned and scrambled the last few metres into some level of cover, hoping it worked.

"That was Davie. Pull over." Nick was working the door handle before the truck stopped. "Davie, mate. It's us. Get in." The other two trucks kept speeding toward the go-cart facility.

Davie's head popped up out of the bush. "Thank Christ."

Nick took a step back. His friend looked like shit. His face was bloody, and the left side of his head was swollen and bruised. He held up the light from his phone and watched Davie hobble out of the bush onto the road. The knees were missing from his trousers, and scrapes and cuts covered his arms and hands. "You look like hell, mate. Get in. Tell me what's happening."

"How the fuck would I know?" Davie pulled himself into the truck and sat back. "How did you find me?"

"Time enough for that later," said Johnson. "How many are there?"

"Four. A couple of gym rats names Andy and," he shrugged, "something else. Peter, I think. Andy is out. Plus Petrovski and Kon."

"That all? You sure?"

"They're the only ones I know about." He leaned back and closed his eyes. So how did you find me?"

Johnson looked back at him and depressed the button on his lapel mic. "Four in there, one unconscious. All hostiles. I'm right behind you."

"I'm staying in this truck if that's okay with you,"

said Davie."

"The three of you are." Johnson slammed his foot on the accelerator, pinning their heads against their headrests.

Chapter Thirty-One

"So how in the hell did you find me, and why couldn't it have been twenty minutes earlier." Davie rubbed his jaw. "Thirty minutes. Ouch."

"You're my man in the chair. And you're important to me, Davie. You really are. But when I found the video where you were grabbed, I also saw Lucy knocked out." Nick took a close look at his friend. He'd been in a battle, that was for sure.

Davie leaned forward and looked past Nick. "Oh, shit. Yeah. You okay, Luce? Sorry, *Lucy*."

She lightly touched the back of her head. "My hair's a mess. Thinking of shaving it all off and starting again."

"But you're okay, though?"

"The hospital said she should be staying overnight for observation." Nick looked at Lucy. "Overnight."

"Couldn't do that knowing Davie was in the back of a paedo-van. Did the scary scar-faced man touch you in your private place, Davie?"

"Just the head and upper body. So you found me, not Nick?"

"No, I found Nick. Nick found you."

"Usual detective trickery, mate." Nick frowned. "I'm puzzled. You said there were four, but one of them, Andy, was out. What do you mean by out?"

Davie smiled and winced. "I reminded myself why I never went out for rugby. He wasn't that smart. They tied me to a chair, and when this Andy guy was the only one in the place, the others were outside, I got him close and head-butted him." He rubbed the top of his head. "So, Lucy, I feel your pain."

Johnson turned off the truck's headlights. "I need

the three of you to shut up and get down. You shouldn't be here, I'll probably get my ass handed to me when management finds out you were, so I can't have you shot, too."

He reached up, turned off the dome light and eased out of the truck.

The three friends sat silently for a couple of seconds before Davie blurted out. "So, it's finally over?"

Lucy chuckled. "At this point in the movie, when everyone thinks it's over, I look at my watch and think, either this is the shortest movie ever made, or shit's about to get real."

"Don't tell me that."

"She's right," said Nick. He tapped the side of his head. "Now is the time to be your most alert."

"Great." Davie slumped in his seat just as gunfire came from the go-kart facility. "Shit." He slumped lower. Nick and Lucy followed. A couple more shots echoed off the surrounding hills.

"Maybe it is over," said Lucy.

The back door was yanked open, and Kon grabbed Davie's left arm and tried pulling him from the truck.

"Fucking hell, mate." Davie swung at him with his right.

Nick leaned over to help and was smacked on the side of the head by Davie's backswing. "Jesus." He pushed Davie's arm out of the way and crawled over him, swinging at Kon's face. Kon's arms deflected most of his blows, and he barely made glancing contact with his target.

Nick heard the other back door open and turned to see who was approaching Lucy's side, ready to take them on. Lucy was gone.

"Shit. You're on your own, mate."

Kon reached his other arm in and held Davie, who was fighting back.

"You go," grunted Davie. "I've got this."

Kon suddenly dropped a metre, letting out a yell.

Nick ran around the back of the truck to see Lucy crack him on the back of the head with a rock and watch him slump to one side.

She tossed the rock into the bush and kicked him repeatedly in the ribs. "You arsehole. My head is killing me because of you. You stupid, fucking arsehole." She brushed her hands off on her slacks. "You okay, Davie?"

He was half out of the truck, upside down and flailing for a handhold. Nick stepped up and helped him out. Davie looked down at the unconscious Kon and toe-punted him in the ribs. "Dickhead." He smiled at Lucy. "Thanks. I'm good now."

"What do we do with him?" Lucy echoed Davie's toe punt. "He's going to be pissed when he wakes up."

Nick shook his head. "You scrambled his eggs. He'll be useless for a couple of days." He crouched down and tried to roll him onto his side. "Help me get him in the semi-prone position so he doesn't suffocate on his tongue."

"That would be bad?"

Johnson appeared out of the darkness. "What in the hell happened here?" He played his torch over Kon's prone form. "Who is this?"

"Konstantin Andropov."

He shook his head. "And who did this to him?"

Davie and Nick simultaneously pointed at Lucy.

She shrugged. "What now?"

Johnson stared at her for a minute. "My ma always warned me about redheads."

Nick nodded toward the facility. "What happened down there? Get what's his name, Petrovski?"

Johnson looked down at Kon again and shook his head. "Just the thug Davie knocked out. The other two slipped past us."

Nick started laughing. "Get in the truck, Lucy. You too, Davie. We're not safe."

Davie scrambled in first, getting a deserved look of disapproval from Lucy, who followed him. Nick rounded off the third.

"Why aren't we safe?" Davie's head swivelled, trying to look out all of the truck windows at once.

"Because the only bad guys caught tonight were caught by you and Lucy. Our federal friends came up short. Petrovski is still out there and will no doubt be looking for us. So far, the only bad guy catching has been by us."

Lucy arched an eyebrow at Nick. "Us? Really? Davie and I held up our end. Who have you caught today?"

A truck pulled alongside, and a couple of guys got out and loaded a slowly reviving Kon into the back seat, wrists secured behind his back. Johnson waited until they left and hopped into the truck. He looked in the rear-view mirror, caught Nick's eyes, and shook his head. He started the truck, put in gear and executed a slow U-turn on the narrow road.

"I want a full briefing back at the house." He rubbed the tip of his nose. "The shit I get into." He accelerated up the hill.

Lucy raised her eyebrows and muttered. "I think dad is pissed." She leaned to her right. "Seriously, Davie. Are you okay?"

"Yeah. Nothing broken." He looked past her to Nick. "I'll be staying at the computers from now on, mate. Nothing personal, but this is just stupid."

"It's a deal. This case is closed now, anyway. We'll take a break. I owe Lucy a better dinner on the beach."

Johnson looked in the rear-view mirror at Nick. "It's not closed yet. We still need to grab Petrovski and any detritus he has hanging around."

"That's a 'you' problem, mate," said Nick. "As far as I'm concerned, this is a closed case. You'll have a manhunt out for Petrovski by dawn, if you don't already. Airports notified, train stations on alert, the whole federal enchilada."

Johnson nodded. "He's not going to leave the country until he gets what he came for. And anyone in his way will be dealt with. I think you're on his list." He rolled to a stop at the safe house. "You're going to tell me more about your case, see if there's anything interesting we can use."

"I'll invoice you."

"No, you'll do it and thank me for the opportunity."

Nick smiled and threw a mock salute at him as he got out of the truck. "As long as there's coffee." A truck stopped beside them, and Jackson, James and MacCready jumped out. "I'll have some of that," said James. "My clock is messed up."

"This has been a hell of a long day for me, too, James." Nick stretched. "I'm happy to hand all this over to you guys and get out of here."

"How did you get involved tracking Petrovski? I thought he was just a South Florida problem." James stepped out of the way as Jackson and Johnson muscled an uncooperative Kon Antonov out of the back of James' truck.

"Kinda got sucked into it on the back of my – our – main case. This was just my bad luck."

Lucy smacked him on the arm. "*Your* bad luck?"

"Ow. Yeah, okay. Lucy and Davie's bad luck I took the O'Shea case."

James stopped Nick. "Who?"

"O'Shea. He hired me to find his daughter."

"Both O'Sheas are in the country? Dammit. I thought she was in Malta and he was in New Zealand."

"They're both here. You've been looking for him, too?"

James motioned MacCready over. "Mac, how cool would it be to grab the O'Sheas on this trip?"

Mac raised his eyebrows. "They're in country? How do you know?"

"Nick has been working for O'Shea."

Mac crossed his arms, a slight smile on his face. "An internationally wanted money launderer? What other clients do you have? Are you working for Ruja

Ignatova, too?" He took a step closer. "Where's O'Shea?"

"The fat, ugly one, or the good-looking daughter?"

Mac's eyebrows were threatening to meet his receding hairline. "Either." he took another step forward.

Nick shuffled half a step back. "Getting into my personal space, mate. Why the interest?"

"Opposite scenario to yours, I think," said James. "We've been trying to nail Petrovski down for almost a decade. Since he got those scars. And, like Capone, we thought we'd get him through his money. We knew Petrovski laundered his money through the O'Sheas."

"Or he used to," said Mac. "That abruptly ended when his daughter fucked off with a large pile of Petrovski's money. But we're still looking for them. Every time we think we've found them, they move. So this is special. Where's the old man?"

"More important, I think, is why is a former federal cop working for an international money launderer?"

"Long story over a beer later. I need to get home. Lucy and Davie are probably ready to call it a night, too. More than me."

Kon yelled expletives as Johnson and Jackson muscled him into the house.

"Hang around a little bit longer. See what this guy has to say."

Chapter Thirty-Two

Kon was dragged into the living room area, pushed into a chair in front of the table and one hand was handcuffed to the rail. His hair was plastered to his skull, and he reeked of stale sweat. He jerked the cuffs, rattling them against the bar.

"What the hell, man?" He gave it another yank. He rubbed his free hand on the back of his head and took it away, examining the drying blood. "I need medical attention."

Nick and Johnson watched from the door. "Let's you and I do this one together, Nick."

"At the table?"

"Just like old times. You brought him down, after all."

"Well, champ, I never interrogated thugs on the job. Just financial criminals with substantially higher IQs than this slug's, and Lucy brought him down. Not me."

"Yeah, right." Johnson chuckled.

"I'm serious. She cracked him on the head." He laughed. "Then put the boots to him. But what the hell? Why not? Let's talk to this moron."

He took one of the chairs across from Kon. Johnson sat to his left. Nick leaned back and wrinkled his nose. "Jesus. We should take this guy out back and hose him down."

"Piss off, mate. You're dead," said Kon.

MacCready and James walked into the room and leaned against the wall.

Kon looked at them, standing behind Nick and Johnson. "Who are these fucks?"

"Manners," said Nick. "Our guests have an interest in Petrovski's location. But since they're guests, they're polite enough to let us talk to you first. If you aren't forthcoming, we'll let them beat it out of you."

"I don't know any Petrovski." He rattled the cuff again. "You've got nothing on me. I want a lawyer."

Nick chuckled. "The go-kart track is owned by a company with you as its only director. It's a crime scene. David Sangster was held and beaten up in there. A van registered in your name grabbed Davie off the street, and *you* knocked out a good friend, concussing her and putting her in the hospital. I've got that on CCTV. That's more than enough to hold you for now."

Kon lunged across the table. Nick and Johnson stood, toppling their chairs.

"Told you. Should have cuffed both hands," said Nick. He smacked Kon on the side of his head with an open palm and grimaced, wiping his hand off on his trousers. "Seriously, mate. We should hose you down."

"Can we talk to him now?" James picked up

Nick's chair and put it back in place. "Sit back in your chair, Kon. Before I sit you down." He laced his fingers together and leaned forward. "We know you know who Petrovski is. We've got footage of you talking together. The scary guy. Scarred face, fake hand. Russian out of Miami. Really coincidental that you have an office at a local Russian-affiliated club, and one of your minions on your payroll met him when he landed at the airport. So, again, where can we find him?"

"You must think I'm fucking stupid. Get my lawyer. I'm not telling you anything about Petrovski."

"We're wasting our time here, James." MacCready rested his hand on James' shoulder. "Let the locals process this fat fuck. We can get enough surveillance info with the data points we have now. This guy will rot in prison."

"You should head back to America now, pigs, while you're still alive. This Petrovski guy is scary.

You might not survive an encounter. Once he has finished off the O'Sheas, he'll turn his attention to you. He won't be gentle."

MacCready threw the other chair against the wall. "Thanks for confirming that he's targeting them."

Kon blanched. He sat back in his chair and said nothing.

"He'll have a trove of information to help us," said James. "He used to launder for Petrovski, and rumour has it he's managing funds for others in the US. You know where he is?"

Kon clenched his mouth shut.

"He's terrified of Petrovski. He's not going to talk." Mac cocked his head and looked at Nick. "You know where O'Shea is, though. Right?"

Nick looked at his shoes for a sec. "Let's get Petrovski out of the way first. O'Shea is a harmless tub of lard who can't hurt anyone."

James stepped up to Nick. "You're on our side, right? Where's O'Shea?"

Davie and Lucy pushed into the room.

"Nick, I've got to get home. I've got work in the morning," said Lucy.

"You should be taking it easy." Nick moved away from James. "How's your head feeling?" He looked over at the feds. "Nice seeing you again. James, good chat. I'll catch you later."

Petrovski followed Peter through the bush north of the go-kart facility. "You know where we're going?"

Peter grunted.

"What kind of bullshit organisation is this? How did the cops find that place so quickly?"

"They're still looking for you. You might want to keep your voice down."

"You *do* know where we're going?"

"I've got a mate a bit north of here. Fifteen minutes. We can grab a ride from them and head back to Kon's place. Get more reinforcements."

"Your friend. Is he reliable? Do you trust him?"

"Jake? Known him since primary school. He's solid as. You can trust him."

"Fine. Then that'll be our base of operations until I accomplish the goal I came here to complete. He knows we're coming?"

"I told him to expect company. I know you're a big shot, but he's only met you once back at Kon's place, then went to the airport with Kon. Let me talk to him first."

"Get on your phone and have every solid man you've got meet us at Jake's house before breakfast tomorrow." He looked at his watch. "Today."

Chapter Thirty-Three

Nick woke with a start. He'd done what he was 'hired' to do, and a smarter man would leave well enough alone, but that Russian was screwing things up.

He called the burner number Terri had given him and it went straight to blind voicemail. So he called the Four Seasons. "Teresa O'Shea, please."

"I'm sorry sir, there's nobody by that name staying here."

"It might be Grace Rawlston, or it might be someone else. Whatever name she's using, please tell her Nick Harding needs to talk to her urgently, and she should call me at this number immediately." He gave them his mobile number and jumped in the shower.

He was making a cup of coffee when his phone rang. "This Terri?"

"Stop bothering me, Nick. I've met with my father. Your job is complete."

"Petrovski has a serious hardon for you. He slipped the cops last night, and I'm pretty sure his sole goal is to track you down, kill you and take whatever money you have. A couple of cops from America are here looking for you, too. I don't condone, generally, what you do, but getting Petrovski's ten million into better hands buys you a bit of grace. Make sure you're out of the country today, okay?"

He listened to silence for almost a minute before she replied. "I'll keep this phone on until I get on the plane. If you hear anything else, let me know. Deal?"

"As long as you're out of the country before the sun sets, sure."

"What about my father?"

"The Americans are looking for him, too. I think their focus is on Petrovski, but your pops is a close second. I'm off to have a chat with him now."

"Thanks. I hope to never talk to you again."

"Likewise." Nick hung up. "One down. I'll see the old guy face-to-face."

He grabbed a bear claw and called Lucy. "How's your head?"

"I'll live. I have to show up at work with a patch missing from my hair, so there's that. What are you doing today?"

"I'm heading to O'Shea's place to let him know the Americans are looking for him and maybe squeeze a couple of bucks out of him. Then I was thinking about buying you and Davie lunch on the waterfront. To make up for the shit yesterday."

"That'll be a nice start. Message me where and when. I've got to run to a meeting."

Davie called him just as he hung up. "How's the head?"

"My whole body hurts, mate. Have you even been beaten up yet?"

"Not this case. I was going to call you. Are you free for lunch? Catching up with you and Lucy. My treat, Make up for yesterday's crap."

"Can do. Let me know where and when. Are you talking to O'Shea today? Warning him about the Yanks?"

"You're getting good at this. I'm on my way over. I'll tell him you said hi. I'll give you a call later."

"See you, buddy. Hope you don't get beat up."

Nick chuckled as he walked out of his apartment door. It was a short drive, and he parked in front of the cafe across from O'Shea's apartment.

Reg opened the door, and Nick entered O'Shea's apartment. He returned to the sofa and his paper, watching Nick and O'Shea.

"I'm going to need you to track my daughter. I think this is the last day she's in Sydney." O'Shea shuffled to the kitchen and turned on the coffee machine.

"Forget it. She was here yesterday. That was your chance to do whatever it was you wanted to do. I'm out, I'll send you my invoice. Terms are 15 days."

"I'm not paying you, you little shit."

"A couple of guys have come to town and are very interested in finding out where you are."

"Are you threatening me? I already know about the Russians."

"Americans. FBI, I think. They are very keen on rounding you up. There are alerts at the airports and all public transit. I think they've got you this time." Nick crossed his arms. "Grab yourself a good meal tonight. It might be your last one."

"You're fucking threatening me?"

Nick sighed. "Not your last meal like you'll be dead. Your last *good meal*. Wow. You're wound tight."

O'Shea glowered at him for a minute. "Is one of

the Americans named something or other James?"

"Yeah. James. He's FBI. And yeah, I'm threatening you. I'll give you the same deal I've given your daughter. Get out of town by sundown. After that I tell the Americans, and the local AFP, what I know."

O'Shea scrambled through the kitchen drawers and pulled out two insulin syringes. "Fine." He took a vial of insulin from the fridge and loaded both syringes. "Last fookin' straw. No fookin' point hanging around, is there? Five minutes after I jab myself, I'll be unconscious. Ten minutes after that, dead. It'll be peaceful." He lifted his shirt and pinched a thick fold of his ample gut. "Nothing you can do to stop it." He hesitated with the needle just touching his skin. "I'll wobble around for a few minutes before I drop."

"What the fuck are you talking about?" Reg jumped off the sofa and ran to intercept O'Shea. "Jesus, old man."

"Well, I'm fucked, yeah? Boy-o here is going to tell them where I am, I don't have the money my daughter shifted off with, so if the cops don't get me, the Commies will. I'm fucked." He pressed the needle into his gut. Reg grabbed both syringes and tossed them on the counter before O'Shea could depress the plunger.

Nick crossed his arms and leaned against the wall. "Maybe you reach out to the cops and get a witness protection deal. I'm sure you've got tonnes of info on all the people you've laundered money for. The cops would love that. They can set you up someplace nice."

"Like Dubbo? Mackay? No thanks. I'd rather be dead."

"Gorgeous beaches in Mackay, you twat." Nick shrugged. "But I don't care what you do. This time tomorrow, I'll give them a call. It's been a slice, O'Shea. Reg, don't follow me. Hope never to see you again."

Nick looked around the spacious apartment. He shook his head. "This place is wasted with you, O'Shea. Eat a salad, for Christ's sake and maybe go for a walk once in a while."

Chapter Thirty-Four

Nick sat in the cafe across from The Four Seasons. He'd been nursing his coffee for almost an hour. He texted Terri's burner: *I think there'll be a Russian army out looking for you.*

He drained the end of his coffee and stood and stretched. He looked at his phone, hoping for a reply. He pocketed his silent phone and was about to turn to the counter to get a fresh cup when he saw a brunette in a floppy hat leave the hotel's front door. He called her number, watched as she glanced at her phone, and dumped the call.

"Gotcha." Nick pulled on a baseball cap and a pair of sunglasses. A pretty ordinary disguise, but it was better than nothing. Hell, it worked for Captain

America. He slipped out of the cafe and followed her from across the street. It was the middle of the morning on a weekday. Pedestrian traffic was light.

She was good. She varied her walking speed. Stopped every half a block or so to look in shop front windows. Good technique to catch out someone on her tail.

Nick was good, too, though. She was easy to pick out on the street and kept her eyes on her side of the street. He mirrored her actions and stayed out of sight as they progressed south on George Street.

He thought she saw him as she crossed George to head east on Martin Place. He stepped into the entrance of a jeweller's shop and gave it a few seconds before stepping out again. She'd progressed up the hill until she had almost reached Pitt Street when she stepped into a small boutique bank on her left.

He trotted to the bank and looked around. He appeared to be the only one following her. He found a bench under a shade tree and settled in for a wait.

His phone chimed. *It's going to be a hot one. Why don't you come in?* He chuckled and stowed his phone. He took another look around to ensure he had no company and entered the bank.

It was cool and warm at the same time. The air was well-conditioned and at least ten degrees cooler than the air outside. But the bank exuded an air of warmth, affluence and hospitality. The carpet was thick and swallowed sounds. The walls and furniture were well-polished dark wood of some sort. If Nick were to guess, he'd say mahogany, but it would be a guess.

A professional-looking young woman nodded at him and pointed to her left. "They're waiting." She handed him a lanyard with a large red V on it.

He slung it over his neck and navigated his way to the desk Terri was sitting at.

A reedy-looking middle-aged man stood as he approached and held out his hand. "You must be

Nick Harding. Grace said you might be stopping by. My name is Nigel McInnes. You can call me Nigel."

"Thanks, Nigel. Yes. *Grace* and I go way back. How are you progressing?" He pulled a chair from a neighbouring vacant desk and sat beside Terri.

"Nigel transferred a few hundred thousand to one of my accounts a week ago. We're just setting up the parameters for a larger transfer." Terri frowned. "I'll need to bring up some funds in my safe deposit boxes. I'll deposit it in my account and wait for you to transfer the bulk of it to that offshore account. You can handle the paperwork?"

"I certainly can. I'll need your box key and account information. Merely a formality, but I need to tick the boxes for compliance."

"Two keys." She produced the keys, wrote down her account information, and slid them across the desk to Nigel. He took the note and slid the keys back to Terri. "You'll need these."

"Ah, right."

"I'll take you down. Mr Harding, can you wait here?"

"Nigel, I'd prefer if he came with us. I may need some assistance. Will that be a problem?"

Nigel looked at Nick, thought for a brief second and smiled. "Of course not. If you'd both follow me."

He led them through a secure door to the back area of the bank. The decor was more utilitarian than the front office but still suitable for an establishment that hosted multi-millionaires. They went through another secure door and into a room lined with deposit boxes.

The room was about 5 meters per side and had a waist-high table about 1m by 2m in the middle.

Terri got her bearings and headed to two large boxes situated side-by-side. She inserted her keys, and Nigel inserted the banks'. They both opened their respective locks, and Nigel opened the doors.

"That's good, Nige. Nick and I can take it from

here."

"As you wish, Miss Rawlston. There's a small green button by the doors on the way back. Pressing them will disengage the locks." He tapped a small faceplate near the door. "The intercom is here. Buzz me if you need me."

"Thanks. Nigel, I need a trolley and a couple of large duffels. Will that be possible?"

Nigel glanced at the boxes and nodded. "I'll be back shortly."

Nick waited until he left and then tried to slide the box out of its recess. He could barely move it. "Damn."

"Ten million, in hundreds, weighs about a hundred kilos. Two hundred and twenty pounds. Fifty kilos per drawer."

Nick nodded. He moved the trolly closer to the box. "This, I take it, broke up the team."

Terri shrugged. The bottom of the hole in the wall containing the safe deposit boxes was half a metre above the trolly. It slid on tracks like a bureau drawer, far enough to open the top lid.

Nick let out a long whistle. "Damn. I haven't seen that kind of cash, ever. Hell, I rarely see a single hundred-dollar bill in my day-to-day, let alone— how many is this? A hundred thousand of them?"

"Yeah, over the two of them." Terri opened the second door and slid the box out. She flipped the lid to an equal amount of cash.

"Goddamn. I really need to know the backstory."

"Petrovski pushed a lot of money through us from a pig butchering operation. That's where people are trafficked from China to a different country in South East Asia to scam people online."

"I'm familiar with the term. That's a good pile of money for a gig like that. About ten times bigger than most."

"Oh, this isn't from pig butchering. We happily cleaned that money for him. He converted it to crypto, we took the cash equivalent and ran it through a bunch of bogus cash businesses to clean it and drop it in his business accounts." She put her hand on top of the cash. "This, however, was gains from a human trafficking - a sex trafficking - operation he spun off the pig butcher scheme. Women - young women - from Thailand, Cambodia and Laos were moved to Europe, ostensibly to be nannies. That's what he told them, anyway. They ended up being sold to wealthy assholes as sex slaves."

"Unpleasant, but not uncommon," said Nick.

"Pops and I agreed, right up front, that we wouldn't launder for gun running or sex traffickers."

"Ah, ethical criminals."

"Piss off. We made that agreement, and the old man reneged on it as soon as he saw the amount. That's the last time he and I worked together. I cashed it out here in Australia and put most of it in these boxes." She smiled. "That wasn't a trivial exercise. Probably why it's taken me so long to do something about it." She unzipped the bags and shook them open. "You going to help?"

"What exactly are you doing here?"

"Taking this to Nigel so I can deposit it."

"And after you do that, he'll return it to a vault nearby. So let's save us the trouble and have him come down with the money-counting machines and do it right here?"

Terri closed her eyes. "Fuck me. I should have thought of that."

"Nigel should have thought of this. I'll go get him."

She dropped the bags on the trolly. "Hang on." She pressed a button by the door and sat on the trolly, waiting for Nigel.

"So, where are you sending this money to?"

"I have an account in Belize." She looked at her watch. "I have a flight to catch. The money will stay in that bank for about thirty minutes before it gets anonymously sent to half a dozen NGOs supporting women and children victims of trafficking."

Nick nodded. "Belize. That one escaped our attention. How long has it been active?"

"It's dormant. Has been for few years. Petrovski set it up and then abandoned it." She smiled. "I relieved him of it. I'm sure he'll get an alert when it fills with money, but it'll be gone before he can do anything about it."

"The first deposit you made, the one you told me Nigel made for you. Was that to the same account?

"Yeah. Why?"

"Petrovski's old account? I think that may be how he tracked you."

She closed her eyes, and her shoulders slumped. "Dammit."

"Half an hour for these other transfer, you say?"

Terri nodded.

Nick grimaced. "Might have to be a bit quicker than that."

"That's about as fast as I can do it. It takes about

five minutes per transaction, and I've got to make six of them."

Nigel poked his head in the door and knocked on the jamb. "How can I help?"

"Rather than schlep all this cash back to your desk, I think it would be easier for you, and more secure if we managed the transaction here. Would that be possible?"

"Not an uncommon occurrence. Give me a minute."

He stepped out of the room. "Not even a minute," he called.

Nick opened his mouth to talk about Terri's transaction timings, but Nigel was true to his word and returned rolling a table with five bill counters affixed. Two junior employees followed him in.

"This shouldn't take more than fifteen or twenty minutes. I can have fresh coffee brought in. We should be finished by 10:30 and have you out of here no later than 11:00."

"Grace and I have some private business to discuss. Is there a small room we can use while you do this?"

"Clients usually prefer to be in attendance when we do the count," said Nigel.

"I know how much is there," said Terri. "Nick and I do need to talk."

"Very well." He led them to a smaller meeting room across the hall. "You can keep an eye on us here."

"Thanks." Nick held the door and followed Terri in. He closed the door behind them. The window in the door provided a clear view of the safe deposit box room and Nigel's efforts. "You're doing the transactions on your phone?"

She nodded. "Adds to the delays."

"Have you used the bank very often?"

"Just the one transfer to make sure it still worked. You're right. I probably tipped off Petrovski when I did that."

"And he'll be tipped off when you make the next transfer in. You'll get some out, but only the first few transfers before he locks it down." He rubbed the back of his head. "Are you keeping any of this money?"

She shook her head. "My ill-gotten gains are held in another establishment, on another continent." She smiled. "Don't ask me where."

"Do you trust me?"

"What are you going to do?"

"Make sure Petrovski doesn't get any of it back." He held out his hand. "Log into the bank account and hand me your phone and the NGO bank details."

Chapter Thirty-Five

Nigel's timing estimate wasn't even close. By the time the counting was completed and double-checked, and the transactions to deposit it in Terri's Sydney account and transfer it to Belize were completed, it was close to 11:45.

Nick stepped out of the bank first, carefully scanned the surroundings, and motioned for Terri.

"Safe?"

"You should get to the airport."

"My flight isn't until 5:00. If Petrovski is smart, he'll have women at the airport waiting for me to go to the restroom and knock me off. I'm timing my arrival as late as possible. Sydney's a big place. I like my chances in the city better."

Nick patted his stomach. "Join us for lunch, then."

"Us?"

"Davie and Lucy and I are getting together. A closing-out-the-case lunch. Not that your old man has paid me yet."

"My treat."

Nick considered this for a minute and nodded. "To the waterfront."

Terri shook her head. "I'd rather not. Too close to the hotel. Ground zero."

"That's a reasonable point. Except that's the last place they'd be looking. How about a compromise? We find an indoor place with dark corners?"

Terri considered and sighed. "Okay. Our regular joint, I guess. Watch my back, okay?"

"Deal."

Nick messaged Lucy and Davie with a twenty-minute ETA.

"Terri, you know where we're going, right?"

She nodded.

"So you walk ahead, and I'll keep an eye on you and anyone paying too much attention to you."

"My very own bodyguard." She looked him up and down. "You any good in a fight?"

He laughed. "Oh hell no." He held up his phone. "But I'm an ace at calling for backup."

"Why?"

They walked side-by-side. "Why what?"

Terri looked over her shoulder and crossed the street. "Why are you helping me?"

"Why did we cross the street?"

"More windows on this side. Easier to catch out black hats. Does that have something to do with my question?"

"I guess you've been looking over your shoulder a lot longer than I have."

She smiled. "Very true. You still didn't answer me."

"Why am I helping you? As I said before. Getting the money into worthy hands."

"But you've already done that." She held up her hands and wiggled her fingers. "Out of my hands now. Before I get on the plane, the funds will be redistributed." She slid her hands back into her pockets. "So, why?"

Nick shrugged. "Finishing the job. Getting you out of here safely."

"That was never your job, Nick."

"Why do you care?"

She walked in silence for a bit. "I have trust issues. How do I know you're not walking me into the arms of the police? You've made sure the money is redistributed. No reason not to turn me in, now."

"Yet you're walking with me, taking me up on lunch. Offered to pay for it, even."

It was Terri's turn to shrug. "You've done me right so far. So many opportunities to be a dick, and you haven't been. Yet."

"Fair enough. We should cross back now. We're getting close to the hotel."

They crossed, dodging trams and pushbikes and met Davie and Lucy just outside the café.

"She's joining us? Is that smart?"

"Davie, mate, when have you ever thought me to be smart?" Nick patted him on the back and pointed him at the café. "You still look like shit. This is the last place they'll be looking, anyway."

Lucy slipped her arm in Terri's. "You're buying, right?"

"That's what he said. You two are a perfect match." She let Lucy enter the café in front of her. "What are you going to do about your hair?"

"I'm thinking about getting a Rose McGowan cut, then let it grow out." She held up four fingers to the server. "In the back, please."

Lucy whacked Nick on the arm. "Look."

Nick stabbed himself in the chin with his fork. He wiped his face off with his napkin. "What? And ouch."

"Sorry. You okay?"

"I'll live. What am I looking at?"

"I think the Russian and a couple of heavyweights just entered the hotel."

Nick turned in his seat. The entrance to The Four Seasons was visible. "When. Just now?"

Terri nodded. "Yeah, I saw him too. This was a huge mistake." She gathered her napkin and stood. Lucy gently took her arm and guided her back to her seat. "Not a huge mistake. Just maybe a little one."

"Maybe not a mistake at all. We're going to sit here until they leave empty-handed. At that point, Terri, you spend the next few hours in the lobby, drinking tea and reading the paper. They can arrange a ride to the airport for your just-in-time flight."

"Oh, that's brilliant." Sarcasm dripped from Terri's voice.

"Seriously. They'll be told you've checked out. They won't be back. That place will be off their list." Nick pointed. "They're leaving already, and they don't look satisfied."

Petrovski and two young men stood arguing on the hotel's front step. Nick couldn't hear them, but the agitation was evident. They stormed north toward Circular Quay.

"Davie and I are following them. Lucy, can you sit with Terri until she gets a car to the airport?"

Davie sat up straight in his chair. "Whoa, whoa, whoa. Follow them? To what end? Call the cops on them. I've already been on their receiving end, and I've got ZERO desire to do it again."

Nick held up his hands. "At a distance. We won't engage."

"It's not like I planned getting beat up the last time, mate."

Terri grabbed her bag and nodded at Lucy. "Lucy and I will be across the street. Give us a heads-up if they double back, okay? Let's go, Lucy. Leave the boys to discuss their next steps."

Nick waited until they had left the cafe before he

turned back to Davie. "Come on, mate. I need your eyes."

His friend scratched the back of his head. "Okay, okay." He pushed his chair away and headed for the door. "We better move, or we'll lose them."

Nick left money with the cashier and trotted to catch up to Davie. "Why the change of heart? Thanks."

"I just want to get this over with." The Russians were walking briskly along the waterfront, passing the Ferry terminals then turning right, back toward the city. "They seem to know where they're going."

The convoy continued south. Petrovski and his two friends were about a block ahead of Davie and Nick. "They don't seem very situationally aware," said Nick. "You could walk right up to them, and they wouldn't even notice."

"Pass," said Davie. "Don't need to get punched again. One of those two was with Petrovski last night. Peter, I think. On the left." He looked at the buildings they were passing. "This neighbourhood looks familiar."

"You've been here before. A few times." Petrovski turned a corner, and Nick and Davie approached with care. "Right around this corner is O'Shea's place. Across from the cafe. They've tracked the fat fuck down."

Chapter Thirty-Six

Nick peered around the corner, then motioned for Davie to follow. A block ahead and across the street, Petrovski and his two friends entered O'Shea's building.

Nick checked for traffic and jay-jogged across the street, Davie struggling to keep up. They reached the front entrance and paused, backs against the wall by the front door.

"We should call the cops."

"We will, Davie. As soon as we get upstairs and make sure O'Shea is okay." Nick peered in the door. The guard desk was vacant. "There was somebody there." He pushed open the door and stepped through the metal detector and around the desk. The guard was on the floor, unconscious. Nick squatted and checked his pulse. It was steady.

"Is he okay?"

"Crack on the head, I guess. He's breathing."

The doors to the penthouse lift opened, and one of the Russians started to step out, then backed in and repeatedly hammered the door close button. Nick dove for the door, but it closed before he got to it.

"Are you nuts? He would have flattened you," said Davie. "That was Peter."

"Call the feds and an ambulance and wait here for them. When they get here, tell them there are three bad guys upstairs and three not quite-so-bad guys."

"I'll go with you."

"You've been banged around enough. And I'm taking the stairs the last couple of flights."

Davie chuckled. "Okay, you've convinced me."

Nick grabbed a lift adjacent to the penthouse service. It went as far as the forty-second floor. He'd take the stairs from there.

The lift ascended quickly. The stairs were at the end of the lift lobby. He entered the stairwell and checked to make sure the door back to the forty-second floor wouldn't lock on him.

He wasn't so lucky on the forty-third floor. The door was locked. He broke the glass on the cabinet holding the fire axe and knocked the handle off the door. A couple of targeted swings at the door jamb broke it open.

He stood for a minute behind the door, steadying his breath, then eased the door open. The hallway was empty. The door to O'Shea's apartment was closed, with sounds of fighting behind it. Nick tested the handle. It was also locked.

He retraced his steps to the stairwell and retrieved the axe.

He swung the blunt, flat end of the axe at the door handle. Three vigorous swings and the door handle snapped off. He reversed the head of the axe and targeted the gap between the door and the door jamb.

After a couple of swings, the door opened.

To Petrovski levelling a handgun at him. "What the fuck are you doing here?"

Nick threw the axe at him and dove behind the sofa. He heard a bullet whiz past his ear. He scrambled to the far end of the sofa and peered around it at floor level. Petrovski's prosthetic hand was pointing the wrong way. It had taken the brunt of the axe.

Petrovski put the handgun on the table by the door and ripped the right sleeve off his shirt. He fumbled with the leather straps and removed the prosthetic.

Nick heard a crash upstairs. Peter came down the stairs headfirst, and Nick heard Reg yelling something. There was another crash, and the second thug dropped from the pool deck onto the table Nick had been sitting at for the past few days. He groaned and rolled onto his back. His left leg pointed the wrong way.

Peter pushed himself to his feet and started back

up them.

"Where in the hell are you, you punk?" Reg stormed down the stairs and met the thug halfway, throwing fists.

Nick lifted his head, and a gunshot split the air above his head, the slug planting itself in the wall behind him. He ducked back down.

"Quit crawling around like the chicken shit you are," said Petrovski. "It's not like you can go anywhere."

"I beg to differ," muttered Nick. He traversed the gap of a few centimetres between the sofa and a chair as quickly as he could and squatted behind the chair. He reached for a large crystal ashtray on the table beside the chair with his left and threw it awkwardly at Petrovski's head.

Petrovski ducked and fired two quick shots as he fell to the floor. The third pull of the trigger clicked. It was empty. Nick scrambled to his feet and charged him before he had an opportunity to reload.

Petrovski twisted out of the way and Nick pulled up short when he heard the 'snick' of an opening blade.

"Mr Nick Harding." Petrovski held a six-inch blade out at waist level.

Nick shifted to his left. "How do you know my name?"

"You have been a pain in my ass since I landed." He looked at the struggle going on between Reg and his muscle. "Peter, finish that up and check on Jake!"

"Not fucking likely," grunted Reg. He and his adversary grappled on the floor, knocking over tables and floor lamps.

Nick skirted more to the left toward the kitchen.

"No, you stop." Petrovski brandished the knife. "I'm going to slice you to ribbons." The left side of Petrovski's face was red with rage, starkly contrasting with the pale, scarred right side. Leather straps from the shoulder harness protruded from the end of his torn shirtsleeve.

Nick threw one of the barstools from the kitchen

at Petrovski.

He easily sidestepped it, taking him closer to the door and farther from Nick.

Reg had his adversary in a chokehold on the other side of the large living area, his legs wrapped around the young Russian's waist. Nick kept one eye on Reg and one on Petrovski. Reg seemed to have things in hand. Petrovski was once again advancing on him.

"You're not getting out the door. When I'm finished with you, you'll have told me where that fat fuck's daughter is," he gestured at O'Shea's prone, unconscious body, "and where that bitch stashed my money."

Reg screamed. Nick and Petrovski both looked at him. Reg still had a hold around Peter's neck, but now he had a knife sticking out of his side. Nick moved to help, and Petrovski took a sideways step and got between Nick and Reg. "No. You're mine. Where is she?"

Nick took a step back. "Where is who?"

"I am tired. I am pissed off, and you broke my hand."

"And you're ugly."

Petrovski grinned and brushed the flat of his knife against his scarred face. "This is beautiful compared to what your face will look like." He shrugged. "But you'll be dead. You won't get to appreciate it. Now where is that bitch who stole my money?"

Nick looked at his watch. "Sipping tea in the lobby restaurant at The Four Seasons, right about now."

"We were just there. She checked out already. She isn't there."

Nick shrugged. "You asked." He took a step closer to the kitchen and the island counter. "I can't help it if you don't believe me."

Petrovski kept his eyes on Nick. "Peter, hurry the fuck up."

Other than a faint wheezing sound, there was no response.

"Peeter! Quit fucking around and get over here."

Nick shifted sideways and looked past the Russian. "Little Pete's not going to be much help." *Neither is Reg*, thought Nick. His friend was on the floor beside Pete, with the knife still sticking out of his side. The blood was slowly pooling below the knife.

Petrovski glanced over his shoulder and looked back quickly at Nick. "Either is your pal."

"Never met the guy before last week." Nick took another step back into the kitchen.

"Where are you going?"

"I'm sure there's a knife back here somewhere."

Petrovski laughed. "With my one remaining hand, I could take you in a knife fight. And I'll get my answers as I carve you up. So do your best, kid."

"I am so fucking tired of being called a kid." Nick got to the other side of the island kitchen and saw the two syringes in the sink, still completely loaded with insulin. The caps had been placed over the needles.

"Looks like your boy is going to need a hospital."

Nick waited until Petrovski turned to look and used the distraction to grab both needles. He pulled the caps off and held them out of sight in his right hand.

"Never met the guy before yesterday."

Nick stepped back from the sink. "I called the police before I came up here. You should probably leave." Nick hoped fervently that Davie actually did call the police.

"They're not here yet. Get a knife and show me what you've got."

Nick stepped out from behind the kitchen island. "You've only got one hand. I can disarm you - ha - without much effort. Or any weapons." He approached him side-on, leading with his left foot, his right hand and the needles hidden behind his thigh. Petrovski led with his left, also. He held his knife with its tip pointed toward his elbow.

Nick backed off a couple of steps. "You look like

you know how to use that."

Petrovski grinned.

"You probably shouldn't do that." Nick waved his hand in front of his face. "Those scars aren't flattering, and your smile makes it all that much worse. Maybe they can sort out the damage while you're serving time."

"I'm going to slice your forehead first. The scalp bleeds like a stuck pig. You'll be blinded. Then I'll selectively nick tendons and ligaments until you can't stand or lift your arms. Even if you tell me everything I need to know about the bitch and my money before I finish, I'll still finish. If you're fast, I'll be fast and make sure you don't suffer. Not too much. If you're slow, I will also be slow."

Nick nodded. "Got it. Very considerate of you to lay out the rules of engagement like that. The forehead first?" He backed off a couple more steps.

Petrovski lifted the knife and moved toward him.

"Got it." Nick ran at Petrovski and dove at his

legs. Petrovski compensated and swung his knife down, slicing across Nick's back as Nick stabbed him in the thigh with both needles while depressing the plungers. One of the needles broke off in his leg as Nick rolled out of the way.

"You're bleeding. Not the start that I wanted, but it'll do."

Nick crab walked away from Petrovski and tried to stand. His hands slipped, and he looked at the marble floor. His hands were slipping in blood. "Fuck." He looked up at the Russian. "It's starting to hurt."

"You'll live if you get medical attention and quickly."

Nick took a careful breath and pushed himself up the wall to a standing position. "Same for you, champ."

"What did you inject me with?"

Nick shook his head. "It's a deadly poison. In a couple of minutes, you'll get very wobbly. In ten minutes, you'll be dead."

"Bullshit."

He pressed his back against the wall, hoping to staunch the flow. "You're feeling it already, aren't you?"

Petrovski leaned against the kitchen counter and looked at his hand. He squeezed the knife handle as tight as he could. He felt weak. The knife was slipping out of his hand. He tried to tighten his grip, but the knife slipped and clattered to the floor. "What was it?"

Nick's vision blurred. He took another deep breath and winced as the cut on his back opened.

"What in the hell is this?"

Nick turned to see Johnson crash into the apartment with people behind him. He looked back at Petrovski, who was now on his knees, looking as white as O'Shea. "Good timing. We all need medical help. Petrovski has overdosed on insulin. Cuff him first and pour honey down his throat. The rest of us

need various amounts of medical care."

Chapter Thirty-Seven

Davie followed the police into O'Shea's apartment. He let out a whistle and headed to Nick. "Damn. This place has been trashed."

"I'm fine, thanks." Nick groaned as his shirt was cut off.

The apartment was crowded. Johnson and Jackson were attending to O'Shea. James and MacCready had Petrovski in the semi-prone position on the floor. Two paramedics were working on Reg while a third attended to the Russian on the balcony with the broken leg. Half a dozen local cops were taking statements from the various people involved.

Nick sat backwards on a chair while a paramedic applied suture staples to the cut on his back. He winced with every single one. "Thanks for calling the cavalry. Ouch. I think we've got everything wrapped up now. Ouch." He watched O'Shea get loaded onto a gurney. "I don't think we will - ouch - get paid for this one." He looked over his shoulder. "You finished yet, Junior Doctor?"

"One more. I'll tape you up, but you need to get to the hospital sometime today to get this sorted out for real. When's the last time you had a tetanus shot?"

"Three years ago. Damn cockatoo tried to take my finger off."

"So you don't need a tetanus shot. Might need antibiotics." He finished with the tape and tapped Nick on the back. "You're good to go."

"Thanks." Nick picked his shirt off the floor and shook his head. A metre-long tear across the back was bracketed with his blood. He stepped around a pile of bloody rags to where two paramedics worked on Reg. "Mate, how are you doing?"

Reg clenched his jaw. "Bloody fantastic. What do you think?"

"Where do you keep your shirts?" He held up his bloody rags. "I need something to wear."

Reg grimaced as he chuckled. "You'll swim in in anything I own." He closed his eyes and took a steadying breath. "Down the hall. Second door."

"Many thanks." Nick cocked his head and looked at the wound in his side. "You'll be right." He clapped the paramedic on the shoulder. "These guys know what they're doing."

He found the smallest rugby shirt in Reg's closet and needed Davie's help pulling it over the wound on his back.

"It hurts?"

"I've got a couple of heavy-duty painkillers in me. I'll be fine."

"It'll be a sexy scar."

Nick laughed. He returned to O'Shea on the gurney. Jackson and Johnson were escorting him from the apartment. "How is he?"

"Concussed," said Johnson. "Still unconscious. He'll wake up shackled to a hospital bed."

"He's diabetic. You'll find insulin in the fridge and needles in the top drawer by the sink."

Jackson waved a paramedic over. "Check his sugar. Do whatever it is you have to do to make sure he doesn't die before we put him in jail." He crossed his arms and addressed Nick. "Hell of a mess in here. We're going to have a long chat about what happened. Where's the daughter?"

"Oh, I don't have any kids, Jackson. Nice of you to ask, though."

"Don't mess with me, Harding."

"Oh, right. You mean the O'Shea girl." He shook his head. "Ya got me. It's a big city. If she's even still in the country."

"When did you see her last?"

Nick glanced at Davie and raised an eyebrow. "We had dinner last night. Right, Davie?"

His friend slowly nodded. "What's the name of that place in North Sydney? The one across from the Post Office?"

Nick snapped his fingers. "The Green Moustache."

"That's the one. Great lamb shank there."

Johnson grabbed his partner by the elbow. "We've got to go. Harding, come by the office in the next day or so and give us your version of whatever this clusterfuck was."

Nick threw him a mock salute and searched out Petrovski.

"You did this?" James stood from a crouch.

"He started it. How's he doing?"

Petrovski tried pushing himself up to a sitting position, misjudging the length of his right arm. He tumbled sideways.

Nick laughed. "He only looks scary. He's literally a pushover."

"He runs mob activity in South Florida."

"Ran, Mac. We've got him." James slapped Petrovski on the side of the face. "You good now?"

"You are way out of your jurisdiction, MacCready." Petrovski made it to his feet this time and scanned the room for his prosthetic. "I'm going to reattach my hand and get out of this spider-infested, upside-down asshole of a country before a kangaroo eats me."

James grabbed his good arm. "We're are here at the invitation of the Australian Federal Police, buddy, and you're coming back to the United States with us." He reached for Petrovski's other wrist and swore. "Shit, Mac. How are supposed to cuff a guy with one hand? You ever look that up??"

Nick laughed. "Davie, come with me to the hospital."

They stepped out of the building into the relative quiet of the city. "Jesus, that was intense."

"I'll get a cab for the hospital," said Davie.

"No, I'm good for now. You head home. I've got to talk to Lucy, make sure she's okay."

"Are you sure?"

Nick slowly moved his arms around, testing his range of motion. "Painkillers are still working. I'll catch up with you later tonight." He stepped off the kerb and crossed the street.

He traced his footsteps back to the cafe. He stood outside, in the shadow of the entryway, and watched Lucy and Terri talking on the hotel patio across the street. Outward appearances seemed like they were just two girlfriends having an afternoon chat.

But if you watched closely, they both spent a good part of their conversation time looking over each other's shoulders, scanning the street. He took out his phone to send Lucy a message when it vibrated with an incoming, from Davie. *You've got a cop on your tail. Not sure if it's local or fed.*

He resisted the urge to look around. *Thanks. I owe you.* He tapped his hand with his phone. "Dammit. I slipped up." He sent him another message. *Keep an eye on him for me. Will be taking a long way around.*

He typed a message to Lucy: *I'm across the street. Don't look. Take Terri into the hotel and down to the parking garage. Text me your brother's number.*

There was a brief delay, then, from Lucy, *Why?*

I'm being followed by a cop.

There was another brief delay, then he received a contact card for Lucy's brother.

He watched and waited until they left the patio and entered the hotel. He checked for traffic and walked up the hill beside the hotel, into The Rocks. He sent text messages while he walked. He received a final response from Bobby and made a quick phone call.

He casually circled the block and entered the hotel from the back entrance. He picked up his pace, ran to the lift, and descended to the parking garage.

Lucy and Terri were not there.

"Dammit." He jabbed the call button to head back

to the lobby, and his phone buzzed with an incoming message.

He read it as he stepped back into the lift. *We're near the exit ramp.*

He stopped the lift door and ran out looking for the exit. It was at the far end of the cavernous garage. Lucy and Terri stood against the wall beside the rolling door. "You two okay?"

"We're fine," said Lucy. "Love the shirt. You think you'll grow into it?"

Nick grinned. "Your brother has checked in. He'll be coming in through the garage. You, Terri, will hide in the boot for a little while as he exits, and then he'll take you to the airport."

The entrance roller door rattled as it raised. A Toyota sedan rolled in and Lucy raised her hand to stop it. She leaned down and looked in the passenger-side window. "Sorry you got pulled into this."

"Why should you have all the fun, sis?" Bobby

got out of the car and opened the boot. It was spacious and lined with a thick blanket. "Not the most comfortable accommodations, but it will be just for a few minutes until we clear this place."

Terri walked to the back of the car and looked in. "Beats the alternative." She raised her eyebrows and looked at Lucy. "Do you have it?"

Lucy pressed a folded piece of paper into Terri's hand. "Good luck. Safe flight."

Terri took one last look at her hiding place and crawled in.

"Watch your fingers." Bobby gently closed the boot. Nick grabbed him before he got back in the car. "Let her out as soon as you're clear of the CBD, and take the long way there. No rush. Her flight is in four hours. Make sure nobody is following her. And go into the airport with her, okay?"

Bobby nodded. "What kind of day rates do I get for this?" He laughed and got in the car. "I'll talk to you later, sis. You keep strange company."

Nick and Lucy stood shoulder to shoulder and watched as her brother exited into the sunshine. They followed the car out of the garage and onto the street.

"So, that's it?"

"What was on the paper you gave her?"

"Nothing important. You owe me a meal."

Nick nodded at the guy in front of them in a suit. He was at the hotel entrance, looking around like he was lost. "I think he's looking for us."

"Cop?"

"I think so." He walked up to the man and tapped him on the shoulder. "Are you looking for me?"

The cop turned, checked a photo on his phone and nodded. "Nick Harding. I'm looking for Teresa O'Shea, but I was told you would know where she is." He looked at Lucy and checked another photo on his phone. "You are not her."

"I am not." Lucy smiled. "Sorry."

"Do you know where she is?"

Nick shook his head. "I have no idea where she is

right now. So sorry. Lucy and I have had a rough week. If you'll excuse us."

"Hang on." The cop proffered a business card. "If you happen to see her, give me a call, okay?"

Nick pocketed his card without looking at it. "No problem." He took Lucy's hand. "I could use a drink. You?"

Chapter Thirty-Eight

Nick and Lucy stood on his parent's doorstep. "Are you sure you want to meet them?"

Lucy looked back at him, smiling. "Absolutely."

"They just got back. Might be a bit jet-lagged." Nick was standing behind her. He placed his hands on her shoulders and looked at the back of her head. "They did a good job. Hardly any scar."

"The hair will hide it. Once it grows in."

"It's only been a week since the stitches came out. Give it a bit of time." He brushed his hand over the softening stubble. "Surprised you shaved it all off."

"Quit stalling." She knocked, and the door was immediately opened.

"I was wondering how long you'd stand there."

Nick noticed the doorbell app on his mother's phone just before she closed it. "How long were you listening to us?"

"Since you pulled up. This must be Lucy. I have a friend named Lucy. You're definitely not her."

Lucy held out her hand. "Great to finally meet you, Mrs Harding."

"You call me Susie." She moved Lucy's hand out of the way and hugged her. "Come in and sit and tell me everything." She glanced at Lucy's head.

"Like where I get my hair done?"

Susie laughed. "If you want." She led them to the backyard patio adjacent to the golf course. "I'm more interested in the adventures you've been on with my son."

"Where's dad?"

"Right behind you." George entered with a tray of drinks. "Not sure what you like, so gin and tonic for everyone." He placed it on the table and sat beside his wife. "So. I read that you two have had some excitement lately."

"Old news, pops. This is Lucy. She said she wanted to meet you two. I told her you were both really boring, but she insisted."

"Tell me about your trip to Italy. I've always wanted to go."

"We found this beautiful place in Tuscany. A large-ish house, but kinda old," said Susie. We've got an offer in on it. You'll have to come visit."

"Sounds nice," said Nick. "Tuscany?"

"Your mum likes the back story more than the house, I think. It was owned by an international criminal at one point."

"About three years ago?" Nick smiled at his father. "Roughly? An Irish guy, maybe?"

"Yeah. How did you know?"

"Just a wild guess." Nick took a sip of his drink. "Pretty strong, pops. Is the doc okay with that?"

His father smacked himself in the chest. "Fit as

a fiddle. So tell us, what trouble have you been getting into?"

They sat that night, again, at a waterfront table at the restaurant on Narellan Beach. The plates had been cleared, and coffee had just been served.

Nick's phone buzzed with a notification. He flipped his phone over, read the message and smiled. He held the phone out for Lucy to read it. "You gave her my banking information, didn't you?" The notification was for a deposit into his business account in the amount of $12,000. "That was the paper you gave her."

Lucy shrugged. "Couldn't let you get stiffed on the job." She sipped her coffee. "Is the amount correct?"

"Close enough. It's not the amount that worries me. It's the source of the funds."

"I'll bet you a hundred bucks that you can attempt to trace that source for days, and it'll all look clean. She's good at what she does."

Nick nodded, absorbing this new information. He put his phone back on the table, face down. "Looks like I can afford dessert. Feel like any?"

"Quite the opposite. I think I need a walk to burn off this meal. Maybe we can have dessert at my place. After the walk."

They strolled up the beach again, toward the parking lot and his car.

"This is nice. You definitely have made my life more interesting, Mr Harding."

"You've come a long way in four weeks."

"Personal growth is good. But I'll have to ask you to keep me out of the heavy business from now on. And maybe give Davie a break, too."

"He's my guy in the chair. I'll make sure he stays in the chair." He looked at her, moonlight reflecting off her face. "You could join my team. I could use someone like you."

"What does 'like me' mean?"

"Smart, tough, quick on their feet."

She squeezed his hand. "I'm good where I am. But thanks." She brushed her hand through her short hair. "You like it short or long?"

"That's your call, Luce."

She shook her head. "No, I want to know how you like it."

"A little bit longer. But really I'm not attracted to you because of your hairstyle."

"Really? So you are attracted to me? So what is it, then? My-" she stopped walking when Nick stopped walking. "What?"

"Company."

Reg stepped onto the beach. "We meet again."

"No way, Reg. I'm on vacation."

Lucy looked past him. "Where's your muscle? I know your weak spots. That wound can't be healed yet. It's going to take more than just you."

"No, no, no." He reached into his back pocket and pulled out a thick envelope. "This is for you."

He handed it to Nick.

He opened it and looked at the stack of new bills. "About ten grand?" He glanced at Lucy, then Reg. "So, how's the old guy doing?"

Reg shook his head. "In the prison infirmary waiting for trial, but I doubt he'll make it to his first court date. He's not well."

"Sorry to hear that." Nick tapped the envelope on his hand, took a deep breath and handed it back. "I can't take this."

Reg looked at the envelope in his hand. "You sure? This is ten grand. It's not chump change."

"He's sure, Reg. Now go away. You disturb one of our dates again, and I'll do you serious harm."

Reg chuckled and backed off. He waved the envelope at them. "Doubt you'll ever see me again. Enjoy your evening, kids."

"Don't call me a -"

"Nick," said Lucy. "Let's get out of here."

<<◇>>

About the Author

Tony McFadden is a displaced Canadian now calling Australia home. He and his wife and two children live near the beaches where he spends as much time as possible writing.

More about Tony and his writing can be found at TonyMcFadden.net/mybooks, Facebook and Twitter (Yes. I still call it Twitter)

Also by Tony McFadden

Hollyweird	⇒ G'Day LA ⇒ G'Day USA
Matt Daly's Adventures	⇒ Matt's War ⇒ Daly Battles: The Fall of Pyongyang ⇒ Target: Australia
The Miami Mob	⇒ Book 'Em – An Eamonn Shute Mystery ⇒ Unprotected Sax ⇒ Family Matters
The Sci-Fi	⇒ Have Wormhole, Will Travel ⇒ Killing Time
Mac D Cases	⇒ Mac D: Private Investigator ⇒ A Step Too Far ⇒ Hunter / Prey
McGinnis Investigations	⇒ The Murder of Jeremy Brookes ⇒ Number Fifteen
Nick Harding Cases	⇒ Batteries Not Included ⇒ Broken ⇒ Dead Tomorrow ⇒ Under the Shadows